Part I Rebirth of Darkness

Wings of Dragons: Resurrection

Wings of Dragons, Volume 2

Morgan Schmidt

Published by Morgan Schmidt, 2024.

While every precaution has been taken in the preparation of this book, the publisher assumes no responsibility for errors or omissions, or for damages resulting from the use of the information contained herein.

WINGS OF DRAGONS: RESURRECTION

First edition. September 2, 2024.

Copyright © 2024 Morgan Schmidt.

ISBN: 979-8227544223

Written by Morgan Schmidt.

Table of Contents

Thank you to my friends, family, coworkers, and students for encouraging me for writing and publishing my ideas. I would also like to thank my wife, Becky, for helping to look over my crazy ideas.

Chapter 1 Past Grief

Ironfire strode angrily into the home of the Ferrolith. The metal dragon leader stomped along the cave floor, his footsteps echoing in the emptiness. The cave was carved out of the side of a hill near the dead land of Mortem and the floor had small pools of water. Some were used for drinking, others for cooling metal for weaponry. The Ferrolith dragons were known for their weapon making because the breath of a metal dragon was liquid metal that could be forged into weapons. They were equal to the Inferoths and Gaiajades in power and veracity. No one could best them nor rule them. Then the Necrodrakes came.

The death dragons killed every dragon in sight. The land of Mortem birthed the monstrosities to ravage the planet of Wyrm, led by Erebos and empowered by Morthauron, the god of death. The Ferroliths were the first line of defense, and were killed by the hands and teeth of the Necrodrakes; except for Ironfire, the former leader of the metal dragons. He fought at the front of the wave; he and other Ferroliths went after Erebos and his generals. Ironfire had been captured, tormented, threatened with being turned into a Silent One. He escaped to regroup with the leaders of the other clans only to be devastated by the death of his clan and which he blamed on incompetence of the other dragons who relied on Auroradraca too much for leadership. Eventually, the Necrodrakes had been defeated and sealed into the land with the magic the other clans were given by Auroradraca but Ironfire was left with nothing.

"They can't all be dead. They just can't be," Ironfire muttered to himself. His large frame echoed in the cave as he looked into the various rooms that had been carved out of the hill. Walking on all fours, his metallic scales reflected the bioluminescent moss that covered the walls.

"Hello! Is anyone here?" he bellowed. "Did anyone stay behind? Any hatchlings hiding? It's safe now, you can come out now. The Necrodrakes are gone!"

Silence met his questions. He looked around more, going deeper into the cave. "This is Ironfire! Come out now!"

The moss spread his shadow across the cave. "They can't all be dead. Someone had to have stayed behind. Hatchlings weren't on the battlefield. Where are you!" he commanded.

The sound of something soft landing on the cave floor echoed in the vast cave. "Who's there?" Ironfire asked. "It's safe to come out now. Don't be afraid." A second sound repeated. "Where are you?"

Ironfire breathed in deep and spat out a string of liquid metal. The cave lit up, revealing the backside of a Ferrolith. The metal hummed with light on the cave floor. Ironfire carefully walked so as to not alarm whoever was in the room. Moss lit up on the walls as he walked in. Ironfire was horrified with what he saw.

"No, no, no, no, no. It's not possible. They couldn't have breached our home," he tried to reassure himself. Ferrolith bodies were thrown about the room like a hatchling who had thrown a fit and ripped apart his meal. Pieces of Necrodrakes, skulls caved in, littered the floor alongside the pieces of Ferrolith. He backed out of the room.

"How'd they get in here? Someone had to survive. Someone just had to. I can't be the last one."

A bright light showed on the back of the cave. It was pure and illuminated the area, revealing how deadly the Ferroliths and Necrodrakes fought. In the center of the room stood Auroradraca, the goddess of light. She stood on her back legs and crossed her forearms, covering her body with her wings.

"You," Ironfire snarled. "You did this. You created these abominations! You killed my clan!"

"Watch your tone, Ferrolith," she responded. "I will do as I wish. You do not get to judge me. Morthauron created the Necrodrakes."

"Why? Why did you allow this to happen? Why are all my clan dead? Why am I still alive?"

"Your clan fought bravely. It's unfortunate that they all perished."

"Then bring them back to life. You are the goddess of life, right? Just snap your talons and fix this mistake."

Auroradraca glared at him. "I cannot."

"Goddess. Of. Life." Ironfire punctuated. "It's literally in the job title."

"Do not speak to me like a-"

"I'll speak to you however I please!" Ironfire snapped back. "You create life. Bring my clan back. Now!"

Auroradraca stood motionless, emotionless.

"Now," Ironfire growled.

"You will not command me."

"Then I renounce you. You mean nothing to me."

"Choose your words carefully, Ferrolith."

"You are nothing to me! Give me back my clan and leave us alone," he demanded.

Auroradraca glared at him. "Renounce me? Renounce me? You fight in my name, make demands of me and then renounce me."

Ironfire locked eyes with her. "I fought for my clan's survival. Not for the graveyard that is now Mortem. Not for this tomb that my home has become. Bring them back."

Auroradraca smiled. "You will make no demands of me. You are my creation, to do with as I please. You may no longer worship me but my connection with you will not simply disappear because of your words. I came to grieve with you, Ferrolith, to mourn the loss of my creations."

"My name is Ironfire, Goddess."

She smiled. "Your clan was one of my favorite creations. I have many more scattered across this world. Many appreciate the life that I have bestowed upon them and fight in my name."

"Spare me your speech, Goddess. Either rid the world of me or leave me be to bury my clan and die alone."

Auroradraca smiled. "You wish to ignore me but make demands of me? Fine. I'll leave you alone but you will not die. I will blind you from the eyes of Morthauron. You will live forever. Your body will be injured but never truly heal, forcing you to find a way to stay alive. You will keep living, doomed to watch as others appreciate what I have bestowed upon them. Goodbye, Ferrolith."

Auroradraca disappeared in a blink, taking her light with her. Ironfire stood in silence. Rage came screaming out of his mouth. Liquid metal painted the wall where she had stood, bringing an orange and yellow hue to the cave. His eyes showed red, his body shaking with anger. The bodies of the dead threw shadows across the room. Slowly, the metal cooled and the cave became dark again.

THE YEARS HAD BEEN difficult for Ironfire. His body slowly began to waste away; staying in his cave, determined to starve himself to death. On a rainy night, Ironfire traveled to find food, giving in to his stomach. He lost his footing on loose soil and tumbled down the side of a hill, landing on a rocky surface. His back legs were broken and misshapen. He laid in pain as the rain fell on him, gagging on water that pooled in his mouth. Every drop felt like a whip across his legs. He turned his upper body and crawled on his belly. The rainwater began to collect into a small stream. He tried to keep his head above water but struggled. He dropped under the surface and waited for Morthauron to take him. His lungs screamed for air. Ironfire opened his mouth and let the water drown him. He pushed against the water and made it to the shore. He vomited out the water and cried.

"Auroradraca, please just let me die. I'll do whatever you want. Just let me perish." Thunder cracked across the sky. He tried to catch his breath as his lungs got used to oxygen again. He tried to move his back legs, pain reminded him of the injuries. "Anything, please. Just tell me what you want." The rain continued to pour and the water level began to rise. Ironfire dug his front legs into the mud and tried to climb up the hill. His back legs slid behind him. Ironfire screamed in pain as the bones realigned back into their original place.

Ironfire knew he could not crawl his way back to his home with broken legs. He needed to do something. Exhausted, he rested his head on the ground. He stared into the mud and grass. A snail crawled in front of him, its long shell giving him an idea. He pushed himself up and turned to look at the right leg. Ironfire moved it gently to make sure the bone was in the right place. He took in a deep breath and blew molten metal on his leg. The metal ate away at his skin and muscle. Rain hit the liquid, cooling it off, and covering the broken leg. He shot out more of his breath to cover the lost tissue. Once his leg was covered, he rolled into the stream, his leg slapping across the surface like dead weight. Steam erupted from his leg as metal solidified and became one with his flesh. He struggled out of the water. He repeated the process on his other leg. After crawling out the second time, he said "Is this what you wanted? I did it. Let me die. Please." Exhaustion overcame him.

DECADES PASSED. IRONFIRE'S body had rotted away and he was forced to replace his anatomy with his breath, enduring pain as flesh became metal. The Ferrolith corpses laid about the cave, the metal scales preserving the skin. His lungs were bits of thin metal pretending to be alive. He took a breath out of habit. Ironfire sat against the wall. He had forgotten what it was like to need to drink water or to crave food. His mind was numb to the world as Auroradraca's curse kept him living an unnatural life. Dust settled on his metallic skin. He missed his clan. He missed feeling things: cold, heat, hunger, thirst. He was alone in his own mind and did not have the will to move. What was the point? He was forgotten by the other clans. No one had come to check on him after the war. He did not have the will to bury the dead. What was the point? He was the only one left. No one would mourn his passing.

YEARS LATER, IRONFIRE was proud of the work he had done. His body had begun to work better as he mastered using his liquid metal breath to rebuild his failing organs. The metal forms of his fallen clan were reforged, by his breath, into hollow statues. He placed them in wooden boxes that he had cut from trees that he had scavenged.

"What are you doing?" Auroradraca said as she appeared in the cave.

"Finally doing what you wouldn't. Bringing back my clan."

"And how do you plan on doing this, Ferrolith?"

"See you gave me this extended life, this punishment for not wanting to believe in you anymore. But it also gave me the time to rebuild the bodies of my clan. You, being the goddess of life, can simply give them life and let me die."

Auroradraca glared at him. "No."

"I have suffered enough. My clan died from your mistake. You will bring them back." Ironfire angrily stared into her eyes.

"No. I have many other creations that appreciate what I have done for them. You have not."

"You have kept me from Morthauron's gaze and the release of death from all this pain you have forced me to endure for centuries. Bring back my clan and let me perish."

Auroradraca stood there, not moving. "You have done nothing to earn a boon from me, Ferrolith."

"My name is Ironfire!" he shouted as he belched out liquid metal at her. She waved her hand, sending the metal toward one of the larger statues. The metal cooled at her touch, transforming into shrapnel, cutting up a large statue. She turned toward Ironfire and rushed toward him in a blink. Auroradraca grabbed him by the throat and lifted him off the ground like he weighed nothing.

"You are nothing to me, Ferrolith, a mistake, a creation that never should have been. If I could, I would end your life myself but I cannot. Don't dare to presume you can hurt or command me. You will worship me, pray to me, or be nothing to me. Know your place in this world." She hurled him to the side of the cave, leaving a dent in the cave wall; his metal body let out a banging sound from impact. The cave turned dark. Ironfire laid on the ground, wishing he had not offended the goddess all those years before.

IRONFIRE THOUGHT HE had seen Necrodrakes coming from Mortem. He was not worried. Most of his body was made from metal after centuries of living. He had finished creating wooden boxes to put his empty shelled clan in. He had been visited by a small group of dragons, each representing the different clans in the area.

"The fight continues. I've done it once but is it worth joining? Could I finally die?"

"It might be," said a cold whisper in his ear.

He stood up, scanning his surroundings. "Who's there? Show yourself."

Silence. "Auroradraca, is this you? Some new mind game to make yourself look good to me?" He paused. "Answer me now."

A tall black dragon separated from the shadows, his face void of flesh. His long horns scraped against the cave roof. His shoulder wings rested on his body, falling to his feet.

"I'm afraid you have the wrong god," the whisper replied.

"Morthauron? Have you come to finally end my life?"

"I cannot due to Auroradraca's curse. I always wondered what happened to the last Ferrolith. You were not among the many in the underworld who felt my embrace."

"How are you able to finally see me?"

"My power grows as the Necrodrakes rise. Death feeds me."

"What do you want from me?"

"Simply to offer you a favor, an exchange of services if you will."

Ironfire hesitated. "What do you offer?"

"Join the upcoming fight with the Necrodrakes. My power will peak and I'll be able to break her curse."

"What's the catch? What do you get in exchange?"

"Nothing much. Simply the statues that you created. I wish to bring back the Ferroliths but in my image; to rejoin Wyrm as I reshape it with my own designs."

"My clan will live again? How?"

"Do you question me as you would Auroradraca?"

"I don't believe you anymore than I would her."

"Fair point. But I'm being truthful to you. Death always reveals the truth."

Ironfire weighed his options. "I die but my clan lives." He paused. "Deal." Morthauron smiled.

Chapter 2 Smell the Flowers

Mudball had been enjoying his life since the Necrodrake battle. He finally got the hang of using his crystals to fire his breath and started to train more in the fighting circle. The young Gaiajade was happy with life. The Gaiajade land had recovered from the invasion of Necrodrakes. Crops were growing and dwellings were rebuilt. Everything was back to normal. Well, most everything was.

Gempath tried to return their life back to routine. Her mate, Oldstone, was the former leader of the Gaiajades. He perished in the Necrodrake war. Mudball tried not to remember having to end Oldstone's life as he was turning into a Necrodrake. No one in his clan knew he was forced to kill Oldstone. The old leader was highly respected and Mudball did not know how everyone would react if they knew the truth. He had told them that he saw the Necrodrakes kill Oldstone, which was true for the most part. He did feel bad for lying to Gempath and what she had to deal with because of Oldstone's death. She was not as experienced of a leader as her mate had been but she was trying. Her old age and the stress of rebuilding the territory were taking a toll on her health.

Mudball ventured out to the fields. Gaiajades were known for their farming skills. Walking on four legs and possessing no wings, one would think Gaiajades would be weak compared to the other clans. Crystals grew on their bodies which, when charged by sunlight, would generate a beam of solid light that could blow a hole through stone.

Gaiajades tended to be a peace loving clan but could fight when needed to.

Tall wheat plants grew in rows across the growing fields. The current crop had grown faster than usual, thanks to Mudball. During the war with the Necrodrakes, he was gifted magic by Auroradraca that allowed him to bring life wherever he went. Most of it got used up when he and his friends poured their magic into the Necrodrake leader's jawbone to defeat their enemy. Mudball was still bothered that it was Rageskin's brother, Redeye, who had been revealed as the newest leader. Even after using the magic to imprison their enemy, he still had a little bit of magic left in him. He mainly used it to help when crops were having difficulty growing. Over the last year, he had gotten pretty good jumpstarting the different growing seasons. He smiled at his handiwork but then he heard two Gaiajades arguing. He came around the end of a row and saw two hatchlings yelling at each other. One was a light green color and the other was a dark brown.

"You're supposed to use your breath to make the planting rows!" the green one shouted.

"No, you're supposed to use your snout crystals," the other argued. They butted their heads against each other, their small crystals grinding against the others.

Mudball walked up to them. "Hey, Flinthead, Stonespark! Knock it off! What are you arguing about?"

Flinthead, the brown one, said, "You're supposed to use your snout to make rows and she says I'm wrong."

"You're supposed to use your breath, dirt for brains," Stonespark insulted. "We are never going to get our chores done if we only use our snouts. Tell him, Mudball." They growled at each other.

Mudball sighed. This is what it must have been like for Oldstone. "You're both right."

The two hatchlings looked at him dumbfounded.

"You can use either method, depending on your abilities. Some Gaiajades have small snout crystals that are not good for digging up the soil, so they use very concentrated breaths to make the rows. Not too deep but not too shallow. Others have large crystals that are perfect for plowing. You do what is best for you."

The two dragons looked at each other, realizing they fought over something silly.

"Now, which of you is good at your breath?" Mudball asked. They looked at each other in embarrassment. "Neither, huh? I've been there. It took me a long time to master mine. Just last year, actually. I was a slow learner. But now, I can use either method, depending on how much I have to do."

"It's gonna take us all day to make a growing row with our snouts," Stonespark whined.

"We wanna play with our friends," Flinthead chimed.

Mudball looked at them, sad little faces looking back. He smiled and readied a stance. His back crystals began to hum. "How far do you have to go?"

Flinthead smiled, "To that rock over there."

Mudball's crystals glowed brighter. He focused on the rock and released his breath. A bright white beam shot out, tearing up the ground in a straight line. He relaxed and his breath stopped halfway to the rock.

"Why'd you stop?" Flinthead asked.

"It's your chore. I showed you how deep you need to go. Now you finish it."

"But how are we supposed to keep dirt from going up our noses?" Stonespark asked.

"Don't breathe it in," Mudball said as he smiled.

The two dragons looked at him and stuck out their tongues. Mudball laughed and stomped his foot, a line of short wheat plants sprouted and raced to the row. He turned around and walked away.

Mudball had lost his family in the Necrodrake war and he wanted to honor them by being a better member of his clan. It was his day off and he wanted to enjoy it. He walked past the growing plantations and found his spot, a meadow with large multicolored flowers growing all around. A path led to the middle in which sat his favorite thing in the whole world of Wyrm was: his flying rock. To his knowledge he was the only Gaiajade ever to fly. Granted, he had clung on for his life while being chased by a Necrodrake Gaiajade but in his mind it still counted as flying. He laid down on the square rock and let out a long yawn. Everything was peaceful and quiet in his field but he kept thinking of his friends. Since the Necrodrake battle, his friends have been busy rebuilding their clans' homes or leading their clan. Rageskin hardly came around anymore to take him flying on his rock. Inferoths were not known for their kindness but Mudball appreciated his friend's efforts.

He laid his head down for a quick nap. As his eyes began to flutter asleep, he caught sight of something in the corner of his eye. He raised his head and looked around. He could not hear or see anything unusual. He laid his head back down and closed his eyes. The flowers made a shuffling sound, like something was moving through them. Mudball opened his eyes again but kept his head on the rock. Flowers were moving on their own. He got to his feet and charged his back crystals, humming with whiteness. He spun around and realized that flowers were moving around his rock and coming closer.

"Who goes there? I don't want to hurt you but I'll protect myself if I have to," he warned. The flowers stopped moving. "Not scary, not scary, not scary," he reassured himself. The flowerheads turned toward Mudball in sync, petals shaking. "Nope, nope, nope. I am not going to be eaten by flowers that I grew." Two flowers, sunflower and rose, met each other, appeared to talk to each other and moved toward him. "Please don't eat me, please don't eat me," he said as his crystals became brighter.

A small dragon jumped into a clearing between the flowers and rock. "Don't shoots us, please," it pleaded, flapping its red rose wings. "Wez friendly. No hurts you."

Mudball powered down his crystals. The sunflower winged dragon climbed out of the grass and stood beside the rose dragon. The sunflower dragon had a brown and yellow body that matched its wings. The scales and skin on the back mounted wings resembled a sunflower in pattern. The rose dragon had green scales on its body with red rose colored wings. The two dragons walked on all fours like Mudball did. He had never seen dragons so small before. Even newly hatched Gaiajades were bigger than these dragons were.

"Who are you?" Mudball asked.

"I iz Thornseed," the rose dragon replied. "And this iz my mate, Petalspear."

The sunflower dragon bowed her head. "Hellos." Both dragons had high pitched voices.

"I have never seen dragons like you before," Mudball said.

"Wez is Florastryx. Wez take cares of plants, " Petalspear replied. "Yourz iz pretty."

"Um, well, thank you. Where did you two come from?"

"Wez come from north," Thornseed answered. "Hads to leaves."

"Why?"

The two Florastryx looked at each other. "Mean dragons. They attacks us, hurts us," Thornseed replied sadly. "Many didn'ts live." Petalspear lowered her head. "Your flowers hides us. So pretty."

"I'm sorry that your clan got hurt. I've seen what bad dragons could do. Could you describe who they were? I might know them."

"Theyz mean," Petalspear said. "Don't likes us cause we not think likes them."

"Are they red in color? Wear lava armor?" Mudball asked.

"Oh noz. Theys have white and golds scalez. Loves sun. Loves Auroraz," Thornseed replied.

"Auroraz? You mean Auroradraca?" Mudball questioned.

"Yez. Hards name to says sometimes," replied Thornseed. "They sez, they sez, we must worships hers or else."

Petalspear cried, "They hurts our eggs, stomp on usses. They large, likes you. Maybe biggers."

Mudball looked at them. "That is so sad. I don't know any dragons like them. We Gaiajades are nice dragons. We wouldn't hurt you. We like plants too."

The pair raised their heads. "Plants? Wez help take care of thems for you," they said in unison, flapping their wings like a hummingbird.

"Hey, watch this," Mudball said. He placed a front foot in front of the Florastyxes on the bare ground. He squinted his eyes and concentrated as his foot glowed lightly. The two dragons starred in anticipation. He lifted his foot and small flowers were revealed. Their eyes grew large, jaws dropped.

"Hows you do that?" Petalspear asked. She looked under his foot. "Is magic?"

"Actually, yeah. Not much but it helps."

The flowers around the flying rock began to move. More Florastryxes came into the open. Their wings had a variety of flower patterns and colors to them. Mudball could not believe his eyes at the number of them. They slowly crawled to Mudball, talking quietly to each other, amazed by the plants that he just grew. Suddenly, a beam of light shot toward the sky, followed by a thunderous roar. The Florastryxes scurried back into the field, their wings blending in with the garden flowers.

"Hey, it's okay, guys. It's just Gempath. She's calling for a meeting of all the Gaiajades. No reason to be afraid."

Thornseed and Petalspear slowly came out of the tall grass. "Gempath? She's nice?" inquired Thornseed.

"Oh, yeah, she's the best. You guys will love her. How about you two jump on my back and come with me. If I can, I'll introduce you to her and see if you can live with us."

They looked at each other. Thornseed nodded his head and the two Florastryxes jumped onto Mudball's back. Each found a different crystal on his back and wrapped their wings around it. "Okay, guys, I have to run so I'm not too late. Hang on." Mudball started into a slow gallop and sped up. The Florastryx bounced on his back.

When he arrived, most of his clan surrounded Gempath. She was an elder Gaijade with looser skin than the younger dragons. The stress of being a leader could be seen on her face, stress forming permanent wrinkles in her skin. Gaiajades grumbled about being called away from what they were doing suddenly.

"Welcome, everyone," Gempath announced. "I'm sorry for calling all of you. I know we have much to do this time of year." The Gaiajades mumbled. She cleared her throat. "I am here to tell you that I will be stepping down as leader." The dragons talked amongst themselves in surprise. Gempath gave them a neutral glare and they settled down. "I stepped in to replace Oldstone after his passing. It has been a year since then and we have managed to rebuild our lives. Age has caught up to me and I can no longer fulfill my duties. I propose a tournament, as is custom to our clan. Those who wish to fight may step up now and announce your intentions. If you do not, then you acknowledge the potential winner as your new leader."

The Gaiajades looked around at each other, waiting to see who would declare first. Gempath surveyed the crowd. A large Gaiajade stepped toward her. His skin was a dark brown and muscles rippled beneath them. He was larger than most of the dragons there. The crystals on his back created lines along his spine. He showed scars from battle against the Necrodrake war. He had claw marks on his sides and two puncture marks on his neck. Each step he took seemed to shake the ground a little. He stood in front of Gempath.

"Do you declare, Coalash?" Gempath asked.

In a deep baritone voice, he replied "Yes." He projected a confidence that made the other Gaiajades hesitate to step up.

"What's happening?" Thornseed asked.

"Hush," Mudball replied. "They are deciding who will fight for leadership."

"I scared," Thornseed said.

"You're safe, little guy," Mudball reassured. "Just don't-".

Coalash let out a roar. The two Florastryxes dug their claws into Mudball's skin. He yelped in pain. The crowd turned around and looked at him. Gempath had a surprised look on her face. "Mudball has declared entry into the tournament." Two more large Gaiajades stepped in to declare. The crowd cheered as no one else stepped forward and the tournament was declared.

Mudball had a worried look on his face. "Oh, my, this will not end well for me."

Chapter 3 Chaos in the Volcano

Rageskin sat upon his throne inside the volcano that was home to the Inferoths. The stone throne had belonged to his father. The ruler of the Inferoths was usually chosen through challenge and combat. His brother, Redeye, would have defeated Sharpfang, their father, and taken leadership had he not become a Necrodrake leader and tried to take over Wyrm. Redeye had slain their father in the Necrodrake battle. Rageskin touched his ebony armor. It was fused to his skin and protected most of him from harm. Inferoths went through a trial of placing and sculpting lava onto their skin to create armor. His armor had been forged with assistance from Auroradraca. He still remembers the pain of becoming one with his armor. A shield was forged onto his left forearm while his right was free to hold a sword. He reflected on the past year since the Necrodrake war.

Rageskin became the de facto leader of the Inferoths. He had shown strength and courage, traits the Inferoths respected. He had been chosen for magic by Auroradraca and had defeated the Necrodrakes using the power-infused jaw of his brother. He led the efforts to rebuild the volcano after it had shown anger from the Necrodrakes invading it. His throne room was set above all, so that he could look down upon his clan. He could see the cave openings that had been hand carved by Inferoths to create small homes. Bridges were set in the sides of the volcano, creating pathways to reach various levels. At the bottom was the lake of magma, always ready to blow but also to be used to create the Inferoth armor. Above it were four bridges that met in the middle at a large circle. The bridges were wide and could allow all the dragons to meet. In the center of the circle, a small pool with magma in it sat. This was where Inferoths would prove their worthiness for battle and become one with their armor.

Rageskin did not enjoy being leader. His father was always ready to defend himself against any challenger. Redeye could defeat anyone at any moment. But Rageskin? He has had to defend his throne twice against challengers who felt he was not worthy of being leader. Both times he got by thanks to his ebony armor. Some claimed he was cheating because the goddess had forged his armor while others felt that he could only win with others helping him. He chose a seasoned warrior to advise on his decisions who happened to be the first Inferoth to challenge him for leadership. A figure came to the cave entrance.

"Rageskin," the figure said as he entered the cave. He had skin colored like burnt rust. His armor covered his chest and forearms. His left wing had a scar that was fused together by magma.

"Blackwing," Rageskin acknowledged. "What is today's newest issue?"

Blackwing chuckled. "The clan gathers below to speak with you."

"About?"

Blackwing took a deep breath. "About you not having a mate yet."

Rageskin rolled his eyes. "Seriously? We have other things to deal with. Fixing trade routes, creating float stones for the water dragons. I don't have time nor need a mate right now."

"May I?" Blackwing asked. Rageskin nodded his head. Blackwing walked toward him. "Your mother was one of the fiercest female warriors we had ever had. She set the bar high of what it means to be a Ferrolith queen. Many of our female warriors want to honor her by being chosen as your mate."

Rageskin replied, "Hooray, more family members to be compared to." He let out a breath of air in frustration.

Blackwing rubbed the side of his neck. Rageskin noticed two puncture marks on it.

"Are you feeling alright, Blackwing?"

"Oh, this," he replied, pointing to his neck. "Nothing for you to worry about, just a scratch from sparring. But you need to remember how the clan felt empowered by your family. They felt we were the strongest of the clans. Now, prides are hurt. Some cling to the notion of strength of self rather than relying on others."

"The battle with the Necrodrakes should have proved to them that we need to be a united society. Mortem has been silent but that doesn't mean other foes couldn't arise."

"You need to lead the Inferoths, either by example or by combat."

Rageskin gritted his teeth in frustration. "Alright, let's go and talk with the clan." Blackwing bowed as Rageskin walked past him. He lifted his eyes and glared at Rageskin as he took flight down to the stone circle.

Inferoths gathered on the stone bridges, arguing amongst themselves. Rageskin took a calming breath and landed by the magma pool. The crowd quieted, all eyes were on Rageskin.

"My fellow Inferoths. I have come to talk with you about some grievances that you have been having."

A tall, dark red Inferoth spoke first. "You are making us weaker by working with the other clans. We rely too heavily on them for our needs."

"Hardfist, I did not hear your complaints when the Gaiajades moved rock to rebuild our volcano. I did not hear your complaints when the Aquanox rerouted the lava for better flow. I did not hear your complaints when the Zeyphrions brought down their extra food when our food storage caves were ruined. But please continue."

Hardfist glared at him. "Your father would be ashamed of your leadership." In a swift movement, Rageskin ran up to him and kicked the side of his knee forcing Hardfist to kneel. Rageskin swung his shield and smashed Hardfist's face. He crashed into the ground with a moan.

Rageskin looked around at the crowd. "Is this what you want from your leader? Huh? A quick hit, a punch to put you in your place? A knockdown whenever you say something I may not like? I'm not my father, I will hear your complaints and concerns. But do not think for a moment that Sharpfang's blood does not run in my veins." He looked around at the stunned looks on everyone's face. "I will still listen to you but don't think you can just walk over me because I'm not like my family. I've led you this long, improved our lives by working with the other clans. I defeated the Necrodrakes, helped to banish them. I defeated and killed my own brother." He paused for a moment, gathering himself. "Are there any other concerns that I need to be aware of?"

A female Inferoth stepped forward. Her skin was a mix of red and black tones. Her armor covered her arms with long spikes coming out of joints. "I agree that you have helped our clan become stronger and better but some of us still respect the traditions of old, one of which is that you must choose a mate. A king must have a queen and the females of your clan have tried to get your interest and prove ourselves worthy of your attention. We are frustrated and want you to make a choice."

"Darkheart, I have noticed all of you trying to get my attention. I-" he paused.

Darkheart gave him a disgusted look. "You have feelings for the Zeyphrion." Rageskin gulped, not wanting to admit it. "Maybe some of us are right about you being too weak to be our leader. If you allow emotions and love to decide who your mate is." He went up to Darkheart and held his sword to her throat.

"You don't know what I want or think."

"You're a male. I can see it. You need to decide soon or you may have some more challenges coming your way." Several Inferoths gave

Rageskin a hard look. Hardfist got up and made a step toward Rageskin. Blackwing held his hand against the larger Inferoth.

"Get out of my way," Hardfist ordered.

Blackwing looked him up and down. "I will put you in your place if you talk to me like that. I am our king's advisor and bodyguard."

"Loser."

Blackwing kicked him in the side of the knee. As he went down, Blackwing held his forearm dagger to his opponent's throat. "I also train our king."

Hardfist crawled on his knees backward. Darkheart said, "Do you propose something, advisor?"

"In fact, I do." He walked and stood beside Rageskin. "I propose that, if our king truly has feelings for the Zeyphrion, then he will bring her to this spot. To prove that she is worthy of his attention, she will have armor grafted to herself. If she fails, she is no longer in contention for queenship and Rageskin will have to choose a mate. However, if she passes, then she will fight you, Darkheart, for our king's hand." He looked at Rageskin. "Your response, King?"

"I agree to this," he said. "Blackwing, you are in charge while I go to see her and bring her back here. Everyone, do your duties while I am gone."

Darkheart smiled as Rageskin flapped his shoulder wings and took off. Inferoths joined him and flew off and about the volcano. Blackwing walked behind Darkheart and placed a hand on her shoulder. "I need you to come with me."

Chapter 4 Up in the Air

Whisper took a deep breath. The ground beneath her was cool as she readed a fighting stance. She held a stone bo staff across the length of her arm. It was a dark gray and molded for her hands. Her wings hung from arms like a silk cape. Zeyphrions were known for their beauty and smaller stature compared to the other dragon clans. They were not known for fighting but Whisper and her mom had begun to change that.

A slight breeze blew through her feathers that ran down her neck and back. Three hatchlings watched in anticipation for her to move. Her prey: wooden dragon dummies. They were painted black, representing the Necrodrakes that once tried to wipe out her clan. She ran toward the first dummy, swinging her leg to its midsection. As it began to fall down, she brought her bo staff down, crushing it to the ground. She turned to the second dummy. Whisper opened her jaw to send out her breath, an invisible punch of air that knocked over her enemy. She looked at the last wooden dummy. It was slightly bigger than the last two and had an angry face painted on it. Her heart began to speed up, her breathing shallow. Voices from her run-ins with the Necrodrakes whispered in her head.

"Zeyphrion flesh, so tasty."

"I don't want to play with my food, I want to eat it."

"You'll make a pretty Necrodrake."

Whisper screamed at the voices. Her breath hit the dummy, freezing it solid. She ran up to it and began to beat it with her bo staff. The dummy cracked with every swing. She yelled and grunted with every swing. Anger began to run through her, causing her to beat the dummy until it shattered into frozen shards. She stood over it, breathing heavily. The face of the Necrodrake she had been seeing in her eyes faded away. She calmed herself and turned toward the hatchlings. She was horrified by what she had done in front of them.

The first hatchling exclaimed, "That was awesome!"

The second hatchling yelled, "First you were like, oof" mimicking Whisper's motions. "Then you were like, smack, then freezing breath, bang, bang."

"When can we learn to use our cold breath?" the third one asked.

"It's a new talent. Not everyone has mastered it yet. When all the older Zeyphrions learn it, you hatchlings will."

"Awwwww," they all moaned together.

"No whining," Whisper commanded. "You are the next generation of warrior Zeyphrions. You must be patient and learn. Now, go home to your parents."

The hatchlings stood up, flapped their arms, and flew off. The floating islands of the Zeyphrions were a sight to behold. Anchored together by vines, the Zeyphrions home floated in the sky. Water, collected from rainfall and clouds, cascaded from higher islands to lower. Each floating rock served a purpose, from growing crops to homes to nesting. Whisper had repurposed the island she was on. Before the Necrodrake war, the Zeyphrions only worried about their beauty and looked down on the other clans. Avoiding conflicts and not fighting was more their style. Whisper took it upon herself to start training her fellow Zeyphrion. Rageskin was a big help in that. Inferoths were fearsome fighters and could hold their own. She wrapped herself with her arms and wings.

Whisper remembered talking with Rageskin about teaching her.

"*YOU WANT ME TO DO WHAT?*" *Rageskin asked.*

"I want you to teach me how to fight. So I can teach others how to defend themselves."

"And your mom was okay with this?"

"Yes. After fighting the Necrodrakes, she opened her mind to us being warriors. She was all 'We can't always run away. It makes us look weak. Plus, the muscles we gain from fighting makes us more desirable to the males.'"

"Yeah, well, um," Rageskin stumbled.

"What?" she inquired.

"Nothing. Yeah, we can meet a couple times a week and train. We will start with the basics and then, uh," he said trailing off.

"Then what?" she said with a sly smile.

"More physical combat techniques."

Whisper gave him a smile. "Sounds good." She started to walk away. "Hey, I didn't know Inferoths can get redder in the face." She flapped her wings and took off.

Over the next few weeks, Rageskin had visited Whisper on her new fighting island to train her. He went easy on her at first but then the training started getting more aggressive. Whenever he would leave a scratch or bruise he would check on her to make sure she was okay or if he went too far. Whisper appreciated the effort and concern that he had. It was a side of Inferoths she had never seen before. It made her look at Rageskin differently.

One day, Whisper was training by herself when Rageskin flew in with something in his hands.

"Hey, Rageskin. What's that?"

Rageskin paused for a moment, giving himself some courage to speak. "Well, you are doing great with your training but you are at a disadvantage against me. The armor."

"Yeah, it kinda hurts when I punch you there."

"It's why my hands are covered." He realized how dumb he sounded. He cleared his throat. "So I had this made for you." He handed her a stone bo staff. "You aren't strong enough yet for a sword or mace but this staff will help you with your strikes. It was made from the side of the volcano. It's strong but light enough for you to swing it." He handed it to her. She took it and gripped it like a bat.

"Wow, this is great." She took some random swings. "Now, I can really kick your tail."

He chuckled. "I wouldn't go that far. But, yeah, it'll be useful."

Whisper hopped in delight. "This is great. Ooo, I got something to show you." She put her weapon down and grabbed a wooden dummy. She placed it and ran back to Rageskin. "Watch this." She took in a deep breath and released her fire. The air shimmered as it cooled. The breath froze the dummy.

"That's wow, amazing," Rageskin said.

"I know, right?" Whisper agreed as a mist came with every syllable. "Stream told me that Zeyphrions used to be able to change the temperature of their breath to freeze and heat things. And I wanted to show-" she paused as she turned around. Rageskin was closer to her than she had realized. His hot breath met her cold breath. The air between them steamed. They looked into each other's eyes.

"So, um," Whisper stammered.

"So, yeah, um, want to start training with the staff?" Rageskin tried to get out.

WHISPER SHUDDERED REMEMBERING that day. She could not decide how she felt about Rageskin. He was a great friend and a brave, smart leader. All the things one could ask for in a mate but they were different clans. To her knowledge, dragons from different groups had never had romantic pairings. She was lost in her thoughts when she heard something shuffle in the dirt. She got into a fighting pose, lifting her staff to eye level. She listened to the wind and found an unusual noise in the air. She looked to her right and struck, a spark jumped in the air. She swung low, aiming for a knee. Her attacker jumped and pushed her to the ground. She landed on her back. She planted her legs and kicked herself back up. She shot her air breath, punching a black shield.

"I yield, I yield," Rageskin laughed.

"Whatever," Whisper said as she relaxed. "What are you doing here? It's not a training night."

"I need to talk to you about something." He sat down on a large smooth rock. She sat beside him. "Being the king of the Inferoths requires a lot from me," he started. "Leadership. Being challenged for it. Decision making for what's best for us. I've done pretty good, I think." He paused.

"What's wrong?"

"I've run into a problem that I can't solve but I don't know how to solve it without causing you pain."

Whisper was confused. "Rageskin, I'm worried."

Rageskin looked up at the sky as his leg bounced in one spot. "I need to find a mate, a queen."

Whisper's eyes grew large. "Oh, my. That is a problem."

Rageskin remained glum. "The females want me to choose or I'll continue to be challenged. They see me as weak for not finding a mate yet."

"So, what do you need from me?"

Rageskin looked down and then at her. "I have enjoyed these last few months. Training, spending time with you. It's not like being with an Inferoth female. You tend to have a physical fight to prove yourself. Then she's yours. No feelings. No love. Mutual fighting. I . . . don't want that. I want the love, the feelings, and -" he stopped. "It's stupid. I'll leave."

"No, don't leave." She touched his hand. Heat rose from his skin, which was normal for an Inferoth. "What can I do to help?"

"You won't like it."

"What do I have to do?"

Rageskin gulped. "Would you be interested in being my queen?"

Whisper paused. Millions of emotions were going through her head. "Yes."

"I was afraid you would say that," he replied. "You will need to become an Inferoth in the eyes of the clan. First, you will need to go through the armor trial. Then, you must fight Darkheart, the main female that wants to be queen. If you survive, then you're my queen."

Whisper sat in silence. Then asked, "How much will it hurt?"

Chapter 5 Troubled Waters

Stream let out a long yawn. His long, serpentine body was wrapped around a pile of stones that he was using to read. A large cave in the Aquanox territory held stone tablets that told the history of their world. He had learned of it during the Necrodrake war when the Aquanox leader, Dreamflow, had shown him. Thanks to the leftover magic he had received from Auroradraca, he was able to read the ancient text. He was amazed at how much had been written and forgotten about. The bulk of the text dealt with his clan and the other three. He had reread the tablets in the first Necrodrake war, trying to figure out how he and his friends could have saved more dragons. So far, he had found nothing except repeated history.

He unwound himself from the rocks, picked up his current read with his mouth, and slid over to the shelves. He turned his head and placed the tablet back in its place. He let out a sigh and moved around the shelves, trying to decide what was next to read. Stream looked above him at the ceiling murals. He had looked at them every time he returned to the tablet cave but never saw anything new, mostly just visual retellings of Wyrm's recent history. He crawled to the last shelf of tablets and looked up. He tilted his head in confusion. There was a new ceiling painting. It showed a Ferrolith with a crack down its body and a mist coming out of it. In the background was a sun and moon on either side of it.

"That's new," Stream thought out loud. "A broken Ferrolith? Injured maybe? And it's at the end of the paintings so it's a new event, maybe? But the Ferroliths are all dead. Ironfire was the last one and he died in the second Necrodrake war. And what is coming out of the mouth?" He looked at the painting closer, stretching his body taller. He noticed that the mist started in the chest and left through the mouth of the Ferrolith. He squinted his eyes, lowered himself, and went to the shelves.

"Where is it? I know I just read something like this. Where, where, where," and then he paused. He felt a book pull to him and turned toward his right. He opened his mouth, bit a tablet, and laid it on the ground. He focused his eyes on the text, rereading the ancient text.

"And the dead dragon's ash left its body as a mist, searching for a new body. We watched as the ash climbed up an unsuspecting Gaiajade and entered the mouth. The earth dragon convulsed and fell to the ground, falling asleep. When he awoke, he did not answer to his name, saying it was not his. In fact, he would only respond to the name of the dragon. Somehow, the dragon's ash had replaced the Gaiajade's. We were appalled by what had transpired and had to end this abomination in the name of Auroradraca."

Stream was confused. "Who was the foreign dragon? Another clan? How did its ash move?" He was going to go back to the shelves when he heard a splashing from the water's edge.

"Stream, you need to come," a young Aquanox shouted. "Big meeting's going to happen."

Stream really wanted to get back to the tablets. "Okay, I'll be there in a minute." The young Aquanox dove under the water. He made a note to himself where the tablet was found and jumped into the water. He heard numerous voices in the water as he swam. Aquanoxes were able to communicate with each other through water. Everyone was talking about the meeting.

"Are they still mad about the water disappearing? It was a year ago."

"Coastal Aquanoxes have it so easy. Let's see them handle the pressure of the depths."

"We demand retribution against the Inferoths."

"Punish the Inferoths!"

"We should leave the clan, start our own."

Stream could not believe what he was hearing. Every tribe in the Aquanox clan got along and contributed to the group. It has been a time since the Inferoth's volcano erupted and boiled the water away, drying out portions of the underwater tunnels Aquanoxes called home. The problem had been fixed with the other clans helping to divert water from other areas back into the Aquanox home. Stream was lost in thought when a wall came into his vision. He opened his back, sail-like wings and made a sharp turn. He cruised to a stop in the water, his heart racing from the near collision. "Okay, no more listening to the messages while swimming. That was way too close," he thought to himself.

Stream made his way to the lagoon that connected all the tunnels in the Aquanox territory. The tunnels came from different directions, some going to the surface, others deeper into the water. Over time and with practice, Aquanox learned which tunnel led them to their destination. He broke the water surface and got his bearings. There were a large number of Aquanoxes at the lagoon. They were a variety of different colors, depending on the depth of their home water. Some were a light blue or green while others were a dark blue color. A large group of them were confronting Dreamflow. The space was open with small stone beaches for Aquanoxes to lay on. Dreamflow sat upon a large, smooth, circular stone that came out of the water. The depth dwelling Aquanoxes were a dark gray in skin color. They were able to withstand the pressure that it brought, muscles rippled under their skin. Their eyes were larger with bioluminescent scales that made lines down their long bodies. Their scales were larger with bony plates going down their spine.

"It's been a year since the Inferoth's volcano erupted and made our water disappear. When are we going to seek justice from them?" a large Aquanox demanded.

Dreamflow responded, "The Inferoths were not in control of their volcano when it erupted. They were battling the Necrodrakes just like we were, Riverbank."

Riverbank snorted steam out of his nostrils. "And they were the cause of the Necrodrakes becoming free in the first place." The crowd around him cheered and agreed.

"That is true," Dreamflow agreed. "But, Rageskin and his clan have helped to rebuild our tunnels and replenish the water. They introduced filter stones to help purify any water that had been polluted from the volcano."

"But they haven't suffered enough," Riverbank retorted.

"That is enough, Riverbank," Dreamflow said with sternness in his voice. This was a side of Dreamflow Stream had not seen from him before. "We have worked with all the clans to become a better society. We were too splintered. Now, you ask me to punish or possibly go to war with our fellow dragons after they have helped us. No, the Inferoths will not be punished. And if you decide to go on your own, you, and any who follow you, will be on your own."

Riverbank glared at Dreamflow. "That's your solution?" He paused, waiting for a response. Dreamflow looked at him. "Fine. I will take mine elsewhere. Find another clan of Aquanox that share the same thoughts as we do. We will head out to the great ocean to the east and see what we find. Maybe another continent where the dragons aren't as weak minded as you." Riverbank and his followers sank below the surface. They left under the surface crowd, leaving ripples in their wake.

Dreamflow addressed the remaining dragons. "My fellow Aquanox. I know rebuilding our home has been difficult but we have made great strides in replenishing the water that was lost. We have improved our relationships with the other clans. But, if you wish to leave, you may. But know that if you do leave and decide to come back, you will be welcomed." The crowd murmured amongst themselves and left for their homes. Stream swam up to Dreamflow, his head poking out of the water.

"That was rough," Stream said.

"Not everyone can remain happy after a major event in their routine. But Riverbank and the others can explore and start new lives if they so choose."

Stream asked, "Are there other clans, besides us and the other three? I've never seen anyone else beside Ironfire."

"We live in but a small portion of Wyrm. There are as many clans as there are elements. The Goddess of Life has populated this world to her delight."

"Then why haven't we seen any of them? Why haven't we seen those dragons before?"

Dreamflow paused. "Dragons tend to be seclusionary creatures. We stay with our own and claim territory as we deem fit. That is probably why we have never truly unified as a whole. The tablet room should have some information about the other continents and clans. I remember reading about one clan where a single dragon could reach up and touch the Zeyphrion's islands."

Stream could not wrap his head around a dragon that large. "Like Erebos was?"

"Larger."

"That's insane."

"And yet they exist in our world. I suppose we are just lucky they haven't come to our part of Wyrm."

Chapter 6 Transmigration

Night fell across the land. Two Gaiajades walked across the barren landscape that surrounded Mortem.

"So, what is out here that is so secretive," the first Gaiajade asked.

"Stonejaw, I have discovered something I bet no one even knows about."

"Really, Rockhead? And what's that?"

"You'll see," Rockhead said with a smile.

They walked around the side of a hill. Rockhead shined his back crystals to illuminate a cave entrance. "See that?"

"Yeah, it's a cave entrance. Not really Wyrm shattering information," Stonejaw sarcastically replied.

"It's what is inside the cave that is life changing," Rockhead said. He walked into the cave first, Stonejaw following, also lighting up his crystals.

Stonejaw said, "Wow, this cave is huge. Who lived here?"

"The Ferrolith leader from the first Necrodrake war."

"No way," he gasped. "Ironfire lived here? How do you know that?"

Rockhead stepped into the back of the cave, his crystals glowing dark. "There's proof back here. You just need to come with me."

"Wait up," Stonejaw said. "Why'd you turn your crystals off? It's too dark here." There was no reply. "Rockhead? Where are you?" No answer. He spun around, trying to get his crystals to glow brighter. "Seriously. Where are you? This isn't funny." He tried to back up and his back foot clanked against something metal. He spun around and saw the body of Ferrolith. He focused his eyes. "Is that a statue?"

"No," Rockhead replied. "It's my old body."

Stonejaw turned his head to Rockhead. "What do you mean?"

Rockhead stood in the dark. A pair of red eyes glowed beside him. "Doesn't matter for you," he said as the red eyes pierced through the shadows. A rusted Ferrolith landed on Stonejaw's back. He bucked, trying to fling the Ferrolith off. The steel dragon opened its mouth wide, two long canines extended out. It clamped down on the back of Stonejaw's neck, the fangs piercing the side of his neck. Stonejaw screamed in pain. His body began to move slowly as a bright glow came from the belly of the Ferrolith. The bright ball moved through the Ferrolith and into Stonejaw at the neck wound. He stopped moving, his legs collapsing. His chest grew bright and stopped.

Rockhead walked over to Stonejaw. He kicked the Ferrolith carcass off, its large canines leaving puncture wounds on the neck. It panged as it hit the ground. Stonejaw suddenly opened his eyes and took in a deep breath like it was his first time doing so. He hyperventilated at first, then controlled his breathing and stood up. He shook his head, blinking his eyes.

"Better?" Rockhead asked.

"This last year has been torture. Being hungry but can't eat. Thirsty but can't drink. Those hollow bodies Ironside made were so numbing. I was close to losing my mind. I'd forgotten what it felt like," he remarked.

Rockhead looked at him. "What's that? Breathing? Smelling? Feeling?"

"Everything," Stonejaw said with a smile.

A deep voice came from the darkness of the cave's back. "While we are grateful for Ironfire and his sacrifice, the metal bodies in which we returned to life were not exactly ideal. Devil is in the details, I suppose. How is our plan working?"

Rockhead turned his head. "Excellent, Melthorn. We have managed to find bodies for our members who were near insanity. Mostly those who won't be noticed if they disappear or act strangely. Most have seamlessly entered the clans without notice."

"And those who haven't?"

"They are causing chaos as a distraction. Vying for leadership. We have even found other clans that are not from the area."

"New clans? Interesting. Do we have names for these other clans?" Melthorn asked.

Two dragons stepped into the cave. The darkness of the cave peeled off of them.

"I found this body to the north. They call themselves the Solari."

"This one is from the Selenthrax, from the south of here," the other dragon said.

Melthorn smiled. "Interesting."

Chapter 7 Desert Sun

The sun beat down on the desert that encompassed the land north of Mortem. The sand was a mix of brown, red, and yellow. Large sand dunes collected as the wind swept down from the mountains of Mortem. Small oases of green littered the desert, providing water and plant life for the creatures that called the barren landscape home. Large stands of cacti scattered the desert. The white cacti were towering with large needles like daggers sticking out and oval red fruit with small spikes hung at the end of the cactus arms.

Small insects buzzed around an oasis. A small pond of clear water was surrounded by moss and grass. Small cacti grew around the edges of the small amount of vegetation. From the warm sand two black Ferroliths meandered into the oasis. Their bodies showed signs of rust, joints grinding from the sand that had wedged itself into them.

""I know it's hot but, but, but I can't feel it. Can't feel anything."," a feminine voice complained.

"Keep it together. Once we find host bodies, life will be better for us," a masculine voice replied. She growled at him in frustration.

"Focus your mind, love. Remember, we find a dragon, place our fangs into them. Then our ash will transfer to their body. Life will be better," the male voice reassured.

"It's so bright. It's so bright after we were alone in the dark for so long. The darkness was alive, playing with my mind," the female rambled.

"I know, my love, but you must remain focused."

"How do you do it? Stay so calm when we can't feel anything, taste anything. Aaaahhh, it's so maddening."

"My love for you keeps those thoughts to the side. After our death at the hands of the Necrodrakes, I was in the dark as well, looking for you. Then Ironfire brought us back and I found you again."

"I need to move my ash before I lose my mind. I can't, I can't, I - I - I," the female let out a roar of frustration.

"Easy, love. There is word of a clan of dragons that call this desert home. When we find them, you will feel better."

"I want to feel something, anything," she growled.

The male Ferrolith looked up. The pond rippled as something sent vibrations through the ground. He moved around the edge of the pond, positioning himself behind a large cactus. A short distance from the oasis, he saw his prey: a group of dragons were marching their way toward him.

They were large dragons, competing with the Gaiajades for who could claim to be the biggest. Walking on all fours, they held a determined look on their face. Their yellow and white scales shimmer in the sunlight. One stretched its shoulder-mounted wings, showing scale patterns resembling sunrays. On their faces were sharp horns, randomly shaped like licks of fire. The largest dragon led the clan, his body was streaked with orange like a fire had been tattooed on his scales. His head had horns that circled around him like a halo.

"Solari!" he shouted. "We will stop here. Rest. Drink of Wyrm's water. Then we will continue our hunt." He thumped his large tail, which had a flame-like tip, on the ground. The land shook from the force, sand misting up into the air. He scanned the area with his gold eyes as they spread out around the oasis. A shout erupted from within the oasis. A young Solari came running back to the leader.

"Skyblaze! Skyblaze!" the young Solari yelled.

"What is it, Brightray?"

"We found some of Morthauron's spawn."

Skyblaze grunted and hurried to the inside of the oasis. He found the clan surrounding the Ferrolithes. The Solari had their wings spread wide, creating a vision of a sunrise. The two Ferrolithes stayed near each other, turning to keep an eye on the Solari who were yelling at them. Skyblaze walked through the line and stood feet from the Ferroliths.

"Are you the spawn of Morthauron?" he asked.

The female Ferrolith growled.

"Answer me. Are you the spawn of Morthauron?"

The male Ferrolith responded, "Not by choice. We were dead and found ourselves alive in these metal bodies."

"Members of my clan have become missing. Are you responsible for taking them?"

The female Ferrolith hissed. "Not taken. Just used to make us whole again."

"You are an affront to Aururadraca, an insult to the purity of life."

"We didn't ask for this. We just want to live again," the male retorted. "Help us."

Skyblaze looked down at him. "Help you? You have taken and murdered one of mine and you ask for help."

The female Ferrolith begged, "We just want to feel again. I want to feel."

"You are unworthy of the life Auroradraca once bestowed upon you. You insult her with your mere presence."

The female growled and leaped toward Skyblaze. She opened her mouth wide, baring her long fangs. A Solari jumped in front of Skyblaze, tackling her to the ground. A second Solari jumped in, helping to pin her down. She tried to turn her head, snapping her fangs at the nearest Solari.

"I wanna live! Let me live!" she screamed. A third Solari walked up, beside Skyblaze, and sat down on his hind legs. He used his talons to force the female's mouth wide open.

"You wish to feel? To live again?" Skyblaze mocked. "We can help you with that but, first, you must be purified." He opened his mouth and released his breath. Gold and red fire shot out of his mouth and down her throat. The metal of the Ferrolith began to glow red. She screamed as the body began to melt, turning into a pool of liquid. Skyblaze turned to the other Ferrolith. Several Solari had him pinned to the ground. He was struggling to get up.

"No, my love! You monsters!" he growled.

"You are the monster," Skyblaze began. "You had died. You should be held in our great goddess' arms. Instead, you are here. I have never heard of a clan of dragons killing others. Why are you here?"

"You are the murderer here. We just want to live." He began to struggle more. "I, grrrr, just want, grrrr, to live!" He pushed himself up, threw his captors off, eyes red with rage. He charged at Skyblaze, mouth wide, fangs extended. Skyblaze swung his tail, connecting on the Ferrolith's side and crashed hard on the ground. The Ferrolith stood up, struggling with the large dent in his side, his legs bent and unbalanced. A Solari came from behind, swinging his sharp tail, and pierced the Ferrolith. Another Solari swung his tail and broke the front legs. Skyblaze walked toward him.

"Abomination," he said as he released his breath onto the Ferrolith. The metal dragon screamed as the body liquified. The Solari raised their wings high. "Solari! We have found our enemy, whispers of moving death given form. We must find the rest of these creatures and cleanse them from the eyes of Auroradraca!" The clan shouted in unison and went about resting and drinking.

Brightray hung back from the rest of the Solari.

"What troubles you, Brightray?" Skyblaze asked.

"I don't understand."

"What don't you understand?"

"They pleaded for help. The female one was clearly in pain. And we," he paused. "We just ended their lives without trying to help."

Skyblaze glared down at him. "They are unnatural. Death cannot create life. Only the great Auroradraca can do that and she sent us on this journey. We follow her word. Are you questioning our mission? Are you questioning Auroradraca?" His eyes were a dark gold.

"No, sir, never," Brightray said, lowering his head.

Skyblaze remained emotionless. "Never question my decisions. We will exterminate these abominations in her name. Now, go. Get water and rest. We continue our journey to the Inferoth's territory." Skyblaze walked away.

Brightray looked at the metal puddles. Pieces of the Ferroliths stuck out of the smooth surface. He shuddered and walked to the rest of his clan.

Chapter 8 Forest Moon

The night took over the sky of Wyrm. The moon lit up the ground while stars dotted the sky. The forest south of the Aquanox territory was populated with large, dark brown trees. The trees were several stories tall with branches that stretched out wide. On the forest floor, bioluminescent mushrooms and moss covered the ground, adding their own light in the darkness. Small furry animals scurried about the forest floor. Insects chirped in the darkness.

In the center of the forest, a large circular clearing made a hole in the canopy above. The moon shone its light, illuminating the grass. Two large, flat rocks laid in the center. Two Ferroliths laid on their sides by the rocks, motionless. The trees around the circular edge began to shake as a clan of dragons moved through the forest. As they stepped into the clearing, the moon reflected off their silvery scales, giving a radiant glow to them. They walked on their hind legs with long tails to keep them balanced. Their forearms were long with wings folded underneath. The neck was long with two long crescent shaped horns coming out the back of their heads. The dragons' eyes were large with blue and silver shaded eyes. They took a few steps forward and stopped.

A large female dragon scanned the area. She looked at the rocks. "Shinestar. Where are you?"

A young female dragon walked up behind her. "I am here, Lunawind."

"Are these the dragons that you saw steal our Selenthrax sister, yes, yes?"

"Yes."

Lunawind looked around. She watched for movement but saw none coming from the Ferrolith. She pointed at a group of three Selenthrax, motioning them to investigate. They released their breath, a thick black shadowy mist covered the area. The rest waited patiently. The mist crept along the ground and rested against the rocks. A misty arm of blackness reached out and felt the Ferrolith bodies. One body rocked side to side. The other Ferrolith made a groan that vibrated against the metal sides. The three Selenthrax flapped their wings, showing their dark underside with constellations adorning their wing skin. The mist thinned out as the rest of the dragons moved closer. Lunawind approached the three dragons.

"This one appears to be dead. The other seems to be alive," one of the three said.

Lunawind stretched her neck closer to the Ferrolith. It hissed at her and snapped its fangs at her.

"Interesting, interesting, interesting," she said. "You're alive but not alive." She traced a talon along the metal body. "You have shape but no flesh. How are you not dead?"

The Ferrolith breathed, paused at each word, "Morthauron. Revived. Us."

Her eyes grew large. "Morthauron made you? He gave you life? How?" The Ferrolith groaned. Lunawind slapped it. "Speak! How did Morthauron give you life!"

"He put . . . our ash . . . in to . . . these bodies." Each word seemed labored.

She looked at him in disgust. "What did you do with my tribe member? Where is she?"

The Ferrolith tried to laugh. "Heh . . . found her . . . here. Friend . . . took her."

"Took her where?" Lunawind demanded, anger in her voice.

"Took . . . body. Ash . . . in her."

"Morthauron gave you the ability to move your ash into a new body. Interesting, interesting. So, why are you dying?"

"Not . . . dying. Just pretending." The Ferrolith's eyes glowed red. He turned his head and leaped at Lunawind. She jumped backward. The Ferrolith barely missed. He started running toward here. The closest Selentrhaxes spew their breath to the ground. The liquid darkness raced to the Ferrolith, exploding from the ground as long spikes. The Ferrolith was pierced in several directions. He tried to move and wiggle his way off the spikes but found himself to be stuck. Lunawind walked up behind him. He rolled his eyes back to see her, snapping his jaw.

"Not very nice, no, no," she said as she traced her talon along the back of his skull. "Not nice being sneaky like that, no, no. We could have been friends, yes, yes, allies. We both worship Morthauron. The god of death now can bring life, yes, yes."

"I don't worship him. He brought my clan back but at the cost of our sanity."

She gave him a deadly glare. "Do not speak ill of Morthauron, no, no. He has a plan for all of us, yes, yes."

"Release me," the Ferrolith demanded.

Lunawind cocked her head. She traced her talons along the seams of his body. She slid her fingers into the holes created by the spikes. Sliding both her hands in the holes, she ripped the Ferrolith in half. There was a brief scream from him. A gray mist came out of the body and faded away. The empty shell fell to the ground as the breath disappeared.

"Morthauron has given us a sign. He has given us a way to continue living after our death so that we may worship him for eternity. Come. We must find the rest of these creatures and learn how they continued to live." The Selenthrax raised their arms, displaying their starry wings. The green clearing was wrapped in darkness. Shinestar looked at her tribe with worry. A pair of green flowers moved backward into the forest.

Chapter 9 Let the Tournament Begin

Mudball sat in his little field of flowers. The Gaiajades were beginning to gather around the fighting circle. The Florastryx started to feel more comfortable in their new home, showing the sheer number that were hidden. Mudball was impressed by how well they hid as well as how friendly and energetic they were. They pounced on each other and played, tackling each other and rolling around. Mudball sat on a flat rock in the middle of the field. Petalspear and Thornseed flew beside him and sat down.

"Are yous still mads at us?" Thornseed asked.

"No, I just," he paused. "I can't back out of the fight. I have to do it. But Coalash is a really good fighter. And so, so, so . . ." He could not find the word he wanted.

"Bigs," Petalspear finished.

"Yeah, bigs," Mudball agreed. "Hey, how are there so many of you now?"

"Wez travels fast," Thornseed replied. "Fastest flyers on Wyrm. Gift froms Tuzu."

"Tuzu? Who's that?" Mudball asked.

"He creates us," Petalspear said.

"Like he is your dad?"

"No, god of plants."

Mudball was puzzled. "I only know Auroradraca and Morthauron. I've never heard of Tuzu."

"Legends says he works fors Auroradracas," Petalspear said. "Helps hers withs plants. Mades us likes hims."

Mudball said, "So there are more dragon gods? Crazy."

Mudball looked around as more Gaiajades gathered. He felt a weight in his chest. He wondered what Oldstone would think of him. The deceased leader of the Gaiajades made Mudball realize that he was not a great fighter, that he needed to train more. Once everything had calmed down from the Necrodrakes, Mudball had tried to learn to fight more. He practiced in the fighting ring but also tried to meet up with Rageskin. It was rough to train with him but Mudball felt like he learned from their encounters. Rageskin had shown him different ways to use his crystals and tail as a weapon. Out of the corner of his eye he saw tall grass shake. He turned around so he could see it better. He was searching for moving flowers when the grass suddenly stopped.

"Hey, Thornseed, do you have a count of your tribe?"

Thornseed and Petalspear looked around quickly, their heads twitching quickly. They counted out loud. "Everyone here," they said together.

"So no one should be in the tall grass? Or have wings that look like grass?"

"Nopes," Petalspear said.

The grass shook again. He saw someone moving. Mudball could make out a dark outline. "Hello," he said. "Who's there? It's safe to come out, I won't hurt you."

The grass stopped. He could hear someone trying to breathe quietly. "Please don't be a Necrodrake, please don't be a Necrodrake, please don't be a Necrodrake." He crept closer to the grass. "Hello?" he asked. "It's okay. I won't harm you."

Soft footsteps walked toward Mudball. The grass bent down and a Ferrolith stumbled forward. She was slightly smaller than Mudball. She kept her head low as her leg joints cracked with each movement.

"Please don't hurt me," she said in a quiet, echoey voice. The sun reflected off her metal scales.

"You're, you're a," he stuttered. "A Ferrolith. But Ironfire said he was the last one. And you're a bit different from how he looked. You don't look -" he paused as he tried to find the right words.

"Alive," she said quietly.

"No, no, no, not that but, um, yeah. Like a moving metal tree or something."

"I've not thought about my condition like that."

"So, sorry, this is weird. I thought Ferroliths were all gone but here you are. Are there more of you?"

She turned her head to not look at him.

"Sorry, sorry. I'm being rude. I've got this big fight coming up and I'm not thinking straight. My name is Mudball."

She slowly turned her head back toward him. "Steelheart."

"Cool name. Do you need help or anything? Lost?"

Steelheart waited to respond. "I'm not lost. I ran away from my clan. I have to do something cruel but I don't want to do it."

Memories of Oldstone flashed in Mudball's eyes. "I understand. Look, stay here. Maybe go back into the grass. Things are kinda tense right now."

The Florastryx slowly came out of hiding. "Oh, this is Petalspear and Thornseed," Mudball said, pointing with his head. "Their clan is hiding out here as well."

Steelheart tilted her head. "So tiny. And pretty."

The two Florastryx leaders beamed with pride. "Has you heards of Tuzu?" Petalspear asked. Steelheart shook her head. "Wez tell you abouts him." Florastryx huddled around her, creating a bouquet of moving flowers.

"Have fun, guys," Mudball said as he headed to the gathering. "Man, what is going on around here? New dragons showing up. Fighting going on. What a day," he thought to himself.

The Gaiajades were standing around the fighting circle. They were yelling and stomping their feet as the first match had started. Mudball wiggled his way through the crowd, thinking of how the fights went. The rules were simple: Knock your opponent out or make them submit. No breath allowed. Coalash rushed at his opponent. The other Gaiajade turned his head, ramming their skulls together. They grunted, trying to push the other. Coalash slid his head to the right, lowered his front leg, and turned his crystals toward his opponent. They slashed along the ribcage and down to the leg. The crowd roared at the move. Mudball gulped as the Gaiajade screamed in pain, blood running down and dripping to the ground. Coalash turned left and got his head under his opponent. He craned his neck, sending the Gaiajade into the air above. Coalash stood on his back legs. As the Gaiajade came back down, he put his front legs into the body and slammed the falling Gaiajade into the ground, Coalash forced his weight into his legs. The Gaiajade thumped against the ground, bones snapping from under Coalash's feet.

"I quit!" the Gaiajade screamed as pain raced through his body. Several Gaiajade rushed to his side to help him. Coalash roared with pleasure with his victory. He turned to look at Mudball and smiled, flashing his long canines. He went into the crowd, walking away with Stonejaw and Rockhead at his side. Mudball looked at him in fright. He moved his tongue along his canines to see if his teeth were as long as Coalash's.

Gempath stood up. "Mudball! Greyquarry! You are up!"

Mudball gave a quiet whine as he entered the fighting circle. Greyquarry strode in. He was a little bigger and two years older than Mudball. His back crystals were irregular in size and placement. He had small spiky crystals that dotted his shoulders and brow.

"Are you ready to go down?" Greyquarry jested.

"How about I just give up now and you win?" Mudball offered. He looked at Gempath who shook her head "No."

Greyquarry charged at Mudball. He yipped and lept to the side. Greyquarry lost his footing and crashed on his side. Several Gaiajades laughed at him. He shook his head, dust flying off. He pawed at the ground with his front legs and ran at Mudball again. Mudball began to back up. He stopped and curled into a ball. Mudball's crystals scratched Greyquarry's underside as he went over. Greyquarry yelped in pain. He landed on his feet and growled in frustration.

"If you want to lose so badly, stop defending yourself!"

"I'm trying. My body isn't listening!"

The crowd chuckled at Mudball's response. Greyquarry got mad. "Stop treating this like a joke! We are fighting for the leadership of our clan." He charged at Mudball who tried to back up. He turned his body so his side would take the hit. His tail swung wildly and smacked Greyquarry across the face. The sound was deafening; the crowd quieted from the sudden slap. Greyquarry stopped. Blood trickled down his face and began to hiss angrily.

"I am so sorry," Mudball began. "I didn't mean to. I really didn't."

Greyquarry's crystals started to glow red. He growled and turned to Mudball. The crowd behind Mudball moved out of the way.

"Don't do it. Don't do it. You'll get dis-," Mudball pleaded as a beam of red breath shot at him. He flew backward and landed on his back with a thump. Greyquarry growled in frustration.

"You stupid coward! Look what you made me do!"

Gempath stood up. "Greyquarry is disqualified. Mudball wins! We will allow both combatants to rest before the final match later tonight." The crowd cheered.

Mudball rolled over to his side and plopped to his stomach. "I am so dead."

Chapter 10 Whisper's Trial

Whisper and Rageskin flew through the open air. The wind wisped by them while the ground hurried along. They had been silent for most of their trip.

"Are you sure you want to do this?" Rageskin asked. "Things aren't going to be the same for you."

Whisper hesitated. "I do. When we were fighting the Necrodrakes, we kept going on about uniting the clans. I think things have gotten better but only just better. Trade is better. The clans work together on projects but we still just do our own thing and only interact when we have to."

"True. But are you sure you want to go through the ceremony? Having lava grafted to your skin?"

"Not really but I will. How bad will it hurt?"

"Like fire is eating you alive. Remember, I had trouble doing it."

Whisper thought about it. "So if I get it on the first try, does that make me more of an Inferoth than you?"

He lowered his head. "Technically, a little bit."

Whisper smiled. "Grrr. I'm angry and wanna fight all the time. Roar!"

Rageskin looked at her. "We're not all like that."

"Ok, name one Inferoth who isn't."

He pondered. Whisper looked at him with inquisitive eyes. "Well?"

"I'm thinking, I'm thinking. Being the leader of the Inferoths keeps me busy. I don't notice everyone's behavior every moment."

Whisper flew underneath him, her arms and wings outstretched. She spun so she could look up at him.

"Name one."

He paused. "I can't."

She smiled.

"Why do you do this to me?"

"Do what?"

"I'm a ruler of a clan. I make decisions, deal with challenges to my throne and leadership. I tend to be angry and aggressive like you said but when I'm around you," he stopped.

"What happens?"

"All that hostility and anger just lessens."

They stared into each other's eyes, lost to the Inferoth's volcano that was approaching them. The heat from the volcano greeted them.

"Um, we are here," Rageskin said.

"Yeah," Whisper replied as she turned so her back was to Rageskin. She had a mix of emotions going through her. Fear. Anxiety. Love?

Blackwing flew from the mouth of the volcano with Darkheart trailing behind him. They stopped mid-flight in front of Rageskin and Whisper.

"My liege," Blackwing said as he bowed his head. "I see the Zeyphrion has joined us. Are you ready for your trial?"

Whisper gulped. "I think so."

Blackwing glared at her. "Very well. Follow me."

Darkheart hissed at Whisper. "If you manage to live through this, I will challenge you for queenhood and burn your pretty little feathers." She turned and flew toward the volcano.

"She's nice," Whisper joked.

"She's my queen if you don't make it," Rageskin said with a solemn look. "Let's go."

They angled down into the volcano opening. The heat from the lava down at the bottom overwhelmed them. Rageskin was not bothered by it. Whisper could feel her skin heat up. Columns rose out of the lava pool, anchored together by stone bridges. Inferoths lined up along the side of the volcano, some watching from their small cave homes. Others were lined up on the bridges, many were female. Blackwing waited in the center of where the bridges met and a large polished cauldron held lava. An elder Inferoth stood by the cauldron, holding a matching ladle. They landed. Whisper looked around, trying to take everything in. Some Inferoths were yelling at her. Others waited quietly. Darkheart was nearby. Whisper tried not to shake from nervousness.

Blackwing held up his hand. The clan quieted.

"We are here to bear witness," he shouted to the clan. "To witness our leader's chosen candidate for queen go through the armor trial." The clan grunted in unison. "To witness a Zeyphrion prove that she is worthy of our king!" The clan yelled. "Or to witness her weakness." Some of the Inferoths cheered.

"You don't belong here!" Darkheart shouted. "You won't be our queen!"

Rageskin stepped toward her. "She has agreed to the test. You agreed to allow her the chance to prove herself. Now, shut it!" His eyes pierced through Darkheart. She smiled and crossed her arms.

Whisper looked at Rageskin. "Any last minute advice?"

"Don't scream. Keep it inside. You'll be seen as weak if you do. Control the pain. Once you can tolerate it, shape the lava into armor or weapons. If you have any of the gift left from Auroradraca left, use it to heal yourself."

"Anything else?"

"Don't pass out. No one will catch you." His face was grim. Whisper looked at the bridge and realized how narrow it was. The lava pool below reminded her what could happen if she did pass out.

Whisper stepped up to the cauldron. The Inferoths watched in anticipation. Darkheart glared at her. The elder Inferoth grabbed the ladle and dipped it into the lava. It glowed bright as he brought it out. Steam rolled off the surface of the liquid rock. Whisper took a deep breath in. Her mind was racing. She knew it was going to hurt. She wondered if her magic would appear and help her. Raising her right arm, she said, "I'm ready."

Inferoths began to stomp in unison. The elder hung the ladle above her forearm and waited. A single drop fell from the bottom and onto her arm. Her skin hissed in anger. Whisper clamped her mouth shut; she closed her eyes to disguise the pain. She felt a warm glow in her chest as it traveled through to her arm. The pain in her arm disappeared. The elder turned the ladle and bright lava layered onto her forearm. Her mind was panicking. Her breathing quickened as a scream tried to escape her throat. Whisper forced the scream down as she smelled her burning flesh. The warmth from her chest reached her injury grew as the pain increased. The pain subsided as the lava began to cool. She used her left fingertips to spread the lava. New pain registered as she shaped it. She knew her healing gift was helping her and thanked Auroradraca in her head for the magic. Her clawed fingers cooled as her gift took away the pain, her talons melting off. She could feel them regrow as fast as they melted. A drip of lava landed on her wing. She almost yipped at the sharpness of it but caught herself. She finished shaping the lava, creating armor that wrapped around her forearm and met where her wing attached. Whisper moved her arm toward the elder. Her arm vibrated from the lasting pain as he inspected it. He reached down into a stone bucket and pulled out a cup of water. He methodically poured it over the hot rock. Steam hissed off as Whisper tried not to yell in pain. He reached and emptied another cup of water. He looked it over one more time and turned to Rageskin, nodding his head. Rageskin walked around the cauldron and leaned into her.

"You did it," he whispered as he raised her armored arm. "Whisper has passed the armor test and has proven herself to be worthy of being my queen!" The Inferoths shouted in agreement. Darkheart and Blackwing flew to the bridge.

"No!" Darkheart growled. "She cannot be queen." Blackwing stood behind her.

"She has proven herself," Rageskin replied. "She will be my queen."

"She is just a Zeyphrion. She is not worthy of being your queen."

"Enough!" Rageskin ordered.

"I challenge you to combat," Darkheart hissed.

"Can she do that?" Whisper asked.

Rageskin crossed his arms. "I'm not happy about it but yes she can."

Whisper looked at him with concern. "Do we have to fight right now? My arm still hurts."

"Ah, poor little hatchling," Darkheart mocked. "Does your little arm hurt? Need to make yourself pretty before you lose? Maybe I'll just disfigure your face so Rageskin doesn't find you attractive anymore."

Whisper felt a fire lit inside her. She hated that her clan was seen as weak and just being pretty. She wanted to end that here.

Blackwing asked, "Whisper, do you accept this challenge or do you rescind your title?"

Whisper locked eyes with Darkheart. "I accept."

The crowd roared in excitement. Many started to stomp their feet in unison. Blackwing held his arms up. The Inferoths quieted down.

"Darkheart has challenged Whisper for the right to be our queen. The winner shall be decided by knockout or submission."

The Inferoths cheered for the rules. Some chanted Whisper's name while others cheered for her opponent. Darkheart lined up in front of Whisper. The Inferoth had a height and size advantage over Whisper. They stared into each other's eyes, waiting for the other to blink. Darkheart spit in Whisper's face. Whisper's cheek burned where it landed. Darkheart chuckled and backed up. Whisper did the same, the side edges of the bridge reminding her of how much room she had to work with. She reached back and pulled her bo staff out from under her purple feathers that flowed down her back. Darkheart grabbed a large blade from a sheath that attached to her left bicep. Blackwing raised his hand up. Both dragons took a fighting stance. He looked at both, giving Darkheart a glance and nod. She smiled and leaped as he lowered his arm. She reared her bladed hand back and thrusted toward Whisper. Whisper raised her bo staff to block her. The weapons clanged, sparks flying off. Darkheart used her free hand to punch Whisper in the stomach. She stepped back, trying to catch the breath that left her body. Darkheart ran up to her, punching her across the face, followed by an uppercut with her blade hand. Whisper fumbled backward to miss the blade.

"I really like this body," Darkheart remarked. Whisper looked at her with a pained face. "It's amazing that the Inferoths don't just take over the clans. So much strength and power." She kicked Whisper in the ribs. Whisper tried to swing her staff as her back arched the kick. The staff slapped Darkheart across the face. She took a few steps back and spat out blood. Whisper tried another swing but missed. Darkheart grabbed her by the wing and tossed her into the air. The crowd cheered at the move. Whisper flapped her wings, trying to regain her balance. Darkheart bulleted into her, driving her shoulder and claws into Whisper. Pain screamed at her. Darkheart wrapped her in a bearhug. Whisper swung her armored forearm against her head, breaking off a horn. Darkheart released Whisper and felt the broken area.

"It took her so long to grow that," Darkheart said.

"What?"

Darkheart realized what she had said. "Nothing, little air dragon." Darkheart flapped her wings and flew to Whisper. Whisper tried to dodge. Darkheart grabbed her by the ankle and tossed her down to the bridge. Whisper thumped against the stone. Darkheart reared back and blew her breath at Whisper. It came out molten and turned into spikes as it cooled in the air. Whisper rolled, barely avoiding the shrapnel.

"That's not Inferoth breath," she thought to herself as Darkheart slammed into her. The bridge began to crack. Darkheart pinned her shoulders to the ground.

She leaned in and said, "I will be queen and we will take over the Inferoths."

Whisper breathed her cold breath into Darkheart's face. Ice formed and covered. Darkheart muttered under the ice mask. She tried to pull it off but found it stuck to her face. Whisper stood up and swung her bo staff. The ice mask cracked from the force. She swung again, catching Darkheart's skull. Whisper swung one last time, uppercutting Darkheart, shattering the ice. Darkheart landed on her back and passed out. The Inferoths cheered for Whisper's victory.

Rageskin walked up to Whisper. "That was awesome. You'll make a good Interoth queen."

Whisper was trying to catch her breath as the adrenaline began to wear off and pain claimed parts of her body. "We need to talk. Something weird is going to happen and somehow she's a part of it."

Blackwing picked up Darkheart and flew away with her. "You needed to win."

Darkheart groggily said, "I haven't had much time with this body. I know everything she knows so imitating her is easy but fighting on two legs is new."

"We must maintain appearances. You were cocky. Melthorn will not be pleased. We must change plans." Blackwing flew out of the volcano.

Rageskin watched as the duo left. "I fear Blackwing may be in on it as well."

There was a commotion at the base of the volcano, where the stairwell for other clans to enter the volcano. Several Inferoth were guarding the entrance as the Solari entered. Skyblaze walked in first, flanked by a Solari who carried empty Ferrolith shells.

"Leader of the Inferoths! I will have words with you!" Skyblaze boomed.

Chapter 11 Knowledge is Power

"I can't believe they just left," Stream said as he slid out of the water and onto the dry surface of his tablet cave. It wasn't really his but he felt like it was. Dreamwave showed it to him and Stream had taken advantage of the knowledge contained in the stone tablets. He looked at the stack of tablets that he left when he went to the clan meeting. He could feel something major was going on but could not put a fin on it. He slithered to his tablets, trying to use his magic to feel for the one he needed. Nothing. He let out a sigh.

"There has to be something. There's a new painting that appeared but I've only been able to find one tablet that sort've explains it but not enough to make sense. Maybe it's a warning of a new war that is coming? Sometimes Auroradraca summons new tablets. At least, I think she does. Dreamwave never really explained where the tablets come from. Or the ceiling paintings." He looked around. Stream had every tablet memorized. Where it was located and what it talked about. He even started to organize them by subject. Nothing explained the painting to his satisfaction and no mention anywhere of other dragon clans.

He slithered through the cave. He scanned the built-in shelves that held the tablets. Each tablet was in its place. Nothing caught his magic. There were less shelves as he ventured toward the back of the cave. The light lessened, with bioluminescent algae growing on the walls that gave just enough to see by. Stream has ventured into this part of the cave several times, always looking for something that he missed, to find a new tablet he overlooked after looking over a hundred times.. He looked at the smooth walls with the occasional crack that spiderwebbed across the surface. Three reading spires came out of the ground. He never really thought about why these were at the back of the cave as there was not enough light to read properly and no tablets.

"I wonder." He closed his eyes and held his breath. His magic gently tugged at skull, pulling him to the right. He turned his head, the tugging pulled him forward. He slid and his muzzle tapped the wall. He opened his eyes.

"It's just a wall. There's nothing here." Something scratched at his skull. "There's nothing at all." More scratching. He turned his head up and down, left and right. Finally, he noticed a small patch of moss growing in a straight line. He traced it with his mouth. "Really wish I had arms," he thought as he got some moss on his tongue, slightly gagging him. As he stretched his body up, he found some of the moss made a square shape. He cocked his head in puzzlement. More skull scratching. He leaned in and pressed the shape with his nose. The square slid back with a grinding sound. Stream lowered himself and slithered backward. The wall shook as it split in half. Each half slid away from the other. Stream coughed as stale air hit him in the face. A soft glow came to his eyes as he finished coughing. Glowing from moss on the walls came from within the large room. It seemed larger than his tablet room and seemed to go on forever. He went into the room and reading spires littered the large space. A pool with crudely cut bricks surrounding it took residence in the middle. The floor angled like stairs in spots, giving the room an uneven look. The walls were carved with shelves which tablets rested on. Stream could not count the number of stone tablets that he could see.

"This is amazing," he said. "How did I not know this was here the whole time? Does Dreamwave know about this place? If he did, why didn't he tell me about it?" His heart was racing at the thought of reading all the tablets before him. He slithered about, glancing at the first tablet he could read, trying to figure out what kind of order, if any, they were in. His mind was racing, not letting him focus. Frustrated with his own excitement, he grabbed a tablet at random and wrapped around a reading spire. It was a large rock that came from the cave floor and flattened at the top. He set it down and took a deep breath to calm himself. The writing was familiar to what he had been reading in the tablet room.

"*The Inferoths have settled in the volcano. Thank Auroradraca they stayed there. Their body heat is too much. Always warming up our waters.*"

Stream chuckled. "Apparently, Inferoths were jerks back then too. Whenever this was." He continued reading. "*All the clans have decided that they would prefer their own territory. The Gaiajades, being farmers, took to the plains between all the territories. The Zeyphrions used magic to lift their islands into the sky. We Aquanox took to the waters to the south. The Inferoths were content with the volcano and the burnt land that surrounded them. The Ferroliths tended to be nomadic and would visit the clans. I hear they are near the lands north of the Inferoths.*" Stream paused. "They were in Mortem? So this had to have happened before the first Necrodrake war." He continued reading.

"*I will miss my friends in the other clans but this is probably for the better. The Solari and Selenthrax are too much to be around. They take their beliefs in Auroradraca and Morthauron too seriously for anyone's liking. Good riddance. And the Florastryx are a bit annoying. Hopefully, they will find a home that is safe for their small stature.*"

Stream read in confusion. "There are more clans in our area? Why haven't we come across them at any point?" He bit the tablet and slid over to a shelf. He grabbed another one and went back to the spire. He started to read it.

"*I had a vision. Morthauron will attempt to create life twice. The first will put their ash into dead bodies to bring life and spread their evil to others. The second clan's ash will become corrupted by Morthauron, bringing unnatural life through theft and blood. Forgotten gods will return.*" He paused. "Okay, the first must be the Necrodrakes. But who are the second ones? Maybe one of those other clans?"

Stream was lost in thought when he heard a splashing of water and voices. He slithered out to the front of the cave. The stone walls began to close behind him. As he entered the cave, he saw two small dragons on the edge of the waterline. They had green bodies with a yellow hue where their back wings connected. Their wings were bright, one being pink and the other being white. They looked scared as they looked at the water and turned to Stream.

"Pleaze, helps us," the pink one pleaded.

"Yes, pleaze," the other repeated. "Helps us froms the crazy dragon."

The water exploded as an Aquanox roared into the room. His skin was dark. He swished his neck back and forth as if an invisible enemy was punching him. He was arguing with himself.

"Stop fighting me," a voice growled out of him.

"Let me go," a more natural voice said back.

Stream recognized the natural voice. "Raindrop? Is that you? Aren't you with Riverbank's tribe?"

The Aquanox stopped. He lowered his head and stared at Stream. "Raindrop? That's his name," the growling voice said. "He would not give that up."

His eyes shifted to panic. "Stream, help me please."

"Raindrop, what is happening to you?"

"I'm happening to him," the growl retorted. He leapt out of the water at Stream. Stream moved to the left. Raindrop splattered on the rock floor. The two small dragons yipped and scattered away. "I'll deal with you two later," he growled as he rose. He hissed at Stream, large canines extending out. Raindrop slid to Stream who shot water at him using his breath. The defense stopped Raindrop for a moment. Stream went up to Raindrop and headbutted him. He shook his head and returned one of his own, stunning Stream. Raindrop wrapped his long muscular body around Stream. Their bodies were intertwined, the mast-like wings outstretched. Stream had been told about the deep water Aquanox being strong from the water pressure but he never bothered to follow up on it. Unfortunately, he discovered the truth of the information the hard way. He tried to take a breath but when he would, Raindrop would squeeze tighter.

"You know, I didn't really want this body but I was desperate," the growling voice said. "I didn't think you Aquanoxes would be any good for fighting. I was wrong on that." He laughed as he gripped tighter on Stream. Stream could not take a breath. His eyes began to roll into his skull when Raindrop screamed. The pink dragon had dug her claws into Raindrop's eyelids, pulling them outstretched. The white dragon breathed a sticky sap into his exposed eyes. Raindrop released his grip. Air rushed into Stream's lungs as Raindrop slithered away and growled in frustration.

"You stupid little pests!" he shouted. His eyes were red and scarred as he tried to look around. "That burns! Once I can see you, you'll make a great snack!" He lowered his head. Suddenly, it went back up.

"I'm blind! I'm blind!" Raindrop screamed, panic in his voice. He started to move about the cave, smashing into reading spires.

"Raindrop," Stream gasped. His muscles still hurt. Every movement felt like he was moving in wet sand. "Calm down!"

Raindrop crashed into a shelf of tablets. The tablets fell to the ground, shattering. Raindrop continued racing around the cave, running headlong into the walls, arguing with himself.

"Help me!"

"Stop it!"

"I can't see!"

"Stupid dragon, stop!"

Raindrop smashed the side of his head into a larger shelving wall. The ceiling paintings cracked, pieces falling onto him. He continued hitting the wall.

"Stop!" the voice growled.

"No!" Raindrop replied.

"Stop it!"

"Get out of my head!"

Stream did not know what to do. He watched as the Aquanox fought himself. Slowly, each slam against the wall weakened. Tablets kept falling and breaking. Raindrop did one last slam against the wall and fell limp to the cave floor. Stream went up to him. Raindrop laid on the ground, bloodied.

"Raindrop? Are you with me?"

Raindrop tried to take a breath. "I got lost from the others. We saw weird shapes in the distance."

"What are you saying?"

"Something from the ocean was coming but I was attacked before we reached the ocean." A death rattle came out on the last word. A silver cloud floated out of Raindrop's mouth. Stream stared at it. As it thinned out, Stream swore he heard a scream.

The two small dragons came out from under a stack of rocks, shaking dust from their wings.

"He okays?" the white one asked.

Stream shook his head.

"Sorrys. Hims a friend of yous?" the pink one asked.

"I didn't really know him but I knew his tribe. They had left not that long ago to form their own clan." Stream paused. "Who are you? What clan are you?"

"Iz Thornroot," the white one said.

"Iz Lilypetal," the pink one said. "Wez Florastryx." She flexed her wings.

"Your wings," Stream said as he inspected them. "They look like water lilies."

"Helps us to hides," Lilypetal responded. "Many bigs dragons. Wez little dragons."

"Why haven't I seen your clan before? Have you been here the whole time and I just missed you?"

"Wez come from lands past scarys black mountains," Thornroot explained. "Hads to leaves cause of means dragons."

Stream said, "You must be north of Mortem. What did the mean dragons look like?"

"Walks on fours like us but big bigs. Bright colors," Lilypetal said as she imitated. "Breaths like fire, very hots. Rude toos."

"No like us cause wez believe in Tuzu," Thornroot added in. "Theys like, Florastryx wrongs. Only Auroradracas. Grrr. Chases us outs."

Stream tried to take in the information. "Wow, okay. That is something new. So why was Raindrop attacking you."

"Wez got lost from clan," Thornroot started to explain. "Wez stop for drinks when means dragons attacks us. Scattered everywheres. Wez hide in river, took us to place where wez found yous friend. He looked hurts."

Lilypetal continued, "He had two holes in necks. Strange metal dragon by hims. Wez tap its. Hollow. Weirds, wez think. He comes awakes. Asks what happens to him. Asks us to takes him homes. Then he argues with selfs. Gets mads. Gets sads. Chases us. Somehow wez found you."

Stream could not believe what he was hearing. He looked over at the damage that was caused by Raindrop. Most of the tablets had fallen and broken into pieces. He had read most of them but no one else would be able to in the future. The two Florastryx hopped up on different piles of broken tablets.

"Sorrys about rock collections," Lilypetal said.

"Wez help to puts backs?" Thornroot asked. "Wez good at helpings."

"It's fine," Stream said as he moved to the back of the cave. He thought about opening the new part of the cave but he hesitated. He really did not know these new dragons. They seemed to be telling the truth but they could be the reason why Raindrop went mad. Stream tried to figure out what to do next. The Florastryx were trying to figure out how to lift up a heavy piece of tablet.

"Are you guys good at swimming?" Stream asked with a smile.

The Florastryx perked up. "Wez good."

Chapter 12 Crown of Grass

Mudball paced back and forth, wearing a path into the flowers. Thornseed and Petalspear sat on a large rock and watched while Steelheart laid on the ground.

"This isn't good, this isn't good," Mudball repeated over and over. He was muttering to himself. "I can't beat him, I just can't."

Thornseed leaned over to whisper, "Friends Mudball is dones for?"

"Probablies," Petalspear replied. "Most definitelys."

"You guys aren't helping him," Steelheart said. "Mudball, is Coalash that good a fighter? If I remember right Gaiajades weren't really into fighting."

"We aren't," Mudball said as he continued on his trail. "I mean, we do when we have to but we don't go looking for fights. Coalash is the best fighter we got. He trains everyone."

Thornseed said, "Hez done fors."

"Cans Mudballs just quits? No fights?" Petalspear said as she raised her arms. "Iz give ups, Iz give ups."

"I wish. You can't just quit. You have to fight, get beat up, and then you can quit."

Steelheart lowered her head and laid flat on the grass. She let out a pained sigh.

"Are you okay?" Mudball asked. "Are you in pain?"

Steelheart had a sad tone to her voice. "Sort've but not really. This body will only last for so long."

Mudball looked at her puzzled. "Your body?"

Steelheart paused herself. She knew she had said too much without thinking. A growl stirred in her chest. "You pathetic, whimpering, sad excuse for a dragon. You can become the leader of your clan but you come to your flower bed and cry and whine about it rather than thinking of a way to defeat your opponent."

The Florastryx hiding in the grass moved away from her, their flower-mimicking wings marking their migration. Mudball stood motionless. Steelheart had been so nice until now. Her eyes glowed red. Mudball slowly charged his back crystals. Steelheart growled, her long canines extending out of her mouth. Mudball's crystals had a bright white glow.

"Steelheart, I don't know what you're talking about but please, stop."

"Your body is so strong but you are so weak minded. Just a child playing as a hero. I-" Steelheart hesitated. Her canines retracted and eyes became a soft blue. She turned her head a little.

"Oh no. No no no no. I can't. I don't want to hurt you or anyone but I want to live, to feel," Steelheart said with sadness and worry in her voice. She turned and ran off.

"Steelheart, wait!" Mudball shouted but she was already too far. "Thornpetal, can one of your clan follow her?"

Thornpetal shook her head. "Orangeblossom, follows," she ordered. A small Florastryx fluttered up, its orange wings beating fast and flew after Steelheart.

Mudball was still in shock. "Why'd she get all mad? I know I just met her but dang, no reason for all that."

A dark green Gaiajade came up behind Mudball. The Florastryx hid as flowers. "It's time," he said. Mudball gulped.

Mudball made his way to the fighting circle. Coalash was already there as Gaiajades positioned themselves to get a good view.

"He's so huge," Mudball thought to himself. "And scary. Really, what can I do?" Coalash stood like a statue. "He's breathing, right? Oh, no, no. This is not going to end well for me." Coalash turned his head slowly toward Mudball. Mudball's chest filled with ice. "I'm so dead."

Rockhead and Stonejaw walked up to Coalash.

Stonejaw said, "She seems to be playing up the role pretty well."

"I don't see any punctures on the neck," Rockhead noted. "She should've taken over the kid. I have learned that one helped to defeat the Necrodrakes."

Coalash looked again at Mudball. "No matter. This body is stronger than all here. Taking over the Gaiajades will be easier than I thought."

Gempath entered at the edge of the circle between the combatants. The crowd hushed.

"Coalash, are you ready?" She asked.

He grunted.

"Mudball, are you ready?"

"No, I'm not. Can we schedule it for next week? I have a slight illness," Mudball thought in his head. "Yes," is what came out of his mouth.

Gempath looked at both Gaiajades one last time. "Begin!" The crowd roared in excitement.

"Is there any way we can just-" Mudball began as Coalash rushed him. Coalash lowered his head and slammed into Mudball. He went tumbling, end over end, to the edge of the circle. Mudball could barely catch his breath. He got to his feet as Coalash swung his tail down at Mudball's head. A loud crack echoed through the air. Mudball went to his belly. Coalash bit down on a back gem and tossed Mudball to the center. Mudball thumped on the ground. As he tried to stand up, Coalash slammed a nose gem into Mudball's shoulder. He gasped in pain as Coalash pushed him around the circle. Coalash raised his head and tossed him above. Mudball was spinning as he came down. The crystals on his tail collided with the side of Coalash's head. Mudball landed, crystal side down, onto Coalash's broad shoulders. Coalash aggressively roared as he tried to buck Mudball off. Mudball's tail kept slapping Coalash at the top of his head, each blow giving him pause. He came to an abrupt stop, loosening Mudball. Mudball tumbled to the ground, trying to get the blood that had rushed to his head moved. Coalash kicked Mudball in the ribs. He went to the ground and slid a few feet. Coalash placed a front leg on Mudball and pressed down. His back crystals began to glow.

"Stupid, little runt," he said. "What makes you think-"

Mudball was shaking from fear. He heard the humming of the crystals go silent. He opened one eye. Coalash had stopped, his eyes looked different.

"Help me," he pleaded.

Mudball was confused. Coalash's crystals began to glow again as his eyes shifted from a brown to a red pigment. "I don't know what you did to this body but you will pay for it, Mudball," he snarled, flashing long canines. His crystals glowed brighter. Mudball wiggled underneath the heavy foot. "Time to-" he paused.

"Mudball, please. This is me. Someone took over-"

"Quiet, you. Why won't you die?"

"Mudball, stop him."

The crystals grew brighter, emitting a louder hum.

"Coalash! Control your breath!" Gempath shouted. "Or you will be disqualified!"

Coalash began to shake his head as he stepped off Mudball. He aggressively slammed his head to each side, arguing with himself.

Rockhead stepped toward him. "Metaleye, control yourself! Be Coalash!"

Stonejaw looked at Rockhead. "Don't use our real names, idiot." He looked around to see if anyone had overheard them. He concluded that with all the yelling no one had or were even paying attention to them.

Coalash's eyes switched from red to his natural brown. He pleaded to Mudball. "Mudball, help me, please." His voice strained in agony. "Someone is in my head. Tell Gempath there are other -".

Stonejaw and Rockhead ran toward Coalash and knocked him down. They rolled him to his side and tried to pin him to the ground. Coalash's crystals grew brighter, cracks starting to form. The humming grew louder.

"Get control, Coalash," Stonejaw demanded. "You can't leave their breaths unchecked."

Coalash looked at them with mixed colored eyes, one red, one brown. "He's fighting me too much." The voice was mixed and Stonejaw could not figure out who was talking. The crowd began to back away from the fight. The humming grew louder, a bright light started to glow under him. His crystals cracked open. Coalash rolled, tripping Stonejaw and Rockhead. He bucked up and slammed a front leg into each of their necks. The light began to encircle them.

Gempath yelled, "Run!" The clan of Gaiajades sprinted away from the fighting pits. Mudball ran toward the flower field. He felt like he was running on air, moving as fast as he did when he flew on his rock. He got to the edge of the flowerfield. He could still hear the humming.

"Mudballs, what's happenings?" Thorseed asked.

"Get behind the rock wall! Now!"

Mudball ran around the rock formation that surrounded the field. He saw Florastryx jumping out of the flowers and over the wall.

Coalash was vibrating with energy. The two Gaiajades struggled under his feet. "You will not take my clan," he said as his crystals shattered. Bright light exploded from where they stood. There was a quick scream as the energy expanded into a circle. The ground under Mudball shook from the force. The Florastryx huddled together like a bouquet mix. Mudball grinded his teeth as the shockwave hit the stonewall. He prayed to Auroradraca that it held. The explosion of energy deafened the area. Dust flew over the top and side of the wall. Pieces of the wall chipped off. Mudball let out a scream as a Gaiajade crystal struck the wall, barely missing his head. It wedged into the wall like it was always there. The Florastryx screamed in fear.

The sky darkened as dust kicked up to the sky, forming a mushroom cloud. Then, as quick as the explosion overtook the area, silence blanketed the land. Mudball coughed dust. He licked his tongue a few times to get it wet. He spat out mud and coughed again. He blinked his eyes to get the dust out.

"Thornseed? Petalspear? You guys okay?"

A pile of dirt shifted and was thrown into the air as the Florastryx fluttered their wings at once. "Wez good," Petalspear coughed out. "Dirtys but goods. Yous?"

Mudball stood on his feet and shook off the dirt. "Same. Good."

Thornseed asked, "What happeneds?"

"I've never seen it but I've heard about it. See, Gaiajades store sunlight in our crystals to make our breath, which is like a solid beam of light." Mudball paused as he coughed out more muddy spit. "If you charge up but don't release you get a build up. Most of the time the energy will go away. Mostly absorbed by plants. But, when you get a crack and lose control." He trailed off as he went around the edge of the wall. The landscape and flower fields were covered in dust. Crops, trees, and flowers were flattened from the force of the wind. Mudball began walking forward. The Florastryx buzzed around him. The smaller Florastryx walked around Mudball. Some flew up and rested on his back crystals. Cracks in the ground showed the direction of the wind. Dust made it difficult to see. The terrain reminded Mudball of a drought that had come through the area a few years ago. Thornseed rested on Mudball's shoulder crystal.

"Booms?"

"Big Booms," Mudball replied.

He continued toward the epicenter of the explosion: the fighting circle. The rocks that had formed it were thrown about in different directions. Mudball could not believe the destruction that Coalash had caused. It was eerily quiet. Even Mudball's footprints made no sound in the loose dirt. He could see figures in the fighting circle. When he was close enough to make out the figures, he froze. The skeletons of the three Gaiajades laid on the ground, stripped of all flesh. Crystal shards littered the ground. Coalash's skeleton was fixed into the ground like someone had stepped on it. The other two skeletons were thrown to the side except the skulls and vertebrates, which Coalash still clung to. The sight made Mudball shake his head in disbelief. Crystals clinked. Mudball looked around to see what was making the sound. He saw a mound of Gaiajade crystals. They started moving as Gaiajades who had linked their bodies together to form a protective shield around Gempath. Their bodies were cut and bruised from taking the force of the blast. Several had large rocks or pieces of crystals in their skin. They winced in pain as they tried moving. Gempath seemed unharmed. She got up and made her way to Mudball. She wore a sad face as she approached.

"Mudball, are you alright?"

"Yeah. A little shaken up but I'm good."

"Thank Auroradraca for our crystals were able to absorb some of the explosion. There would be casualties." Gempath's face went from sad to puzzled. "Who are these little dragons?"

"I iz Thornseed. This iz mate, Petalspear. Wez leaders of Florastryx."

Gempath looked at them. The Florastryx were so tiny compared to the Gaiajades.

"Thornseed said they like to help with crops. Like growing and stuff," Mudball interjected. "And they are really friendly."

Gempath had a suspicious look on her face. "You deem them to be allies of the Gaiajades?"

"Oh, yeah, definitely," Mudball agreed. He thought it was weird why she asked him that question. A look of realization came to his face. "I'm the new leader, aren't I?"

Gempath nodded her head. She looked over to the fields that had been affected by the blast. "Can you Florastryx help with cleaning up and restoring our crops?"

Before Thornseed could respond, a pair of green Florastryx flew in. They were breathing hard.

Petalspear asked, "What is the matter?"

One gasped, "Pales dragons comings from belows us."

"Pale dragons?" Gempath asked.

"Pales likes moons. Blacks breaths. Means. Talks of goings to lands in air."

Mudball said, "The Zephrions. But who are the pale dragons?"

"Crazy dragonz. Theys follows Morth, Mortar," the Florastryx tried to say.

"Morthauron," Gempath corrected.

"Yes, yes, hims," the Florastryx agreed.

Gempath and Mudball looked at each other with concern. "This cannot be good," she said. "We will need to have everyone on alert in case they come through our territory."

"Yeah, yeah. Good idea," Mudball agreed, concern in his voice.

Gempath squinted his eyes. "Is there something else?"

"I met another dragon right before the tournament. She's young like me. She looked like a Ferrolith but wasn't. I can't really describe her. She freaked out and ran away." Gempath looked at him with disappointment that he had not told her about this new dragon. "Also, there was a weird mark on Coalash and the others that died. Like something had punctured their neck twice.

"We face new enemies and questions. Mudball, you need to decide what we need to do."

His eyes grew wide. "I keep forgetting I'm in charge now. Um," he trailed off. "Gempath, what would you do?"

She smiled. "I would say we need to alert the other clans of this new threat. Maybe you should since you and your friends are good at bringing everyone together."

"I like that, I like that," he agreed. "But who will be in charge of everyone while I'm gone?"

She looked at him with a you-know-that-answer face.

"Gempath, can you be in charge while I'm gone?"

"Of course, Mudball."

"Wez come toos," Petalspear said. "Mes and Thronseeds helps friend Mudballs. Wez tell clan to listens to great leaders Gempath." The two took off to spread their orders to the other Florastryx. Gempath gave a slight chuckle.

"These Florastryx are something," she mused.

"Yeah," Mudball agreed. He looked up at her. "Did Oldstone have it this tough when he became leader?"

"Oh, it was much worse," she mused.

A look of concern came over his face.

"He had to battle another so that I would be his mate," she smiled.

Chapter 13 A Difference in Philosophies

The tension in the Inferoths' volcano rose higher than the temperature of the lava. Numerous Inferoths held spears and swords toward the Solari in a tight circle around them. The Solari waited, showing no aggression. Skyblaze scanned the volcano.

"I wish to speak to the leader of your clan. Where is he?" he demanded.

Rageskin looked down from the bridge he stood on. Whisper looked at him.

"Any idea who they are?" she asked.

"No. But if he wants to talk, we will talk," he replied. He spread his shoulder wings and flew down to the ground. Whisper was still sore from the fight she just had. She could feel her magic healing her but still ached. She opened her arms and followed him.

Rageskin landed behind his clan that faced and surrounded the Solari. Rageskin made his way through the Inferoths and saw the intruders up close. He took in their massive size. He knew the Gaiajades were large but these dragons could match up. Skyblaze looked down on Rageskin.

"You are the leader of these dragons?" Skyblaze asked.

"I am."

"So young and small compared to your brethren. Are you sure you lead them?"

Whisper landed beside him. Skyblaze looked her up and down, taking note of how she looked different from Rageskin.

"I have proven my worthiness for leadership of the Inferoths," he said. "I am Rageskin. Who are you and why are you here?"

"I am Skyblaze, leader of the Solari," he replied, arrogance in his voice. "We are here because there is an evil afoot in these lands." He moved his long neck to point at the Inferroth carcasses. "Are you protecting these creatures?"

"I don't even know what you are talking about. I've been a little busy dealing with clan matters. You come into my home and make accusations? That tells me a lot about your clan's beliefs."

"You raise arms against us but ask for calm actions? We are followers of Auroradraca. We go where she sends us and we have been sent here. Are you followers of the great goddess of life?"

"We are."

"That is good. I feared we may have come across some . . . uncultured dragons," Skyblaze said with smugness in his voice.

"We believe in her. Even had a few conversations with her."

Skyblaze squinted his eyes. "Watch what you say."

Rageskin replied, "I don't need to. You are in my territory. I have been contacted by Auroradraca in the past. She even saved my life. My actions have proven my worthiness. My armor," he said as he spread his arms, "was a gift from her. So what is your business here?"

Skyblaze kept a blank face. "You have spoken with our goddess? You lie. We are not worthy of her divine voice."

Rageskin became irritated. "State your business or we will forcefully ask you to leave." The Inferoth guards raised their weapons.

A Solari bit one of the Ferrolith carcasses and raised it up. Skyblaze said, "On our journey through the desert lands, we came across these unnatural creatures. Dragons in metal bodies attacking others. Biting them and taking over their bodies. They are a blight in the eyes of Auroradraca. Probably followers of Morthauron." He said the last words with venom in his voice. "We found these two carcasses outside your volcano. You harbor these creatures."

"We have had experience with creatures of Morthauron, the Necrodrakes. I find it interesting that you and your clan have never fought the Necrodrakes. Not even mentioned in the stories."

"We are nomadic. We go where Auroradraca commands us."

"Convenient."

"Are you implying we are cowards?"

"I'm implying that you say Auroradraca sends you places but not when you would have helped her cause."

"Maybe you don't pray to her hard enough. Maybe you and your clan were being put through a trial, to prove your worthiness of her attention."

"More like cleaning up her mess. She allowed the Necrodrakes to exist."

"Rageskin, watch your words. She does not make mistakes."

"Maybe you weren't involved with the Necrodrake War because you were not worthy of protecting this world."

Skyblaze raised his wings, joined by others, creating a sunset with their patterns and colors. "We are worthy of her. We will search your docile for these creatures and eradicate them since you are too busy to bother."

Rageskin raised his ebony sword and placed the tip under Skyblaze's chin. The Solari growled. "I think not. Take your clan and leave my territory. Leave the carcasses."

Skyblaze lowered his wings. The other Solari followed. "We will leave. Our fight is not with you. Auroradraca sent us to your clan. Now, she must want us elsewhere. To purge these lands of Morthauron and his followers. Pray that we are on the same side next time we meet." Skyblaze turned and left the volcano, followed by the other dragons.

Whisper placed a hand on his shoulder. "Are you okay?"

"Yeah," he replied. He turned to the Inferoths that were standing by him. "We cannot leave the entrance open anymore. Have a team place the hidden pressure points again so that only we know how to move the entrance rock. Expand our sweeps of our territory. We are missing things. Someone entering our territory without us noticing. These new creatures are making their way in. We need more information." The Inferoths lowered their heads and flew off. Others joined them to begin work.

"That was impressive," Whisper complimented.

"I guess it's a perk from leftover magic," Rageskin replied. "Leadership can just come naturally."

"So, now what?" Whisper asked.

He paused. "Go back to my throne room and think of the next steps." He stretched his wings and took flight. Whisper followed. Inferoths flew about the volcano, going in various directions. They landed in the throne room.

"So, it looks like the clan is getting ready for war," Whisper remarked.

"Some habits don't die," Rageskin responded automatically. An awkward silence rested between them. "So, you're my queen now." He let out a small chuckle.

"Yeah, I am," she said. "With everything going on I haven't had a chance to let it sink in. Wow. I'm a queen."

"Who would've thought that a self important, prissy Zeyphrion would help rule the most vicious dragon clan on Wyrm."

She smirked at him. "Last time I checked you came to me because the females here are too mean. Leave the ego outside the cave, Mister Grrrr I-am-angry-all-the time." She laughed at her mockery of his voice. "I put melted rock on to prove my toughness."

"Oh you're going to go there," Rageskin noted. In a high pitched, feminine voice he mocked, "At least I didn't need a special gift to help heal my delicate soft scales of the big mean melted rock."

She curled her lips. "Jerk."

"Princess."

"Queen actually."

They broke out in laughter. It felt like the weight of the day had lifted off their shoulders. Rageskin tried to calm himself so he could speak. "We need to focus."

"I can't just enjoy the moment. I'm queen. I mean, I would've been when my mom died but still."

Rageskin looked at her. She felt like all her happiness deflated. "You're right. I mean, there are these Solari dragons roaming around and now maybe Necrodrakes?" She shuddered at the thought of them being back. An Inferoth flew up to the cave opening and left one of the carcasses.

"We have taken the other one to look at and try to figure out what the Solari leader was talking about," he said. "I felt that you may want to look this over yourself."

"Let me know if anything is discovered," Rageskin said.

The Inferoth crossed his chest with one arm. "At once, Rageskin," he said and flew off.

"That thing is weird," Whisper said.

Rageskin looked it over. He traced his talons over the various lines that drew scales into the metal. He picked it up and was amazed how light it was. Whisper stepped closer and looked it over.

"The detail on this is incredible. It's like-" she paused.

"It's a Ferrolith. The scale markings. The tail. It's like someone made a replica of a Ferrolith but hollow. There's nothing in here." He moved the legs and found them to be as flexible as his own. "It's not as large as a Ferrolith, though."

"Maybe it's a hatchling?" Whisper suggested.

"I don't know. We only met Ironfire and he was old and pieced together. In fact," Rageskin continued looking over. "This looks a lot like how Ironfire had pieced himself together. Remember, he said that he had to replace his body parts over time? This is like what he could've looked like if he was done properly."

Whisper looked at him disgusted. "Like if he replaced himself all at once, he would look like this?"

"Possibly," Rageskin said as he examined the mouth. There was a crude nub that resembled a tongue. He noticed that it did not have any teeth. "Weird. If this was alive, how would it eat? No teeth. I'm guessing no guts," he said as he banged on the belly, hearing a hollow sound.

Whisper looked closer at the mouth. She noticed two holes on each side of the upper jaw. She put a claw into one hole. She yipped as a large canine sprung out of each hole. Rageskin looked surprised and gave a chuckle.

Whisper was examining her claw for blood. "What are you laughing at?"

"You have had lava poured onto your skin, fought for your life, and dealt with the heat of the volcano. But you screamed at that tooth."

"You would've reacted too, you jerk."

"Probably not. King of the Inferoths and such." He looked up at her. Whisper stuck her tongue out. "I bet Stream has information about these somewhere in that tablet room of his."

"Wouldn't be a bad idea to see him," Whisper said. "Plus I need to check on my clan, make sure everything up there is good."

"Plus show off your new armor and status," Rageskin added with a sly smile.

"And show off my arm and that I'm a queen, yes," she agreed, rolling her eyes.

They laughed at the conversation. Behind them a large stone toward the back of the room began to move itself from the wall. It ground against the floor.

"What's that?" Whisper asked.

"I don't know. Someone is behind the rock. Quick, over here," Rageskin as he grabbed Whisper by the arm and pulled her behind a large stone column. It was a naturally occurring structure and wide enough to hide the two of them. Rageskin peered around the edge. A large rock was pushed out of the wall and to the side. Blackwing and Darkheart stepped out from the hole. Two Ferroliths followed behind them. One was shaking and had difficulty walking.

"I don't know if I can last any longer in this metal body," it said with a feminine tone.

"The pretty little air dragon will be easy to take. She will be tired from fighting me," Darkheart said. "Rageskin will be more difficult. He has armor that is different from the rest of them."

"It was forged with the help of Auroradraca," Blackwing said. "This one was there when he arrived in it for battle."

"Ironfire really screwed us with this deal," the second Ferrolith said.

"Quiet!" Blackwing retorted. "If it hadn't been for Ironfire, we would still be stuck in the darkness." He knelt down in front of the second Ferrolith. "You remember the darkness, don't you?" The Ferrolith tried to turn his head in shame. Blackwing grabbed him by the jaw. "The Necrodrakes killed all of us. We followed Auroradraca to the end, to protect Wyrm from those creatures. And what was our reward? Nothing. Absolute darkness forever. Now, if you want to return to that, please, remove yourself from the body you are in now." He let go of the Ferrolith, its head hanging in shame. "That's what I thought."

Darkheart said, "We are going to leave you two here for Rageskin and Whisper. If we can control the leaders of the Inferoths, we can advance our plans. Already, Coalash is fighting for control of the Gaiajades. The strongest clan is here and soon we will rule them."

"Remember," Blackwing said as he walked toward the hole in the wall. "Get a grip on the body and sink your fangs into their necks. Your ash will transfer to their body. You will gain their memories and self.

You'll be able to act like them without letting anyone know you aren't them. Got it?"

The two Ferroliths shook their heads in agreement. Blackwing and Darkheart started to pull the rock behind them. "We will meet with Melthorn. Come see us when you have succeeded." The rock slid seamlessly into place. The two Ferroliths searched the cave.

"Rrrrrrrrrah! Where are they!" the female screamed.

"Hush," the male said. "Probably out ruling people. We will find a hiding place and jump on them when they aren't looking."

"I'm so tired of this life. I want to feel it again. Ironfire was an idiot to put us in bodies that we couldn't feel."

"He didn't know Morthauron would make us kill others in order to live."

"I'm ready for it. That pretty little Zeyphrion. Going to be so nice to have a body that can fly."

"Agreed."

"Do you think it's true?" the female Ferrolith asked. "That some of us aren't able to drain the ash from their victims and go insane?"

"I don't know and I'd rather not find out. Now go and find a spot to hide," the male said.

The two metal dragons clanked against the stone floor. Rageskin could not see where they had gone. Whisper looked at him with fear in her eyes.

"What do we do?" she whispered.

"They'll be expecting us to come in from the opening. We should-."

Before he could finish the male Ferrolith sprang onto him. The weight of him caused Rageskin to fall backward. The Ferrolith slid out his fangs and snapped at Rageskin. Whisper tried to swing her armored arm back but the other Ferrolith leaped onto her back. She tried to swing but the weight pulled her down. The Ferrolith tried to bite her.

Rageskin used his arms to keep the Ferrolith from biting him. He drew a leg under the dragon and pressed his foot against the metal stomach. With all his might, he launched the Ferrolith into the air and slammed the metal dragon against the wall. Rageskin swung his onyx shield and it clanged against the female Ferrolith. She went flying off Whisper. Rageskin helped her up. The male Ferrolith leapt again at Rageskin. He raised his shield as the male opened his mouth. He sunk his fangs into the shield and got stuck. Rageskin started stabbing him with his sword.

The female Ferrolith bull-rushed Whisper. Whisper leaped up and straddled the metal dragon. She dug her talons into the shoulder. Sparks jumped out as she got a grip. The dragon bucked, running around the cave to get Whisper off of her.

Rageskin stopped stabbing as he realized the sword had no effect on a creature without organs. The Ferrolith tried to release its fangs out of the shield. Rageskin yelled as he ran forward. He smashed it into the wall, denting the wall with the Ferrolith. He ripped his shield from the Ferrolith, tearing the two canine teeth and a part of the jaw. Rageskin moved back from the wall. The Ferrolith fell to the ground. He growled in anger as he realized that his teeth were missing.

"No! No! What have you done? I won't be able to live! I can't, I can't stay like this? How could you? Rawwwr!" he angrily yelled as he ran to Rageskin. Rageskin took a step back, grabbed the holes in the Ferrolith torso his sword had caused, and tossed him toward the front of the cave.

Whisper tried to hang onto the steel dragon she was riding. The dragon slammed its body against the cave wall. Whisper let out a gasp as the air escaped her. She let go of the dragon and fell to the ground. She got her footing and turned to face the dragon. It slammed into her before she was ready to attack. She dug into the holes that she had made. She released cold breath onto the Ferrolith. Ice covered the neck and traveled over the head. The dragon slowed down as the ice crept over the leg joints and into the holes. Whisper pushed herself off and reached for her bo staff. She regained her balance and swung upwards under the dragon's jaw. Its fangs went flying in different directions. It stumbled to a stop by the other Ferrolith. Rageskin went beside Whisper.

"You okay?" he asked.

"Yeah. Thanks again for the bo staff. It's been helpful."

"No, no, no, no!" the female Ferrolith screamed. "My fangs! You broke my fangs!"

"Let us help you," Whisper said. "Maybe we can figure out something."

"No," the male Ferrolith replied. "It's too late. Our minds will unwind in these bodies. If you could have only let us have your bodies."

They turned toward the entrance of the cave. The light from the lava invited them. They looked at each other in silent agreement. The two Ferroliths sprinted out of the cave and leaped off the edge of the bridge outside the cave. Whisper and Rageskin chased after them. They watched as the Ferroliths disappeared down toward the lava pool. The two dragons splashed and let out a quick scream. The distance was far but the screams made Inferoths nearby stop what they were doing. Several Inferoths rushed to Rageskin's side.

"Rageskin," one of the Inferoths started. "Are you alright? What happened?"

"Darkwing and Blackheart are traitors. They allowed those two dragons in to kill me and Whisper."

"What are your orders?"

"Find the traitors. Chain them up. Keep an eye on the lava pool in case those bodies react with it. We don't know what type of magic those bodies may have had."

As he finished, two smoky wisps floated in front of him and continued. He swore he heard one of them speak. "Stop us."

Whisper asked, "Rageskin, are you alright?"

"Nothing. Thought I heard something."

"I need to see my clan. I'm worried."

"We will. Then we should meet with Stream. Maybe he will have more information."

Chapter 14 Resurrection of Knowledge

Stream swam through a connection tunnel. They led all over the Aquanox territory and allowed them to venture from one part of their underground kingdom to another as well as other dragons' territory for trade. The water pushed him in the direction he wanted to go. He shifted his back sails to steer himself. The two Florastryx clung to his tail. It had hurt at first as their small talons dug into his flesh. They had said they were fast but apparently they were not ready for Aquanox speed. Stream ejected out of the tunnel and floated into the waiting water. It was a large lake near the living caves. He looked back at the Florastryx. They hung onto him but they were not moving. He swam to the surface and raised his tail above the water. The two Florastryx gasped for fresh air. He raised the rest of body to the surface. The small dragons climbed onto his long serpentine back and rested on his sails.

"Thought you guys could swim," he joked.

"Thats waz fasts," Thornroot said between breaths.

"Yous doz this all times?" Lilypetal gasped.

"Yeah," Stream replied. "Didn't you guys use those tunnels to find me?"

"Wez could nots controls wheres wez went," Thornroot said as he breathing normalized. "Chased by yous friend. Very scareds. Likes calms waters. Like this," he said as he patted the lake. "Safes."

Stream started moving through the lake, heading toward a sandy beach.

"Wherez we goes?" Lilypetal asked.

"I have to see Dreamflow. He's our leader and needs to know what is going on. He might have some information."

Aquanoxes swam around him, going about their day. The Florastryx laid on top of Stream with their wings open. Stream looked back. It looked like two plants had stuck to him as he swam. This was a common thing and no one paid attention to his flowery companions. He swam toward Dreamflow's cave. The water level slowly lowered as he got closer. Stream sank his head into the water. Aquanox sent messages through the water. Most of the messages were pretty mundane.

"Lilypad is becoming such a fast swimmer. Might outswim her brother."

"I can't wait for the Inferoths' floating rocks to come!"

"The kelp from below is so delicious. Blooming season is upon us."

"I haven't heard from my son yet from the coast. He joined Riverbank's group."

Stream paused at that.

"No one has heard from anyone that left. I hope they are alright."

Stream paused for a moment. After fighting Raindrop, Stream had not even thought about the fact Raindrop had been part of that group. Did the rest of them come in contact with whatever infected Raindrop? Were they going insane as well? Or did Raindrop kill them all? The Florastryx only mentioned seeing him when they got lost from their clan. Was their clan affected? Were these two afflicted like Raindrop? No, they were running for their lives when he met them. They were afraid of him and he was trying to kill them. Infect them? Not knowing things bothered Stream. He read so much with the tablets in the cave but felt like he had not learned anything useful

Stream traveled up a tributary that led up to Dreamflow's cave. His cave was similar to everyone's. Maybe a little larger as he met with other Aquanox often and they needed space. He slithered out of the water and looked around. Bioluminescent moss lit up as he ventured into the cave. The walls were smooth from years of water coming through. The Florastryx stretched and flew off Stream. They found reading spires and sat on the flat tops.

"Dreamflow, are you here?" Stream said, echoing through the cave. He looked around, looking for signs of him being there. "Dreamflow?"

"Friend goes missing?" Lilypetal asked.

"He's our leader. He tends to be busy. We probably just missed him."

Stream looked on the floor. There was water slowly moving from the back of the cave. Stream followed the trail, moving his head back and forth for where it was coming from. The Florastryx flapped their wings beside him. Water slapped against the cave floor. As he went toward the back of the cave, the floor rose out and plateaued, forming a circular pool. Dreamflow was hanging out of it, his head under the water. Water splashed out again. Stream rushed over, bit his backfin, and pulled back. Dreamflow looked at him with surprise. Stream released him.

"Dreamflow, are you okay? What happened?"

"I'm fine, I'm fine. I've just been doing an experiment. I was hoping to send messages through water that the other clans could hear. The distance is much larger compared to local water messages. This pool concentrates my messages to where I need it. But, sadly, no one has responded back. Probably busy."

Stream was astonished by what he said. "The other clans couldn't understand us if we spoke to them through water. That's why it isn't working."

"The right vibrations," Dreamflow said, lost in thought. "With the right vibrations, they could. Lava is a bit tricky-" he paused. He noticed the Florastryx. "Who are you?"

"I iz Thornroot. This iz mys mates, Lilypetal."

"We iz Florastryx. Wez help Streams," Lilypetal continued.

Dreamflow looked at them with curiosity. "You are so small."

"Wez know," Lilypetal replied. "Helps us to hides from yous big dragons."

"Interesting." He paused. "And you talk oddly."

"Way wez talk?" Thornroot said insulted. "Youz dragons speaks weirds. Wez talk normal."

Dreamflow smiled and chuckled. "Another clan. Are there more of you?"

"Oh yes, manys," Lilypetal replied. "Wez got losts from clan. Founds Stream and friend."

Dreamflow looked at Stream. "Friend?"

"Raindrop came back but something was wrong with him. Like he was arguing with someone else in his head. He," Stream paused. "We fought and he hurt himself badly. He died. His body is in the tablet cave."

"I'm sorry," Dreamflow said. "Did he say anything that may explain what happened to him?"

"Not really. These guys found him and led him back here. Well, more like chasing them. He talked like he was arguing with himself and his emotions kept changing. Even his eyes changed colors."

"Necrodrake?"

"No, not even close. It was . . . tough to watch. Any ideas?"

Dreamflow was in deep thought. "The tablets never said anything like this."

"There was a new ceiling painting. It showed a Ferrolith and a mist coming out of its body. Then I came across a tablet that told a story about a dragon's ash entering a Gaiajade and causing him to act crazy. Seemed odd when I read it. Think that has anything to do with it?"

"I have not read that. Your magic allows you to read old language. It may have been a tablet that I couldn't read. Or perhaps a new one Auroradraca sent us?

"Is she the one sending the tablets and the ceiling paintings?"

"I don't know for sure. I've always just assumed she did. Her own way of informing us."

Stream said, "Is there only one room in the cave? Anything hidden or more tablets hidden away somewhere?"

Dreamflow looked at him. "Why do you ask?"

"I discovered a room, hidden in the back. I found a pressure plate like the Inferoths have and a wall opened. There were a lot of tablets in there. Looks like no one has been in there for a long time."

Dreamflow smiled. "Of course you would find it. I'm not surprised. Not after the war."

Stream looked at him puzzled.

"I was told stories of a cave that contained lost information: The cave of Futurarteon. Everyone had different directions of where it could be found but no one could find it. When I was your age, I swam for miles, following every clue that I was given. Nothing. I gave up after a while and just assumed it was just a story. I never mentioned it to you because I didn't think it was real. Most had forgotten about it when I did ask. Hmmm. Never imagined it would just be right under my fins."

"Who is Futurarteon?"

"I don't know. I've asked every clan, thinking maybe they knew. Asked our cousins in the oceans. Some knew of a story about an Aquanox who could see the future. Others said it was a forgotten dragon god or just another name for Auroradraca. One even said it was a bedtime story and never existed. No one knew, a name forgotten to history, I suppose."

"Maybe Tuzu knows," Lilypetal chimed in.

"Tuzu?" Stream asked.

"Ours god," Thornroot replied. "Helps Auroradraca with plants."

"Another dragon god," Stream said. "But how do we not know of him? Is it a him?"

"Yes, hims," Thornroot said.

"Another mystery on top of what happened to Raindrop," Dreamflow said. "I will send someone down for his body for a proper burial. You should look into your new tablet cave. Perhaps something in there will help us."

"Yes, sir," Stream said.

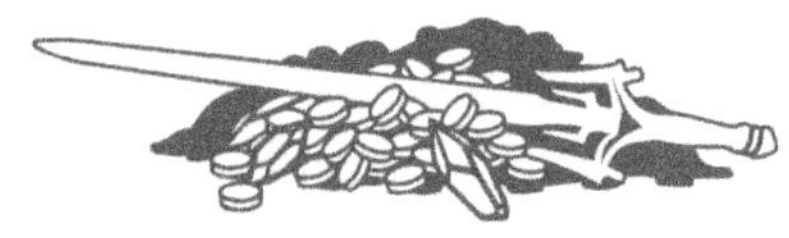

AFTER A TIME, STREAM and the Florastryx returned to the tablet cave. Raindrop's body had been removed. Stream saw someone had attempted to stack the broken tablets into piles.

"Youz okay?" Lilypetal asked.

"Yeah, it's just," Stream lost himself in thought. "He killed himself. Right here. Every time I come in here that's all I'm going to think about." He saw blood on the cave floor. "He needed help and now he's dead."

"Wez sorry," Thornroot said. "Deaths nevers easy. Wez hope thats our clans isn'ts deads."

"I didn't think about that," Stream replied. "You two should leave and find them."

"No worries," Lilypetal said. "Wez help friend Stream. Tuzu puts us heres for reason."

"If you are sure," Stream said.

"Wez sure," the two Florastryx said in unison.

Stream slithered to the back of the cave, trying to refind the pressure point he had found earlier. He followed the moss and pressed it. The rock wall slid open and the moss glowed. The cave was huge and Stream did not know where to begin. The two Florastryx followed on either side of him. Their eyes were large with excitement.

"Doez this room ends?" Thornseed asked. "Iz huge."

"I'm sure it does but I can't imagine what kind of information is here. I could spend weeks here."

"No foods heres. Wez would goes hungries," Lilypetal remarked.

"I didn't mean it literally," Stream chuckled. "But I need to figure out where to start though. I need to meet with my friends. Update them and see if they have had similar issues." He tried to feel his magic, see if it could pull him in some direction. He closed his eyes. In his mind he could see a soft ring of blue fire toward the back of the cave. There was writing in the center but he could not read it.

"*Say my name,*" a voice in his head whispered.

Stream opened his eyes, caught off guard by the voice. He looked at the Florastryx. They were wandering about and exploring. They did not seem to hear what he did. He closed his eyes again. He saw the fire circle again.

"*Believe in me,*" the voice said again. He jumped at the second message. He swallowed and moved forward. He followed the water to a large wall. It had runes carved into it, creating a circle. Stream had not seen these markings before and tried to use his magic to decipher them. He followed the runes to the center where one rune appeared.

A word popped into his head. "Futurarteon." The runes glowed brightly and the ground began to shake. The water boiled and made waves. The Florastryx hid behind a reading spire. Cracks formed in the wall and light burst out. Stream turned his head and closed his eyes. A hum grew louder as the light intensified.

"*Believe in me,*" the voice said louder.

"I do," Stream said. He felt a rush of air slam against him. Once it stopped he opened his eyes. A soft glow lit up the cave. A large dragon towered over him. It had a long serpentine body with its lower half curled up. Its tail had long white feathers that ran the length of the end. The massive wings sprouted from the shoulders and seemed to stretch across the ceiling. The arms made the top part of the wings. The underside of the wings were blue and gold mix lines of color and leathery while the outside were covered in white feathers. Another set of smaller wings came out under them. They reached forward with claws at the end. The center scales were gold and looked like metal plating. Blue scales covered the rest of the body. At the neck, two heads sprouted. The left head had gold scales while the right head had blue scales. Each had a set of horns that curled backward. The left head had horn tips that turned inward while the other had outturned horn tips. Around the heads were small feathers with a variety of colors. Sharp spikes went down the back of the heads and converged where the necks met and continued down the body. The two heads looked down at Stream. He shook slightly from fear.

"We are Futurarteon," both heads said in unison. "The goddess of knowledge and future."

"I thought, I thought," Stream tried to say but stammered. "I thought Auroradraca and Morthauron were the only gods."

"Our sister has a bit of an ego," Futurarteon replied. "Her creations birthed us with their imagination but she caused them to forget. She bound us with our own power and we have waited for one to free us."

Futurarteon looked at Stream with curiosity. "You are not afraid of us. Nor bow down."

"Sorry," he said as he lowered his head. "I did not know you existed. And I've met Auroradraca so having a god before me isn't new."

They smiled. "You are a special one. You have magic in you. We can sense it."

"Yeah, from Auroradraca."

"We know. Everything that has happened in this world since we were imprisoned is now available to us. Hmmm. Much has changed in this world since we last lived in it. Tell us, Stream. Do you know of Freeriver?"

He shook his head. "No, I don't. And how do you know my name?"

They smiled. "Goddess of knowledge, Little one. Remember?"

Stream felt embarrassed. "Sorry."

"It is alright. And, please, have your friends come out. We do not intend harm on you. Only knowledge and answers that we can give."

The two Florastryx came out of hiding. They stayed low to the ground and stayed close to Stream. "I iz Thornroot. This iz mate Lilypetal."

"Hello, little ones," Futurarteon greeted. "We see that Tuzu's creations are still alive in this world."

The Florastryx perked up. Lilypetal said, "Youz know Tuzu?"

"The god of plants? Of course. He would often work with us on creating the seasons and what plantlife should grow."

"Do youz knows where he iz?" Lilypetal asked.

Futurarteon paused. "We do but we cannot tell. The future is being created by your actions and his fate is tied to it. Anything we tell you may either hinder him or help him. We do not barter in fate."

The Florastryx looked worried. Stream said, "I don't mean to sound rude but who is Freeriver?"

"She was the last Aquanox or any dragon to know of us. We spoke to her. Taught her to read and write in stone. To tell of the past and future. She was seen as crazy by the Aquanox of the time. Speaking of gods that didn't exist. She was locked away in our cave. Our connection was strong with her until her death. We were forgotten, which allowed Auroradraca to seal us in the runes. We have tried to influence events. Provided tablets and paintings to hint at the future. But could not interfere."

Stream came to a realization. "You're the one creating the tablets. I thought it was Auroradraca this whole time."

"Of course our sister would take claim to our work but we knew that it would happen. Cannot change what has been determined. We will answer what we can for you, Stream. We must leave soon before Auroradraca senses our presence."

"I have so many questions but I don't know which to ask." He thought for a moment. "Why do me and my friends still possess our magic? Shouldn't they have gone away by now."

"This we can tell. You and your friends are direct descendants of the founding dragons of your clans, first created by Auroradraca, using stolen magic. Over time, more of your kind were born and the magic lessened."

"So she just awakened in us something we already possessed but not aware of?"

They nodded their heads in agreement.

"Wow. Just wow. Okay. Can you tell us of this new threat that seems to exist? The Ferrolith and their ash."

"We are restricted. We can tell you that the Ferrolith have been corrupted by Morthauron. He wants to create his own creatures, overturning Auroradraca's actions and decisions. Death should not create life. That is the cycle and he means to break it. Do not allow the Ferrolith to evolve."

"Evolve? What does that mean?"

Futurarteon gave a concerned look. "She has noticed us. We must leave to hide before she finds us. Pray to us, young dragon. Pray to us and we will help as allowed." They turned into a mist and disappeared.

Stream, Lilypetal and Thornroot were stricken with fear.

"This nos goods," Thornroot said. "No goods at alls. What wez do, Streams?"

"We need to find my friends. I have a bad feeling about all this."

Futurarteon: The Distant Past

Futurarteon sat on top of the mountain that had been recently created by order of Auroradraca. A light breeze blew through the snow that littered the ground. They closed their eyes. They could see the future, all that could happen and those that never will, and retain the knowledge for others to be aware of. The sun reflected off their gold shoulder scales. They wrapped their feathery and leathery wings around their shoulders, letting them fall down their body. The outside feathers reflected the sunlight, giving a soft glow to them. Footsteps crunched the snow behind them.

"Hello, Auroradraca," they said, not looking at her.

"I will never get used to your abilities, dear sisters," she responded. There was an awkward silence between them.

"Have you thought about what we said the last time that we met?" Futurarteon asked.

"Yes. And you must know what I have come to ask of you."

Futurarteon stood in silence. "We have seen the path that your decisions will take you down, how it will change you, how it will end you."

Auroradraca kept a neutral face. "The future is fluid and ever changing. My creations on Wyrm will change my fate."

"That is a decision you must make. Do you wish to still use our essence to change the future?"

"You know the answer to that question," Auroradraca said with anger in her voice.

"*You will have our essence but we will not be forgotten as you wish to happen. We will continue to influence in ways that you cannot see, to exist in this realm even if we are not part of it. That is the future that we see.*" They slowly turned their heads toward her. "*Do you wish to continue down this path, knowing that it may bring your own demise? Even after breaking your promises?*"

"*Give me what I ask of you,*" she ordered.

They stared at her unblinking. "*The future will continue its course. No action you take will sway you from your destiny in the end.*"

"*I will see about that,*" Auroradraca said with fierceness in her voice.

Chapter 15 Breaking the Cycle

Melthorn paced in front of the other Ferroliths. He scanned each one, noting the variety of dragons that stood before him. Several Ferroliths were still in their old metal bodies. They were slowly breaking down, rust grinding in their gears. A couple Ferroliths, still in their metal bodies, were chained to the wall, their minds gone crazy. Melthorn stood in front of them like a general.

"Each of you had a task. Find a new body. Infiltrate. Return. We have had time for all of you to find bodies and yet," he stared at the ones chained to the wall. "And yet, we still have some who haven't found a body and have lost their minds."

"It's difficult to find a dragon who won't be missed," one Zeyphrion spoke. "Many of these clans are close to each other and know when someone goes missing or is acting odd."

Melthorn turned to her. "And yet you have a body. I found this Gaiajade wandering by himself. He was easy to inhabit. And some of you have not even properly removed the ash of your host body! Ironfire did what he did so that we could live again and, yet, some of you have taken it for granted. Do any of you want to go back to the void that we were resurrected from? I will gladly return anyone who does not follow my orders."

The dragons stood in silence. Many remembered wandering for years in the nothingness of the afterlife. There was no sound or direction. It was easy to walk forever in one direction and never find the end. Just an endless void of nothingness for centuries.

"Now, do we have updates?" Melthorn asked.

"All the clans are accounted for," a small Gaiajade said. "Our numbers have thinned some. Coalash, Rockhead, and Stonejaw have all perished."

Melthorn was not pleased. "What happened? We had the strongest amongst them."

"In the fight for leadership, Coalash lost control and, for lack of better words, blew up. These Gaiajade crystals can be difficult to learn. It isn't like blowing out your breath weapon."

"I don't care for excuses. What of the Aquanox and Zeyphrions?"

An Aquanox slide forward. "Both have proven difficult to infiltrate. These water dragons rarely leave their watery homes and the air dragons stay up on their islands. The metal bodies proved to be useless in those territories."

"And yet I see a handful of both here. Dumb luck, I suppose. Ironfire should have just left you in the darkness. Grrr, what of these new tribes? Solari and Selenthrax."

"They have torn our metal bodies apart and seem to think as one," the Aquanox stated. "Getting one of them has proven difficult. We only have one of each."

Melthorn stomped his feet in frustration. "And the ash was probably lost in the process. Please tell me that we at least control the Inferoths."

Darkheart and Blackwing stepped forward. Blackwing spoke. "The Inferoths have proven to be more difficult than imagined. We did not take into account the induction of a queen. I had to improvise. I thought placing this one into Darkheart, a strong warrior, would give us control of leadership. The Zeyphrion was stronger than anticipated."

"Idiots! All of you are just idiots! At least our enemies don't know of us." Melthorn read the crowd. "Correct?"

"The Inferoth leader may have a suspicion but not of our nature," Darkheart replied. "But we did leave behind a couple of our clan members to take the leaders over."

"And?" Melthorn asked, anger in his response.

"We have not heard back from them. We snuck in and left quickly before we could-"

"You left them? And just disappeared," Melthorn said, annoyed. "No follow through or, I don't know, give assistance to them."

"We thought you would want us here," Darkheart responded. "Rageskin and Whisper were distracted and," Darkheart stopped as Gaiajade breath shot past his head.

"And nothing! We need the Inferoths to be under our control, our leadership. Their bodies are perfect for war and you just left, wanting to talk with me, not making sure or even helping, which would have been a better use of your time than being here, giving me excuses. Anyone else have some important information to share with me?"

A timid Gaiajade stuttered "Same with the Gaiajades, they may, they may know about us or something. Steelheart never did her part to stop the challenger to Coalash."

Melthorn charged his crystals. They glowed a dark red. "If you weren't kin, I would kill all of you again. We can't take over if our numbers simply dwindle and we can't influence leadership if we aren't inside dragons that they trust for advice." He powered down. "Leave me. I need to think."

The bioluminescent moss in the cave flickered on and off. The Ferroliths looked around. The darkness at the back moved forward. A tall dragon stepped out of the shadows as if it was a part of it. His scales were a deep black with gray chest armor down his middle. He walked on two legs as his wings folded onto his shoulders, talons clasping at the neck, and dragging on the floor. His eyes were an angry red. Gray horns circled his head like a crown. He walked through the cave, looking at each dragon. A chill entered the cave, fear went through each of them. He stopped in front of Melthorn.

"And who are you?" Melthorn snarled.

"Such rage. Who knew what potential you would have."

Melthorn charged his crystals. "I won't repeat myself. Who are you?"

The dragon smiled. "I am your creator. I am the one who brought you back from the void and placed your ash in metal bodies."

Melthorn's face fell slack from disbelief. "Morthauron?"

The dragon stared at him. "In the flesh. As it were." At his feet, shadows move about on their own, moving like water in cracks toward each dragon. Morthauron stepped beside Melthorn and looked at the crowd.

"I have listened to you. All of you. Your fears. Your dreams. Your frustrations. Life moved on without you. Heroes of a great war, only to be forgotten as your bones turned to dust. Auroradraca using you for her own amusement. She cared so little for your clan. So much so she forced Ironfire to be blind to my sight. An insult to a mortal being. To never know the peace that death brings. To only be tormented by life. But, then, finally, I was able to grant him death. He asked for a boon: the return of his people."

The crowd murmured. Melthorn said, "I apologize for my rudeness, Morthauron. The void was not peaceful for us. Many of us still remember the fear of being lost for centuries and don't want to return to that."

Morthauron stroked a crystal on Melthorn's back. "No apologies needed. If anything I should atone for the torment that the Ferroliths had to endure. I am sorry for that, my child. The void is unapproachable for me. There is another that controls it but his name has been forgotten. But, I offer a solution." He tapped his talons on the crystals. "I look amongst you and I see no clan. No identity, a mixture of dragons who don't know who they are or what they could be. In bodies that are favored by Auroradraca. And at some point in your mortal lives, I will bring you my touch again."

Several dragons shuttered in fear of dying again. "I can provide you with new bodies. Ones that are stronger. More fearsome. And immortal. All you need to do is believe in me and accept my gift."

The dragons talked amongst themselves quietly. Morthauron looked around the room, patiently waiting.

"I believe in you, Morthauron," Melthorn said, turning to him. "Auroradraca threw us to the side. You found us and gave us a second chance to live. I'll be your first disciple."

Morthauron smiled. "Excellent." He opened his wings. His scaled armor glowed softly. He reached out his hand, long knifelike talons jutting out from his fingers. He pressed a talon against Melthorn's head. Blackness spread from his talon onto Melthorn, covering him with an eggshell. Grunts of pain and bones snapping could be heard under the shell. The crowd watched with a mix of horror and curiosity. After a few minutes, the shell split open. Melthorn was curled in a ball, with his arms wrapped around his legs and head down. Three long tails unwound from the body. They were covered with spikes down the sides ending with a curved barb at the end.

"Arise, my reclaimed apostle. Keep your name but embrace your true being."

Melthorn stood up, his black and red highlighted leathery wings stretching outwards. Small hooked nails lined the bottom. His scales were thick down the middle like armor leading up to sharp plates at the shoulders. The body scales were black with red streaks. Long dark horns rose from above his red pupiless eyes. His talons were long and sharp.

"How do you feel, my child," Morthauron asked.

"Strong. Whole," Melthorn replied. He flexed his hands. The talons scraped together making a metal sound. "What is our clan name?"

Morthauron smiled. "Eclipsire."

Melthorn made a low guttural sound as a whip-like tail went on either side of him and the third rose up like a scorpion's tail. Morthauron turned to the dragons

"Do you believe in me? Do you believe that I can grant you an everlasting life?" He raised his arms out. The dragons began to chant his name. He smiled.

"Hmm, this is a new feeling," Morthauron noted as energy rose within him. "Yes, pray to me. Yes, yes." Black tendrils left his body and encased all the Ferrolith who chanted his name. The chanting quieted as all the dragons were covered.

Steelheart hid in a corner by a tunnel entrance. "I can't believe everyone agreed to this," she thought. She hoped that Morthauron could not see her. A tendril slithered toward her. "I don't know what to do. I can't be a part of this." An orange winged Florastryx landed by her feet.

"Friend, follow mes. Founds secret ways out. Comes, comes," he said quietly. She looked at the clan as she heard shells rip open and growling as Eclipsire rose up. Tails shook, making an eerie sound. Steelheart nodded at the Florastryx and they took off down the tunnel. She could hear what was happening echo down as she ran.

"Rise, my Eclipsire! Rise and take what is yours! Drink the blood of your enemies to live forever!"

Roars flooded Steelheart's ears. She wanted to cry but knew that she was not physically able to.

Chapter 16 A Threat of the Moon

Night claimed the world Wyrm. Nocturnal creatures came out to hunt and find prey. Rageskin and Whisper flew above the blackened land. The moon reflected off the lake that had been created when a Gaiajade transport tunnel had collapsed and filled in with Aquanox water. Nearby the lake was the remains of a Zeyphrion island that had crashed into the land thanks to the Necrodrakes destroying the magical air that allowed their islands to float far above the surface. It allowed the air dragons to remain safe from the dangers below. Whisper kept moving her right arm up and down as they glided through the air.

"Stupid, frigging thing," she mumbled.

"What's wrong?" Rageskin asked.

"This armor keeps throwing my balance off when I fly. The bo staff is flat against my spine and balanced. But there's just enough weight on my arm to make me lean to the right. Really annoying."

Rageskin looked at her and shook his head.

"What?" she said.

He shifted his back wings so that he was on his side. He pointed at the onyx armor that covered his body. He spun so that she could see how it spread to his back and onto the base of his wings, gesturing with his hands where his armor was.

"You know what?" she said as she looked down. She paused with fear on her face.

"What is it?" Rageskin asked.

"It's probably nothing. I could have sworn I had seen movement on the ground. Like a black mass that moved but it's probably nothing. Trick of the light or something."

"Are you still having flashbacks of Necrodrakes?"

She sighed. "Yeah but not as bad as they used to be. The training helped me to focus my mind but still, every so often, something just triggers my fear." She lost her thoughts to the winds that glided them up to the islands. "How do you manage it? You went toe to toe with your dead brother, watched your dad die? How do you sleep?"

"I don't sometimes," Rageskin responded. "Some nights I can still hear someone talking to me, taunting me. As if the volcano itself was speaking with the voices of the dead. It was a lot at first. One minute I'm an armorless soldier no one wanted to be seen with, a disgrace. Then, suddenly, I'm someone held at the highest level of respect through combat and death of kin. I never thought I'd be king. Part of me was hoping to die in a great battle long before I ever became a king."

Whisper looked at him with sadness and pity.

"My dad was the toughest warrior ever. My brother was second to none. I was never going to be king so I accepted my place and tried to earn the respect of the Inferoths, even if I couldn't get armor on me several times."

"But your all mighty and beautiful queen got it on the first try." She smiled at him.

He smiled at her. "Yeah, yeah. Anyway, I never thought I'd have a mate, let alone a queen. Being an Inferoth who couldn't get lava poured on him doesn't really make you desirable."

They flew in silence for a moment. "My mom wanted me to choose a mate. To find the most handsome male and have many hatchlings with him. I sometimes spent days watching males dance for me, to impress me. I pretended to care. I didn't want to insult them. They tried really hard to win me over. But I just didn't, I don't know, care."

Rageskin took the new information in. He did not know what a mating dance looked like or how to even perform one. The thought of dancing made him shiver.

"You okay?" Whisper asked.

Rageskin realized she saw him shake. "Nothing. Just lost in thought."

"Must have been a deep one," she remarked. She paused. "I'm honored that you chose me to be your queen. I never really saw us as a royal couple at any point but it feels. . .". She tried to find the right words. "Right. We have some kind of connection."

Rageskin smiled and turned so he was on his stomach.

"Do Inferoths feel love?"

Rageskin looked at her surprised. "Yeah but probably not like how Zeyphrions do."

"Explain."

"We show strength to each other. We protect each other and fight to improve each other's fighting skills. I would bring you a fresh kill from a hunt and you would look it over to see how clean or gory it was. We sacrifice for the clan over our own wants and needs."

Whisper thought about it. "Have I shown you love, the Inferoth way?"

As Rageskin was about to say something, a large bug flew into his mouth. He choked and gagged on it.

"Are you okay?" Whisper asked.

Rageskin spit out a gooey mess. "How are there bugs this high up?"

"We must be near the islands. Probably fell off the edge."

Rageskin continued to spit and hack the pieces of bug out of mouth. "Do you have these things on purpose? They're disgusting."

Whisper chuckled. "We use them on crops to keep away any pests that find their way here." Rageskin stuck his long tongue out to examine it. He tried to brush remnants off. Whisper smiled at him.

They landed on the first island they came across. It was smaller compared to the others. A small pond rested in the center. Small bushes grew around the edge with a couple of green trees growing near. Other islands could be seen in the distance. Rageskin took the sight in.

"I'll never get used to this," he said. "Floating islands strung up with magic air."

"You live inside an angry mountain," she replied. "I think that's more impressive."

"*Release me,*" a whisper came to Rageskin, distracting him.

"You hear me," Whisper asked.

"I'm sorry, what?"

"I said you live in a volcano. That's cool. Are you okay?"

"Yeah. I thought I heard something but it must've been the wind going through my head armor. Where's your clan at?"

Whisper looked around. The islands were quiet. The moon reflected off the pond's surface. Whisper listened to the wind around her. She picked up on a shift in wind direction. She saw a group of Zeyphrions flying toward them. They came into view and landed on the island. Dancewing swung her arms and landed near the dragons. She gracefully moved her wing flaps to seem like she was twirling a dress. Two males and two females landed on either side of her. The males were taller than her but shorter than Rageskin. Dancewing brushed her talons through her short head feathers.

"Whisper, my sweetie, you've returned," Dancewing said as she wrapped her winged arms around Whisper. "And you brought the Inferoth king with you."

Rageskin bowed his head. "Dancewing, it is an honor to be up here on your islands."

"Honor accepted. To what do I owe the pleasure of hosting the fire dragon leader?"

Whisper started, "Mother, there is a new enemy out there."

Dancewing's face grew solemn. "Necrodrakes?"

"I don't think so. But they seem to somehow take over other dragon bodies. Even their minds it seems."

"First they want to eat us, now be us," Dancewing remarked. She looked at Whisper's arm. "Whisper, Sweetie, what is that?"

Whisper realized that her forearm armor was showing. "I was going to get to that."

"What did you do?" She turned angrily to Rageskin. "What did you force her to do?"

"He didn't force anything," Whisper retorted. "I chose to do this."

"You chose to mutilate your beautiful scales? It doesn't even match your fleshtone."

Rageskin interrupted, "Dancewing, if I may explain."

"Shut it!" Whisper and Dancewing said simultaneously.

His eyes widened and he put his hands up.

"Sweetie, what did you do? And why? You will never get a male now that you're damaged."

Whisper looked at her purple scales burned with red scar tissues. "I don't need a male. Rageskin made me his queen!"

Dancewing looked at her with angry eyes. "He. Did. What?"

"Rageskin asked me to be his queen. I went through a trial to prove my worthiness and even fought an Inferoth female to earn the right to be queen."

Dancewing shook with anger. "You are lying. You cannot be an Inferoth queen."

"I am. Mother, you agreed to help our clan to evolve past being dragons seen only for their beauty. You let me learn to battle and teach others to fight. We even let the males out and contribute more to our clan."

"I didn't mean for you to go out, get uglified, and become royalty of another clan."

Rageskin tried to speak. "Dancewing, if I may. I was facing a traitor from within. A member of this new enemy posed as a challenger to be my queen. I asked Whisper because I could trust her and believed that she would be successful. The armor on her forearm is a symbol of her worthiness. She would not need to get more to prove herself. Many were impressed that a Zeyphrion was able to pass the armor test."

Dancewing squinted her eyes. "I'm still not happy that I was not included in the conversation. And that I missed my hatchling's trial and fight."

"I apologize for that. It wasn't intentional. Time was of the essence. If I hadn't gotten Whisper to help when I did, I would have been forced to be with a traitor who would probably take over my clan."

"You are a young king but you are right. I shouldn't be so angry. I'm trying to change but I guess I'm still stuck in my old ways." She lifted Whisper's armored arm. She looked at it with determined eyes. "It's smooth and sleek. And beautiful in its own way." She looked it over some more. "I'm not happy with how this has transpired but I approve of your decisions." Dancewing let go of her arm and went back to the other dragons.

Whisper leaned into Rageskin. "You had no idea that Blackheart was a traitor."

"Nope but your mom doesn't know that. It's close enough to the truth."

Dancewing looked at Rageskin. "You do realize that this puts you in line to rule the Zeyphrions. Once, I pass on my queenship to Whisper, you will be her king. She will be in charge and you will only rule if she dies or doesn't have a female heir. And you must prove yourself worthy of being a Zeyphrion leader."

Rageskin had not thought about how his relationship with Whisper would affect the Zeyphrion monarchy. "Will I have to do a dance to be accepted?"

Dancewing and Whisper looked at each other with a devilish grin. Rageskin was worried. Dancewing walked up to him.

"Answer me. Monarch to monarch. Are you going to treat my daughter properly?

"Yes."

"Are you going to protect her?"

"Yes."

Dancewing looked him in the eyes. "That's good enough for me." She turned and walked away.

Rageskin felt confused. "So am I an honorary Zeyphrion?"

"No. But you have my trust and, with that, the trust of my clan." Dancewing went to speak with the other Zeyphrions. Whisper went back to his side.

"I was not expecting that," he said. "I really thought I'd have to perform for you."

"I really hoped you were going to," she said with a smile.

"*Say my name.*"

Rageskin looked around. It wasn't very loud but he knew he heard someone talk to him. "Is there anyone else here beside your mom's group?"

"Just us. Why?"

"Someone keeps whispering to me. I thought it was the wind but it keeps happening."

Before Whisper could say anything, a darkness rose around the edge of the island. It crept toward them like a mist. The dragons came together in a circle, placing their backs against each other. The mist spread open as several Selenthrax flew onto the island. They landed on their back legs. They stood like the Zeyphrions but were much larger. Even Rageskin felt small to them. They raised their arms, showing the blackness with white scales accenting it to look like a night sky in their wings. They were covered in white scales with hints of blue. Crescent horns adorned their heads. Their tails were long and curved as they rested on the ground. The largest of the Selenthrax scanned the island.

"Very pretty place, yes, yes, this is," she said. "Very pretty."

Dancewing went toward the Selenthrax. "What business do you have here? This is our territory."

She looked down at Dancewing. "Such a pretty little dragon, yes, yes. Feathers and all. I am Lunawind, leader of the Selenthrax. We mean no harm, no, no."

"State your business," Dancewing repeated.

Lunawind turned her head to the right and then the left, like something was shifting in her skull. She repeated the motion. She reached out her right hand, a long claw pointing to a young Selenthrax. "Shinestar, bring forward our finds, yes, yes."

Shinestar walked forward, carrying the metal carcass of a Ferrolith. She placed it on the ground. It was torn open. Lunawind took a step forward and caressed the broken edges with a long talon. "We look for this, yes, yes. A new dragon perhaps. Maybe a child of Morthauron, yes, yes. Do you know of its?"

Whisper and Dancewing shook with fear. Rageskin stepped beside them. "We have not seen this before. It's a bit unusual. What do you know about it?"

Lunawind cocked her head. Her eyes glanced from Rageskin to Dancewing. "You are not of this clan, no, no."

"I am an ally to them," Rageskin replied. He gripped his sword harder.

"Ally. I see. You lie for your allies, yes, yes?"

"No lies. We haven't seen this dragon before nor you. But we do know of Morthauron."

Lunawind's eyes grew large. "You know of the great Morthauron, yes, yes? We have searched to be seen by him but Auroradraca has cast a shadow upon us, silencing our prayers to him, yes, yes."

"We have dealt with both of them in the past," Rageskin stated.

"You have met Morthauron?"

"We dealt with his Necrodrakes. Destroyed them. Sealed them to Wyrm's land."

Lunawind hissed at him. "You destroy his creations, no, no. You lie. All you lies."

Rageskin raised his sword and stepped toward her. "You have overstayed your welcome. Go back to where you came from."

Lunawind let a low growl rest in her throat. "We will leaves, yes, yes. I will let you have the carcass. Maybe it helps you remember things. We will find these dragons, yes, yes. Maybe returns, yes, yes. These islands are an eyesore of the night sky that is the skin of our god." She turned and the others followed. Shinestar hesitated. Before they left, Lunawind said, "Morthauron bless all of you with his kiss," and proceeded to jump off the island. They opened their arm wings and floated to the ground. Shinestar was the last to leave.

"Her vengeance will be patient. I'm sorry," Shinestar said with sadness in her voice and leaped off the island.

Rageskin looked over the edge. He could see the Selenthrax floating to the surface. He turned and said, "They're gone."

Dancewing released her breath like she had been holding it in for too long. "Whisper, what do you know about this, this, this thing?"

"It's the enemy we were trying to tell you about. Somehow they are able to transfer their ash from these bodies into living ones," Whisper explained.

Dancewing's eyes grew full with concern. "That's impossible."

"If Morthauron created this creature, then it could be," Rageskin said.

"Have you been visited by Auroradraca? It's happened before," Dancewing asked.

"Not yet, which is odd considering what we are dealing with," Rageskin said.

"You think she created this thing too?" Whisper wondered.

Rageskin was examining the carcass. "The ones we ran into jumped into my volcano, killing themselves rather than go insane. And the Solari brought us an empty shell as well." He traced a talon along deep grooves in the carcass, noting how much larger they were compared to his.

"What happened to that one? And the Solari?" Dancewing questioned.

Rageskin ran his talons into all the grooves. "I think Lunawind happened," as he pantomimed a ripping motion. Horror came across the Zeyphrions' faces. "They are a new clan. Seemed to be a little extreme with their love for Auroradraca. We need to find Mudball and Stream. Something bad is coming. We must unite the clans again."

Chapter 17 Reunion of the Hearts

Mudball sat in the middle of the wooden raft with Thornseed and Petalspear looking over the edge into the water. He had decided the quickest way to get around was to use a trade cave. Gaiajades created underground tunnels that allowed them to visit all the territories without worrying about the weather or crops being ruined by the sun and heat. The small river that flowed in the cave led to other tributaries and tunnels. Mudball remembered hurrying through this tunnel, being chased by a Gaiajade-turned-Necrodrake. The tunnel had collapsed and created a lake above ground. Since then, the Gaiajades and Aquanox worked together to open the tunnel and reroute the river. It was the same day he had learned to fly. He smiled.

"Friend Mudballs," Thornseed asked. "You okays?"

"Yeah, I'm fines," Mudball replied. "Fine. Just remembering stuff."

"Wez sent ours clans aheads to meets us at ends of tunnels," Petalspear said. "Theyz send messages for others to returns."

Mudball gave them a confused look. "How?"

"Wez send pollen into airs. Others smells its. They zooms backs to heres," Thornseed said. "Yous can't smells it?"

"I guess not. That is pretty cool. The Aquanox can do something like that but with water," Mudball noted.

"Wez been getting messages," Petalspear said, sniffing the air. "You knows a Rageskins and Whispers?"

"Oh, yes! Theyz are my best friends," Mudball responded excitedly. "They are. I've been around you guys for too long."

"You finally sounds normal," Thornseed replied. "Clan members finds thems. Big stuffs goings on."

"I have another friend named Stream. Are any Florastryx with him?"

Petalspear sniffed the air, following a pattern that only she could see. Mudball sat in awe as the tiny dragon seemed to move from one pattern to the next. "Yes, Streams has clans with him." She paused. "Friends beings led to tunnel's ends. Wez meet at lakes."

Mudball cheered on the inside. It felt like forever since he had last seen his friends. He wished it was under better circumstances. He wondered if they had run into these new weird dragons. Out of the corner of his eyes he thought he saw something move in the shadows. The tunnel was lit by moss but there were still dark areas along the solid dirt path beside the river. His heart raced a little. He focused energy into a back crystal, brightening up the tunnel. He could not see anything beside large rocks that littered the area.

"Somethings wrongs?" Thornseed asked.

"Maybe. Probably nothing. Thought I saw something moving but I guess not. Are there any Florastryx in here besides you two?"

Both of them sniffed the air. "Faint smell. Maybes couple wents through heres earliers?" Petalspear noted.

Mudball kept looking around. He felt something was off. Behind him the water started to move to the sides. Something was moving toward him. He tried backing up but forgot how small the raft was. The raft lifted a little under his weight. He moved back to the middle. The crystals lit up brighter, a humming coming from them. The Florastryx got into a fighting stance, spreading their wings wide, trying to make themselves look bigger. The water calmed as something went deeper into the water. Mudball's breathing slowed as he tried to listen. Suddenly, the water surface exploded as Stream jumped out of the water. Mudball screamed and fired a breath at him. The shot missed and hit a large boulder on the edge of the water. The raft tipped up and over as Mudball fell backward. The Florastryx flew into the air.

"Mudball, it's me!" Stream shouted. He looked around but did not see him. Worried, he dove back into the water. Mudball was kicking his legs, trying to get to the surface but was sinking quickly. Stream wrapped around him and pulled him up. They got onto the riverbank. Stream uncoiled around him and lunged for the raft. He bit and pulled it to the bank. Mudball coughed up water and tried to take a breath. He gave Stream a frightened look.

"Stream! Don't do that ever again! You scared the life out of me," Mudball whined.

"I'm sorry. This river has some fast undercurrents. I was going faster than I thought."

"Yeah, well." Mudball paused. He could not see his little friends. "Thornseed! Petalspear! Where are you!"

"Wez are Thornroots and Lilypetals," two pink and white Florastryx said in unison as they climbed out of the water. "Thornseed and Petalspear aren't withs us."

"Wez good, Mudballs," Thornseed said. Their wings stuck out of the ground from the quick holes they had dug. "Hides goods, wez did." The pair climbed out of their holes. They saw the other Florastryx.

"Thornseed! Petalspear!"

"Lilypetal! Thornroot!"

The four dragons greeted each other with head rubs.

"I see you got your own Florastryx," Stream said.

"Yeah, there's a whole group of them waiting for us at the end of the tunnel. Did you catch their names? They're almost the sames."

Stream looked at him.

"I know, I know. I've been around these guys for a while now."

The four Florastryx turned and looked at Stream and Mudball. "Wez are eggmates. Shares parts of names."

"Siblings," Stream realized.

"Wow, that is so neat. Hey, Stream, I have had some weird stuff happening. What about you?"

"Oh, I have had an interesting last day or two. Let's get you guys back on the raft and I'll push you to the end. Did they tell you if Rageskin and Whisper were on their way?"

"Yeah. Pollen messages. Kinda like you but not as wet."

Stream chuckled. Mudball and the Florastryx gathered onto the raft while Stream bit into it and pushed.

THE DRAGON GROUP EXITED the cave after tying up the raft. The land where the dragon territories converged was a sight to behold. A large meadow of various flowers decorated the flat land. The large lake that was created during the Necrodrake war was a bright blue and reflected the cloudless sky. Nearby rested the ruins of a Zeyphrion island that had fallen. The Zeyphrions were not able to recreate the magic that once resided within and lifted the island many centuries before so it stayed as a reminder to those who were lost to the Necrodrakes. Mudball and Stream stared out into the lake.

"The last time I pulled you out of water, you were a lot lighter," Stream joked.

Mudball looked at him and blurted, "It's muscle!" Stream chuckled. "Really it is. I've been training."

"Why do we always end up here?" a familiar voice shouted behind them. They turned around to see Rageskin and Whisper. The four dragons went to greet each other halfway. Whisper delivered hugs while Rageskin looked on.

"We have so much to tell you guys," Mudball said excitedly. "I've met some new dragons and made friends with them. Oh, oh, and I fought for leadership of the Gaiajades, and,-".

"Slow down, Mudball," Whisper encouraged. "We have a great deal to tell you as well." Thornseed and Petalspear landed on Mudball's back crystals.

"And who are you?" Whisper asked.

"I iz Thornseed. This is mys mates, Petalspear. Wez are leaders of Florastryx."

"So tiny and," Rageskin began.

"And pretty," Whisper continued. "You look just like the flowers around us. Have you been here this whole time and we missed you?"

"Wez come from norths, past scary mountains," Thornseed replied. "Big, scary dragons no likes us theres. Wez come heres for safeties."

"Mudball verys nice," Petalspear said.

"Of course he is," Whisper said. "Is your whole clan here?"

The meadow around them began to move about as Florastryx sprang into the air. The meadow seemed to migrate as they moved about.

"That's a lot of little dragons," Rageskin remarked.

"But they are so useful," Mudball said. "They help with crops, to help them grow. And they are speedy and can send faraway messages."

"That explains the little one that stopped us as we were flying," Rageskin noted. "I hadn't seen one before and he was hard to understand."

Mudball remarked, "You gets used to its." The other three stared at him. His cheeks turned a little red from embarrassment. Then they all started to laugh. The Florastryx joined in, not understanding the joke but wanting to be included.

"I've missed you so much," Whisper said. "You were always funny and could cheer me up."

"What's been happening to you guys?" Stream asked. He noticed Whisper's arm. "I assume it has something to do with Whisper's armor?"

Rageskin told the group about how he asked Whisper to be his queen, her trial, and fight. Rageskin told them about Darkheart, Blackwing, and the two Ferroliths that attacked them.

"And then there was this new clan. Came right into my volcano. Solari," he finished. "They seemed to enthusiastically worship Auroradraca."

"Theys the means dragons that mades us leaves," Petalspear interjected.

"And then there was another group that made it to my islands. Selenthrax. They seemed the opposite, worshiping Morthauron," Whisper continued.

Stream began. "I discovered a hidden cave with tablets. One made reference to a new clan made by Morthauron from the metal dragons. Sounds like the Ferroliths did something to get him to bring them back. Something to do with transferring their ash from these metal bodies to living. But I met one and he went insane." He shuddered, remembering how Raindrop acted.

"And I think there were some Gaiajades who were possessed or whatever it is," Mudball added. "They were acting weird during a leadership battle, which I won by the way, and ended up exploding."

The three dragons stared at him in disbelief. "You charge your crystals for too long and don't use your breath: Kaboom!" he explained, adding sound effects. "Wait, you two are married? Like a couple? How does that work?"

"I am king of the Inferoths and she's my queen by ceremony."

"How are you going to have kids?" Mudball asked.

Whisper shook her head. "We will worry about that later. What do you mean, you're the leader?"

"Gempath wanted to step down as leader and we had a tournament and I accidently volunteered to fight and I kept winning somehow, I don't know how but I did, but then Coalash went all crazy like he was fighting himself, like in his head-"

"Slow down, Mudball," Stream asked. "Coalash was fighting himself? Explain."

"Like he was talking, then someone else was talking but it was his mouth moving and then he used his breath, which you can't do, and exploded and I won." He looked at them. "What?"

"That's what happened to me," Stream said.

"Dreamwave exploded and now you're the leader?" Mudball asked.

"What? No. An Aquanox acted like someone else was in his head, fighting for control. It," he paused. "Didn't end well for him."

"So these Ferroliths are sneaking into each clan and taking over bodies. I still don't understand how this is happening," Rageskin said.

"I know," a metallic feminine voice said. The group turned around. Steelheart, along with an orange Florastryx, showed up.

"Steelheart, you're back. What happened?" Mudball asked.

"You know her?" Stream asked.

"She's like the ones that attacked us in the volcano," Rageskin commented.

"And the empty shells," Whisper noted.

"Yeah, she showed up one day and we just hit it off. Then she ran away."

Steelheart lowered her head. "I had to. I was ordered to take over your body and throw the fight with Coalash so he would be leader but I couldn't." There was sadness in her voice. "I just couldn't. You were so nice to me and just accepted me like this and." She stopped. "Oh, Auroradraca, I want to cry but I can't." She started to bang her head on the ground. "Make it stop," she would say as she lifted her head. "Make it stop!"

"Orangeblossom, whats is happenings?" Thornseed asked.

"She's beens doings this all ways," Orangeblossom replied. "She gets mads and hurts selfs."

Steelheart stopped what she was doing. "I'm sorry but you just don't understand what it's like."

Whisper calmly said, "Try us. We have seen some stuff. We want to know so we can help."

Steelheart looked at Mudball. "They're my friends. You can trust them, Steelheart."

She scanned the dragons. "Centuries ago, there was the first war with the original Necrodrakes. The Ferroliths were wiped out by them, me included. After that, there was only blackness. I tried to find my family but there was nothing. There was no direction, no noise, nothing. Then someone grabbed me and I woke up in this metal body. Ironfire made a deal with Morthauron to bring us back when he died. But this body is nothing, I can't feel anything and it's so frustrating. I know there's ground under me. I know the sun is hot but it means nothing to me. We had to find other dragons, bite them, and transfer our ash into them. We can access their memories, their breaths, everything is available to us but their ash is forced out. Sometimes it doesn't work and I've seen my friends fight for control of the body they attacked."

She paused. Memories raced through her mind. "I left you, Mudball, because I didn't want to hurt you. I can feel my sanity leaving me day by day. It's been so long being in this body. I . . . . went back to my clan, just hoping that maybe there was another way. I want to cry so bad." She stopped.

The four dragons looked at each other. "Tell us what happened. It's okay," Whisper encouraged.

"I hid in the shadows. Everyone was angry and frustrated, especially Melthorn, our leader. And then Morthauron showed up." The four dragons' jaws dropped. "It was so scary to see him in the flesh. He gave us a choice to have new bodies that were our own, to live forever. Everyone accepted and they, they, they, changed into something horrific. They were renamed the Eclipsire. Now they have to drink blood to stay immortal."

"How did you not change?" Stream asked.

"I didn't accept it. Orangeblossom got me out of there without being seen."

"Any ideas what their plans were?" Rageskin questioned.

"No, I don't. Melthorn wants to rule everywhere, I think. But I don't know how they are going to do it."

Rageskin began talking, using his fingers to count off his thoughts. "We have the Solari. The Selenthrax. The Florastryx seem to be allies. Now, the Eclipsire. Enemies on all fronts. Morthauron seems to be gaining power like he did with the Necrodrakes. Has anyone been visited by Auroradraca? Seems like she would have shown up to guide us or something."

They looked at each other. Mudball said, "The Florastryx talk about a god name Tuzu that they believe in."

Thornseed was excited. "Oh, yes, the greats Tuzu, god of plantlife. He works with Auroradracas with flowers and trees. He creates us in his images."

Rageskin blinked his eyes, trying to wrap his head around the idea that there were other gods. "Have you met Tuzu?"

Thornseed lowered his head. "Nos. Wez pray buts never hears from hims."

"It's okay, Thornseed," Rageskin comforted. "We've met Auroraradraca. Sometimes meeting your god doesn't go the way you want it to. Plus, I've never heard of Tuzu. Just Auroradraca and Morthauron. Are there gods that we don't know of?"

Stream licked his lips. "I may have been visited by a forgotten god."

"This is a bit much now," Mudball remarked. "Was it Tuzu?"

"Her name is Futurarteon, goddess of knowledge and future. I met her in a hidden cave behind my tablet cave."

"The brainy dragon found the smart god," Mudball noted. "Makes sense."

Stream thought about what he said, then nodded in agreement. "She implied that Auroradraca imprisoned the other gods, used their powers to fight in the first war and to not let Morthauron create life."

"Think she messed that one up," Whisper said. "Did she say anything else?"

"It might be helpful but the reason we can still hold onto the power Auroradraca gave us during the war is because we are descendants of the founding dragons."

They stared at Stream. Mudball reacted. "We what now?"

"We have hung onto our magic powers because of our ancestors. That's why no one else can have it."

"That is, wow, something," Whisper replied. "Was there anything else? Another surprise?"

"She disappeared before I could ask her the list of questions in my head," Stream said. "Said Auroradraca sensed her and disappeared."

"This is insane," Mudball said. "What should we do? Gather up everyone? Fight all three clans or just the scary dragons? I don't want to fight scary dragons again."

"Calm down, Mudball," Rageskin said. "We cannot panic. Our people didn't listen to us before because we were just kids lost to the background of our clans. Now, we have experience and leadership that everyone should respect."

"But what do we do first?" Whisper asked.

Around them, the flowers began to move around them. It was slow at first but they began to move in a circular motion. Thornseed watched as they moved. Florastryx escaped the moving meadow. "Hey, guys, this no goods, I thinks." The group turned around and watched as the flowers and grass merged together to create two separate hill-shaped piles. Rageskin took a fighting stance and raised his shield. The first hill split down the middle. Two large wings spread open, branches acting as a humerus and limb bones, the skin made of lily pad leaves. Flowers covered the backside of the wings. Large legs appeared, made from tree trunks and roots for claws. Down the chest were bark plates surrounded by green leaf-shaped scales across the body. The head had several thorny branches growing out of it. Various flowers dotted the neck and head.

The other hill opened. One wing was covered with healthy growing plants with green leaves alongside yellow and purple plants. The other wing was a yellowish-brown with red berries and dark purple and red flowers. The scales were green with purple trim. The body with the green vegetation appears muscular and healthy while the other looked malnourished. The head continued the duality of the body: one side was covered with green and purple scales while the other side was a skull. At first glance, the two giant dragons could pass as twins. The small dragons stood mesmerized by the sight.

"Guys, any thoughts? Anything at all?" Mudball asked.

"They're gods," Stream said. "It's the same as when I was visited."

"Friendly?" Whisper wondered out loud.

"They don't look scary," Mudball said. The second dragon god turned its face. "Nevermind. Yup, scary."

The giant dragons said nothing. They looked at the group. Thornseed stepped toward the giants. He seemed so small compared to them. "Tuzu?"

The first giant looked at him. "Yes, mys childs," he said in a gentle voice. "I is Tuzu, god of plantlifes." The Florastryx lined up around Tuzu and bowed their heads. "My childrens, I is so happys that yous haves survived withouts me."

Rageskin leaned over to Whisper, quietly saying, "He talks just like them. That's crazy."

"There are two gods in front of us and that's your first thought," she said back.

"No bows, no bows," Tuzu said. "Please, stands ups and rejoice in mys return." The Florastryx bounced about him in happiness. The other god sat quietly, her face showing no care. Whisper stepped forward.

"I'm sorry for not praising or acknowledging you," she said, addressing the second god. "We do not know who you are."

The god turned her head toward Whisper. She took several large steps and leaned her head toward Whisper. Whisper tried not to move. Forgotten god or not, she did not want to make her an enemy by doing something offensive. The god sniffed her. She reached a front claw toward her, long sharp needle-like talons tapping Whisper on the shoulder. She could feel a sharp pain as the talon cut her slightly. She felt the warmth of her magic move to heal her. The god retracted her claws. "Interesting," she said. Her voice sounded like two talking at once, one happy the other sad. "Interesting," she repeated. "You have magic within you, small one."

"Yes, a gift from Auroradraca. To help defend Wyrm from Morthauron's creations," Whisper explained.

The god puffed some air like she was amused by a lame joke. "Oh, yes, dear sister Auroradraca. Ever manipulating others. How things never change. Probably made all of you forget about the other gods in the pantheon. But, despite being her creation, I find you . . . pleasant." Whisper swore she saw the skull side smile. "I am Exalithor, goddess of healing and disease. Tuzu is my twin."

Stream said, "Is Futurarteon a sibling of yours?"

Tuzu exclaimed, "Oh, yes! Verys much sos! Haves you seens thems? Theys so mysterious."

"I have," Stream responded. "They tried to tell me what happened to you. That Auroradraca made everyone forget the other gods but the Florastryx seemed to remember Tuzu so I don't understand why no one else remembered you."

"Ours sisters means," Tuzu replied. "Blocks us in other realms, blinds us to ours followers. I exists in alls plants, my little dragons remembers throughs them but Auroradraca too powerful, stops mes."

"She used us," Exalithor said. "Used our powers. Then hid us from Wyrm."

"What do you mean," Stream asked. "Used your powers?"

Exalithor and Tuzu looked up, like an unseen someone was talking to them. "We must go," Exalithor said. "Futurarteon is telling us that Auroradraca has detected us. We must leave and join them."

"Please don't goes," Thornseed pleaded. "Wez finally finds you."

"Frets nots, little ones," Tuzu said. "Wez will returns."

"Be careful. Auroradraca is furious at the return of the gods. Other gods wish to return and are angry at her. War is coming for all of you."

Both gods closed their wings to resemble giant mounds of plants. Then deflated and flowers fell to the ground. The group stared at the flowers as they soaked in the information.

"Stream, do you have any ideas?" Whisper asked.

"This is a lot. I don't even know where to begin."

A Florastryx with thin purple flowered wings came zooming in. He breathed hard. "Rageskins, comes quicks," he gasped. "Volcano unders attacks." The Florastryx landed and fell to the ground from exhaustion.

Rageskin picked up the purple dragon. "Thank you, little one." He placed the Florastryx near the lake edge. Other Florastryx went to help their kin. "You guys gather the clans. Prepare everyone for battle. I have to handle this and can move quicker without you."

"I'm coming," Whisper said.

"No, you need to get your clan organized."

"But-"

"I said no. Help get everyone ready." Rageskin flapped his wings and took off.

Tuzu: The Distant Past

Tuzu *walked about the forest he had just created. As we walked, grass and bushes trailed behind him. Walking on all fours, he came to a clearing in the forest. Trees had fallen from a recent storm. He looked over the uprooted trees, his leaf-like scales shimmering from the sunlight that invaded through a hole in the canopy.*

"Nos, Nos, nots goods. Poor trees. Tuzus wills help yous." He closed his eyes, his branch head horns glowing. Spores flew out of the horns and landed on the trees. Small colorful mushrooms sprouted from the trees. "Nice. Very nice," he said, happy with his work. He stretched his wings, their lily-like skin dropping dew that had been collected that morning. He shook off the water. Small flowers and weeds grew where the water droplets landed. He continued to walk through the forest, plants responding with growth spurts as he ventured through. He came out of the forest to a field of tall grass and flowers. A breeze hit his face. Tuzu closed his eyes, enjoying the feeling of coolness. A bright light got his attention.

"Hello, Tuzu," Auroradraca greeted.

"Hellos, hellos," Tuzu responded. "Dids yous likes the new forests I mades?"

"Oh, yes, Tuzu. They are exactly what I wanted for my newest creations."

"And the crops for Gaiajades?"

"They are perfect. Tuzu, I need to ask something of you."

"Oh, okays. Oh, waits I has somethings to shows yous." Tuzu began to search through the flowers. The flowers responded to his presence and opened up to what he was searching for. He picked it up with his mouth, carried it over to her and set it down with a beaming smile.

"What is this?" Auroradraca asked as he picked it up. It was a small dragon made from dirt with flower colored wings. "What have you been up to, Tuzu?"

"Wells, I beens helping yous with plants and such and I hads an idea for dragons. They will help serve yous and mes with plants around Wyrms. I justs can'ts brings to lifes like yous."

She examined the little statue. A sly smile came across her face. "This is beautiful work, Tuzu. Just beautiful."

"Thanks. I prouds of thems."

"I will gift your creations with life but I must ask for something in return."

"Whats does yous needs?" Tuzu responded with happiness in his voice.

"In the centuries to come an event will threaten Wyrm, possibly ending all the life you and I have made."

"Oh, nos."

"Yes, Futurarteon has seen it themselves."

"What cans I do to helps?"

"I need a portion of your essence. I will merge it with my Gaiajades so that they can champion against the evil that will arise."

"But if I does thats I wills be forgottens, banished to others realm."

"That is the price that must be paid so that Wyrm can survive. Will you willingly give me some essence for the future? Your plants will continue to live on. As will your Florastryx."

Tears came to his eyes. "Florastryx is theirs names? And you'll release mes after threats gones?" Auroradraca smiled and nodded her head.

"Okays. For safeties of Wyrms I gives myselfs to yous."

"Thank you," Auroradraca said with a sinister tone to her voice.

Chapter 18 A Change in Thought

Rageskin rocketed to the Inferoth volcano. The land, littered with thorny trees and red dirt, raced below him in a blur. Many thoughts went through his head, thinking of the worst case scenario, trying to prepare himself for what he would find. The volcano came into view and he slowed down. He could see figures moving on the ground. Bodies scattered on the landscape, both Inferoth and an unknown black dragon. He feared the Necrodrakes had escaped but he could not smell their rot. At the base of the volcano, he could see a single Inferoth surrounded by four dragons. He adjusted his wings and bulleted toward the closest dragon. He raised his sword and shield. He rammed his sword into the shoulders of the first, skewering it on the blade. His momentum slammed his shield into the next one, slamming it and himself into the volcano side. He ripped his sword out of the first, sending blood everywhere. The second dragon hissed and struggled to get out from under the shield. He reared back and drove his sword into the dragon's head.

"Help!" the Inferoth pleaded. The two dragons were trying to claw their way through the plate armor on his neck. Rageskin roared and spewed liquid fire onto the two dragons while the Inferoth ducked. The dragons screamed in pain, trying to shake the breath off their skin. The Inferoth punched upwards at the closest dragon, driving his wrist mounted spike into the dragon's jaw. The second dragon dropped to his knees, trying to remove the liquid fire. Rageskin swung his sword, removing the dragon's head. The body fell to the ground with a thump. Rageskin looked at the Inferoth as he got up.

"What happened?" he asked.

"Near the break of dawn but still dark, we were attacked while most of us were asleep," the Inferoth explained. "These dragons were," he paused, trying to find the words. "Something is wrong with them. They would bite onto the necks and drain the body of blood. At first, they simply snuck around but as the sentries became aware of them, we were roused to the call of battle. It did not go well without you to lead us. We killed many but they had abilities we hadn't seen before. A breath of a poisonous gas that made you choke so they could attack you. And don't look into their eyes. They take over your mind or something. I watched my brothers stop flying after staring into the eyes. They fell into the lava pool." He paused, fighting back tears. "I'm sorry, my king, for my weakness."

Rageskin put a hand on his shoulder. "It's alright. Let's get inside and save who we can." They ran to the side entrance, pressed the pressure plate, and waited for the rock door to slide open. They ran up the stairs, readying their weapons for battle. They reached the top and looked around. The battle had ended. Several Inferoths were attending to the wounded. A tall Inferoth landed beside Rageskin. He saluted Rageskin with his arm across his chest.

"Talonblood," Rageskin began. "What can you tell me? I received some information from Sharpclaw."

"Darkheart snuck a group of this clan in during the night," Talonblood said, pointing to a black corpse nearby. "We were able to drive away most of them but these dragons took zero prisoners. They simply drank the blood or made sport with our minds somehow. As the sun rose, they retreated as if the sun hurt them. Some of them shared names of Inferoths who have disappeared like Darkheart."

"Unfortunately, they are the missing Inferoths along with other clans. Morthauron corrupted the Ferrolith clan into these creatures called Eclipsire," Rageskin explained.

"*Death to them all,*" the voice whispered in Rageskin's ear. It was louder than before. He looked around to see if another Inferoth landed by him.

"What are your orders?" Talonblood asked.

"Continue helping the wounded. Determine how many we lost. Seal off all known entrances: only the volcano's mouth will be our way in or out."

"*Don't be weak,*" the voice whispered. "*Bring death to them.*"

Rageskin could feel an anger build in him. "Are there any Eclipsire still alive?"

"*Release me!*" a voice demanded from above him. Rageskin could see on the armor bridge an Eclipsire struggling with three Inferoths. Rageskin flapped his wings and went to the bridge. The Eclipsire had his arms pinned between two of them while the third tried to hold down the wings. The Eclipsire stopped struggling when he laid eyes on Rageskin. The black scales on him were wet with blood. He snarled, exposing his long canines.

"Explain yourself," Rageskin demanded. "Why did you attack us?"

"We only want to live. Live the lives that were stolen from us," it hissed. Its three tails vibrated on the ground. "You were on the way. Why attack you? Convenience."

"*Kill him,*" the voice whispered.

"We will continue across this land, taking what we want," the Eclipsire said. "Your land. The floating islands. Blood for immortality."

"*Avoid his eyes. Kill him.*"

An unfamiliar rage built inside Rageskin. "Chain him up. We will figure out what to do with him later."

As the Inferoths started to move him, the Eclipsire's tails came to life. Long barbs came out of the ends, each stabbing the Inferoths in the necks. They instantly fell to the ground. Rageskin froze for a moment, taking in what happened.

"*Kill it. Kill it. Kill it now!*" the voice screamed at him.

The Eclipsire turned to Rageskin, his tails moving on their own behind him, his canines growing longer. "I wonder how royal blood tastes," it said as drool escaped his mouth. He leapt toward Rageskin. He raised his shield. The Eclipsire splattered against it but dug its long sharp talons into the rock. It pulled backward, ripping the shield off Rageskin's skin. Rageskin lurched forward, losing his balance. Pain flooded his arm from the armor being ripped off. The Eclipsire threw the shield off the bridge and ran at Rageskin again. He swung his sword but the Eclipsire sidestepped at the last moment. It slashed at Rageskin's calf. He winced in pain as he spun his left arm back.

"*Rip them off,*" the voice said.

Rageskin grabbed the middle tail and removed it from the Eclipsire. It wiggled in his hand, trying to stab him. He threw it over the edge into the lava pool. The Eclipsire fell to the ground. Rageskin put his weight on the back of leg and grabbed the other two tails.

"*Do it.*"

He pulled back and ripped off the two tails. The Eclipsire screamed in pain as Rageskin stabbed the wing base with the tails' barbs. He placed his other foot between the shoulder blades, reached down to the wing base, and gripped it. He grunted with effort as bones began to break. He twisted his wrists, breaking the wings off. Blood ran out the new holes in the Eclipsire's back.

"*End him.*"

Rageskin dropped his left knee into the small of the back, wrapped his left arm around the dragon's neck and pulled back. The Eclipsire snapped at him, trying to bite whatever was closest. Rageskin swung his armored right arm as the dragon opened its mouth. It chomped down on the arm, teeth shattering into a million pieces. The jaw was stuck in the forearm armor. Rageskin pulled his arm back quickly, turning the

Eclispsire's head in an unnatural direction. He released his grip on the dead dragon and the body slumped to the ground. Rageskin stood over it, hate in his eyes.

"*Sacrifice it to me.*"

Rageskin looked at the Eclipsire as other Inferoths showed up to check on him. He grabbed the Eclipsire by the ankle and tossed it into the lava pool. The volcano seemed to shake with pleasure. He saw the three Inferoths being checked on. One dragon shook his head. Rageskin felt something come over him, an anger building inside him

"*Show no mercy.*"

"Show no mercy to these creatures," Rageskin commanded. "Death on sight."

LATER IN THE DAY, RAGESKIN sat in silence in his cave. It had been a long day of recovering bodies, preparing them for the lava pool burial, and searching the volcano for more Eclipsire that may have hidden in the magma tubes. He tapped his claws on his stone throne. A million decisions went through his head. He wanted to go to war with the Eclipsire but no one knew where they went. He sent scouts to check out the former Ferroliths home to see if it was their base of operations. He wanted only to grieve for his lost clan members but he needed information. The dead outnumbered the living. The volcano seemed quieter than usual. He failed his clan, to protect them, to keep them alive.

"*You're weak,*" the voice said.

"I'm not. I just want what's best for my clan."

"*And your decisions have killed them.*"

"They have not!" Rageskin screamed as he stood up. "Who are you?"

Silence. The volcano shook slightly. "Who are you?" Rageskin repeated.

"*I do not like being ordered by Auroradraca's creations,*" the voice finally said.

"I'm too angry to care. Deal with it. I repeat, who are you?"

Silence. The volcano shook more.

"*You do not command me.*"

"I. Don't. Care. Who are you?"

"*I am a prisoner of an agreement, a lie used to bolster Auroradraca's own power. I have waited for my time to return. To have followers like my dear sisters and brothers.*"

"I didn't ask for your sob story and grow impatient. Who are you?"

The lava pool started bumbling. "*I am Draegar, the god of war and the afterlife. Release me. Allow me to fuel your vengeance against the Eclispire and any who would raise a claw against us.*"

"And how do I release you?"

"*Believe in me. Say my name.*"

Rageskin began to open his mouth when Talonblood entered the cave. "Rageskin, the Solari have returned." He gave Talonblood a look.

"What do they want?"

"To help us with the Eclipsire."

Rageskin left the cave and flew down to the edge of the lava pool. Skyblaze and several Solari waited for him.

"I see you have been visited by these abominations. We came across them as we had left your home. They avoided us, fearful of our light," Skyblaze remarked.

"I'm not in the mood right now. What do you want?" Rageskin snapped back.

"We have a common enemy, these creatures of Morthauron. They should not exist in the world of the great Auroradraca. They are an eyesore to existence. I hope to gain more knowledge of them since they no longer seem to be in their metal bodies."

"They are called the Eclipsire. They want blood so they can live forever. They attacked us. Now we fight back."

"Do not be angry with me, my friend," Skyblaze said arrogantly. "We are on the same side."

"To be honest," Rageskin said, looking around. "I'm not really a fan of Auroradraca right now. She let this happen and we are not friends by any means."

Skyblaze squinted his eyes. "Morthauron created these beasts."

"Yeah and she made Morthauron angry at the world and look where it got us."

"You were punished for lying to us. You knew what that carcass was and didn't tell us. Auroradraca simply allowed them to find your home as punishment for slighting her favorite clan."

"If you are wanting to ask for my clan's help, you better choose your next words carefully," Rageskin warned. "We may be fewer in number now, compared to your clan but we have a lot of fight left in us." Inferoth flew down and backed up Rageskin. Skyblaze scanned the scene.

"We came once, extending a wing to be allies. You felt you had to do things on your own. We will leave and continue searching for these Eclipsire. Perhaps you will pray to Auroradraca for guidance and you will see the error of not joining us. May she bless you with her wisdom." Skyblaze turned to leave when Rageskin spoke.

"How do you feel about other gods?"

"There is only Auroradraca. She governs all, bringing life to all. Her will is law."

"I don't think Auroradraca will be the one that I pray to."

Skyblaze's face turned angry. "There is only Auroradraca. You will not speak blasphemy of her. She gave you life. She is your only true deity."

Rageskin raised his sword into the air. "Draegar. The Inferoths pray to you for guidance in how to rid our land of our enemies." The volcano began to shake violently. The lava pool boiled, spewing liquid rock across the inside. A large dragon head rose out of the large lava pool, spikes rising up like daggers, his eyes glowed a molten gold and anger. Two large bone-colored horns reached out from the back of his skull. His underjaw was lined with black whiskers from the chin to the long neck. The space between his eyes were bone with runes written into them with a crown of jagged horns. His scales were a mix of red, black, and yellow, giving the appearance of chainmail. Large bone plates covered his shoulders like pads with pieces added to cover the chest. He wielded in his hand a long rock ax handle topped with two metal ax heads, the top one larger than the second. Draegar stretched his shoulder wings, cutting through the sides of the volcano, sending boulders outward, lava bleeding from the wounds. Flames swirled around him as black smoke escaped from his nostrils.

The Inferoths looked at the god in awe. The Solari looked on with a mix of hatred and fear. Rageskin looked up at Draegar and back to Skyblaze.

"Run," he growled deeply.

Draegar released a war scream that sounded like a bomb going off. The Solari retreated out of the volcano. Rageskin looked on with a wicked smile on his face, eyes glowing a dark red.

Draegar: The Distant Past

Draegar swung his double-headed ax into the mountain, carving out the insides, muscles rippling underneath his scales. The war hungry god and the underworld enjoyed the destruction that he was causing, venting out frustration that grew within him like a cancer. The ax cut deeper and deeper into the mountain until magma bubbled to the surface. He breathed hard, a growl under each one. A sense of satisfaction came into him.

"I think someone will be mad with you for destroying their mountain," Auroradraca said as she walked across the lava that pooled beneath her.

"They can deal with it. I made it into a volcano." Draegar glared at her. "What do you want?"

"I just came to see how you were doing."

"That is a lie. You want something. If it's to start a war, I have a few ideas."

"Maybe in a few centuries but you are correct, I do need something from you. Something will happen in the future and I will need your essence to combat it."

"Why not just have me fight it?"

"I have my reasons, Draegar. Will you give me some of your essence?"

He glared at Auroradraca. "I do enjoy my time on Wyrm. Your creations are excellent in their worship and beliefs in me. I do not wish to give up my essence to simply be forgotten, all to what, benefit yourself?"

She looked at him, trying to hide her frustration. Auroradraca looked at the volcano, an idea coming to her. "I will make a deal with you, Draegar. Give me a piece of your essence and I will have you reside in this volcano. As I create new dragons, I will have a clan just for you. They will worship war, build armor from this volcano from the lava you are trapped in. They will have no peers in regards to fighting and violence. In fact, I will place your essence into the leader of this clan when Wyrm will be threatened by enemies that Futurarteon has foresaw. What are your thoughts on this arrangement?"

"And the underworld will be cared for and I'll be released once this threat is taken care of?"

Auroradraca nodded her head.

"Deal."

Chapter 19 Dark Alliance

The tunnels under the Inferoths' volcano were hot to the touch. As the Eclipsires ran through them, the temperature slowly cooled the further they ran. They clung to the ceilings and walls to allow them to run swiftly without tripping over each other. Several were bathed in Inferoth blood which dried on their black skin. After traveling for miles they came to a fork, splitting to the right and left. Melthorn looked at the two tunnels with caution. He knew from stolen memories that some tunnels to the Inferoths were dead ends while others led to other clans. None of the Eclipsires had stolen bodies from a dragon that knew the way.

"Which way, Melthorn," a thin Eclipsire asked, licking the blood from its talons.

"I'm thinking," he replied. He took a deep breath. A sweet scent met his nostrils from the right while the left held a sulfur smell. He tried to think of what would be producing clashing scents like this. The thin Eclipsire pointed to the right tunnel.

"I hear footsteps. Large ones."

Melthorn pointed to the Eclipsires directions to hide back in the tunnel. He took a position with two other dragons in the left tunnel. The sulfur smell attacked his nostrils. The footsteps grew louder. He readied his talons, growing them longer, for a strike. He could hear talking amongst the incoming targets. He waited, wanting to know what was coming.

Silence. He held his breath.

"I can smells you, yes, yes," Lunawind warned. "If you are looking to attack, the darkness is ours to command. Show yourself and we may shows mercy, yes ,yes."

Melthorn weighed his options.

"Decide or we decides for you, no,no," she said.

Melthorn stepped out from the tunnel. He was tall but Lunawind looked down on him.

"Beautiful, dark dragon," Lunawind said. "Are we friends or are we enemies, no, no?"

"All depends," Melthorn replied. "What do you want?"

"Wants? Hmm, what we always want. To draw the eye of Morthauron. To worship him, yes, yes. Morthauron will praise us, yes, yes. Do you believe in him?"

"That is something we share except we have met Morthauron."

Her eyes grew large. "Do not lie to me, no, no. I have heard these lies already, yes, yes."

"I would not dare lie to another clan, a potential ally, who sees Morthauron as the savior of Wyrm."

"How did you meet him, yes, yes?"

"He came to us. To right a wrong committed by Auroradraca. He rebirthed us in his image."

"We have been searching for him, praying for a sign. We found this cave and now found you, yes, yes. Must be the sign?"

"Did he create your clan?"

Lunawind snarled. "No, Auroradraca made us, no, no. Then she didn't want us. Morthauron would want us if she didn't keep us from him, no, no."

"Doesn't seem like anyone wants you around."

Anger flashed across her face. "False dragon. You were given the gift of life by Morthauron but you don't worship him like we have yes, yes. You are unworthy of his attention." Behind her, several Selenthrax were opening their mouths, preparing to unleash their shadow breath. Eclipsires appeared behind Melthorn, a green gas seeping from their mouths.

"We have fought in his name, trying to bring down his enemies. Drinking of their blood for immortality. Do not speak to us like we are unworthy of him."

Tension filled the cave. Each clan waited for the other to attack first. The tunnel began to shake like an earthquake was happening.

"Immortality was ours to receive for worshiping him, false dragon! You don't deserve to worship him until the end of time when he will rule all, no, no."

From the right tunnel came footsteps. A figure seemed to blend into the shadows and then out. The dark dragon stepped between the two leaders. He put a long clawed hand on each and petted them.

"Now, now my children. There is no reason to squabble amongst yourselves. I love you both of you," Morthauron spoke in a calming voice.

Melthorn dropped to a knee, the Eclipsire joining him. Lunawind stood in awe.

"Morthauron, you see us, yes, yes?" she asked, a tear leaving her eyes.

"Yes, my lost child. Auroradraca blinded me from many in this world, keeping me from gaining power. But now, I have you two and your clans. Perhaps more in time."

Lunawind and the other Selenthrax dropped to the ground, their four legged bodies not allowing them to properly kneel. "We live to serve you, Morthauron."

"Stand, all of you. Unlike my former love, I appreciate you and don't need you to bow down." The dragons began to stand. Morthauron turned to the Eclipsire. "My first born. Did you and your clan find your path to immortality by the blood of your enemies?"

"We have. The Inferoths were a perfect choice in testing our new bodies with combat and death. But some of us did fall."

"Alas, your immortality is not without consequence. You must always drink the blood of others to stay alive and your bodies can be hurt. Being creatures of the dark, Auroradraca's sun will hurt you."

"The price is worth it to live again," Melthorn replied.

"What of us?" Lunawind asked. "We wish to worship you forever. How do we become immortal?"

"Patience, my moon dragons, patience. The world changes as we speak. Forgotten gods have begun to return, putting Auroradraca in a panic to maintain control of this world. When the dust settles, I will rule all." The tunnel shook, dust coming from the ceiling.

"Ah, I see my brother Draegar has awoken. Rejoice, for the god of war and the afterlife has returned. I have tasks for you both. Melthorn, take your clan to the surface and end the other clans that once stopped me from claiming this world. Lunawind, you will need to help your fellow clan with the sun. Be creative. And a warning, my children. There is a clan called the Solari. They believe Auroradraca should be the rightful ruler. End them. Once all of Auroradraca's children are gone, you shall receive your rewards."

The two clans began chanting, "Morthauron! Morthauron! Morthauron!" Shinestar watched as her clan fell into what she considered madness. She slowly backed away from them and ran down the tunnel, hoping to find the other clans to warn them.

Part II War Drums

Chapter 20 Shattering of Spirits

Whisper was not happy with the way Rageskin had spoken to her. She was his queen and she felt disrespected. Yes, Inferoths are brazen and blunt but she thought he would talk to her as an equal. He chose her to be queen. Asked her to go through the trials and was worried about her and encouraged her. She was proud of herself for surviving the armor trial and showing that a Zeyphrion could fight. Her own feelings seemed to be fighting with themselves. Was she Zeyphrion or an Inferoth or both? Could she separate the two or would she make her clan more like the Inferoths? The Zeyphrions had taken to the fight training naturally, which had impressed her. They were being seen in a more positive light in regards to battle. Yes, they have not had a major enemy since the Necrodrakes but still. She shuddered at the memory of the dead dragons.

Whisper was also trying to sort out her feelings about Rageskin. Yes, they were a royal couple but was she falling in love with him? Was he falling in love with her? He is usually calm but during their training he always seemed awkward. Could she love such a stubborn headed dragon? Could she see herself growing old with him? Or battling for her title all the time? Maybe she could convince the female Inferoths to leave her be. Centuries of culture and thoughts erased in days? Probably not. But could love change the Inferoths?

She flew through the air toward her floating islands. She wished she could have left Stream and Mudball under better circumstances like they used to. Playing in the forest. Teasing each other playfully. Now, there are enemies everywhere and they are talking of war plans. Stream had some good ideas. He always seemed to. She hoped that when this fight was over he could give her some ideas of how to rule the Inferoths without insulting them.

The floating islands came closer to her. She could see Zeyphrions practice fighting with each other. She smiled, happy that they took it seriously. She landed on the first island. Dancewing was ordering some dragons around when she saw Whisper.

"Oh, sweet daughter, I am so glad that you have returned."

"What's wrong? Did something happen?"

"No, it's just." Dancewing paused. "I'm too stuck in my old ways. You and Rageskin showed me that I am not what our clan needs in order to be stronger."

"Mom, what are you saying?"

"I am handing over leadership of the Zeyphrions to you, Whisper."

"Mom, I can't-."

"Hush. You are such a strong dragon and I am simply holding you back and, quite honestly, I'm holding our clan back. Look around. All the females Zeyphrion are fighting just as you taught them. The males, despite my objections, took to standing guard at the edges of our islands to protect us. Our world is changing, and I have to admit, I cannot lead the change for our clan. You must."

Whisper tried not to cry. She was not ready for that. "Mom, I don't know what to say."

"Say nothing. Look over your clan. Help them to be ready for the fight ahead of us. They showed so much potential during the battle and fighting with the Necrodrakes. Now, you have the ability to lead us into the future, whatever it may hold. Come." Dancewing led Whisper to a tall boulder with a flat top. The Zeyphrions took notice of them and stopped fighting.

"Zeyphrions! We enter a new chapter in our clan's history. We face new enemies and challenges. I fear that with me as leader we may not survive. But, Whisper has shown that she is more than capable of leading us into the future. I resign as queen and pass it to Whisper. Follow her as you have me!"

The Zeyphrions began to chant Whisper's name and raise their wings to her. She started to cry. "Go to your cave and gather yourself," Dancewing suggested.

"In a minute," Whisper said. She put an arm up and the crowd silenced. "My fellow Zeyphrions. I am blessed and humbled to be chosen as your leader. You have listened to me. Began training to fight. To allow the males to be seen above the island ground and make them more part of our lives. We face new dangers and I have much to share with you. I hope that you will trust me and continue to believe in me. Thank you." The crowd cheered and continued chanting her name.

She turned to Dancewing. "Thank you, mom."

Dancewing smiled back. "Hush now, you earned it. Now, go. Rest up from your flight. I think I can handle things for a little longer." Whisper hugged her and quietly said, "Thank you." Whisper released her and flew off. Tears went down her face. She could not believe what just happened. Zeyphrions waved at her as she flew by. "She must've told everyone before I got here ahead of time," she thought. "That was way too easy."

She landed at her cave and walked in. The colorful bioluminescent moss glowed at her entrance. Her thoughts swirled around as she laid down on a slab of rock that was covered by soft plants. She closed her eyes and tried to quiet her brain. She crossed her talons across her chest. Her breathing slowed down. "I'm queen of two clans," she realized. "Two clans that could not be any more different." She smiled, thinking how ridiculous it was. "Grrr, me fire dragons, you weak pretty dragon. Growl, you angry dragon, me beautiful. Now we friends." She laughed at her joke. She let out a breath and relaxed. "Grrr," she mused as she felt the threat of sleep creep into her mind. Her chest began to warm as her magic clicked on. She opened her eyes and sat up, checking herself for injuries. She did not see any.

"I was pretty like you once," a voice said.

Whisper turned and saw Exalithor sitting on a pile of rocks. Whisper gasped, being caught off guard by her presence. Exalithor sat with her skull face turned toward Whisper.

"I apologize for scaring you. It's been long since I have truly interacted with mortals. I suppose our meeting earlier counted but such is life." She turned her head to reveal her unharmed side.

"I must be the one to apologize, Exalithor. I disrespected you by gasping."

"It's fine, little one. I've gotten used to my appearance over the centuries."

"May I ask what happened?"

Exalithor paused. "Auroradraca happened. Have you been blessed by her presence?"

Whisper shook her head. "When the Necrodrake war happened. She gave me my gift of healing to infuse into the jawbone of their leader."

Exalithor chuckled. "A gift? Is that what she did with it?"

Whisper looked at her confused.

Exalithor looked at her. "I do not know what stories you have told or what your clans believe but I imagine Auroradraca painted herself in the greatest of light. So great she made all of her creations forget the other gods." Whisper could hear anger in Exalithor's voice at the end. "Auroradraca and Morthauron came to this planet, populated it. Overtime, they needed help shaping their world and called upon their siblings to help. In return, we joined them as part of their pantheon. I helped her creations to heal themselves but also to protect themselves. Plants that could both help and harm. Creatures that were venomous. Balance." She paused. "Auroradraca became greedy. As her creations believed in her more, more did her power grow. The rest of us were fine and content. We had a purpose to our immortality but she wanted more as did Morthauron but she was the first to become greedy. She had an idea for dragons, each blessed with a magic to found their clans, to protect against a future she would not accept. She stole a piece of essence from each of us, giving it to her creations."

Whisper thought about what Stream had found out. "I'm a descendant of that first creation. My power came from you."

"Yes. Auroradraca made it seem like she had blessed them with their abilities. But she stole a piece of me and made her creations forget me. Weakened, she trapped me in another realm. I waited until either one of her creations remembered me or she became distracted enough to allow me to escape. My twin, Tuzu, saw a moment of weakness in her and we escaped."

"Are you mad at me for having your stolen power? Do you want it back? I'd willingly give it back to you."

Exalithor looked at her. "I should be angry but I have been watching you. You are unique. I do not want it back but I do want you to believe in me. And when the time comes, you will assist me in bettering this world."

Whisper tried to decide how to interpret those words. Something seemed cryptic about them. "Okay." She blinked her eyes and Exalithor was gone. "I hope I don't regret what I just agreed to." An explosion could be heard outside her cave. She got up and rushed outside. A cloud of smoke could be seen in the distance. Zeyphrions stood on the edge of their islands, looking toward the Inferoths territory. Whisper spotted her mother and flew down to her.

"What happened?" Whisper asked.

"I don't know for sure but I think Rageskin's home just blew up. I hope they all escaped before it blew."

With the arrival of Exalithor, Whisper felt it was not anything natural. "Maybe they are under attack from the Eclipsire."

Dancewing looked at her confused. Whisper said, "Morthauron's newest attempt at creating life."

"Not again, not the Necrodrakes."

"No, Mother, not like the Necrodrakes. These dragons are alive and drink-". She was interrupted by a couple of male Zeyphrions who were holding a Selenthrax who struggled against their grip.

"Let me go," she demanded. "I need to speak with your queen. I have to warn her."

"I recognize you," Whisper said. "You are with the Selenthrax."

"Yes. My name is Shinestar. Our queen, Lunawind, has gone crazy. She's made a deal with Morthauron and the Eclipsire to take over Wyrm. I couldn't be a part of it."

"What does she plan to do?"

"I don't know for sure but it involves harming all the clans. I don't want to be a part of it. Morthauron has gone crazy as well. He's appeared to us. Promised us eternal life in exchange for killing everyone else."

"And you swear you are not a part of whatever she has planned," Whisper demanded.

"I swear to you. Cut my wings off and throw me off your island if you don't believe me."

Whisper tried to think of what Rageskin or Dancewing would do. She wasn't ready for tough decisions like this. She was barely queen for a minute. "You show anything remotely treacherous and I will take you up on your offer personally. Let her go. Get everyone organized, hide the eggs. We will go to the surface and meet up with the other clans in the tunnel systems like before."

Whisper looked at Shinestar. "Do you know anything? Attack plans? Targets?"

"The Eclipsire have a weakness to sunlight and my clan prefers the night. Lunawind is crazy enough to try something to block out the sun. Morthauron ordered her to think of a way to do it."

Whisper thought about it. "That's impossible. How would you be able to?"

"She's crazy. She'll do anything to please Morthauron," Shinestar said, worry in her voice. She looked around at the islands. "So beautiful up here. And large, I didn't really notice before." She paused. "Oh no, she would. She would, she would, she would, she would," Shinestar rambled.

"What? What would she do?" Dancewing asked.

"Get your clan off the islands now!"

Behind them a beam of solid black shot through an island and continued through. The island exploded and went falling to the surface. There was the sound of something charging and another black beam destroyed another island. Boulders rained down on other islands as it fell. Lunawind appeared, flapping her wings to stay afloat in the air.

"Our cousins don't like the sun, no, no. We will take care of it, yes yes," Lunawind informed. Below the islands, several Selenthrax were gathered, pointed their heads up, and fired solid blackness as a group, their breath uniting as a single cone-shaped shot. Zeyphrions tried jumping off islands before beams of black ripped their island home apart. Some were hit by falling stones that shot out from explosions, hitting them fatally. Others tried to escape, only to find themselves in the jaws of Selenthrax. Island after island sunk to the ground. Whisper tried to find as many Zeyphrions that she could, to lead them off the island. They followed her toward the edge.

"Go! Go! Find the tunnels near the Gaiajades!" she ordered. She looked around. "Mother! Where are you!" She saw Dancewing carrying an egg. "Mother! Hurry!"

"I'm," but before Dancewing could finish a beam of black engulfed her, leaving behind a hole. The island buckled and large pieces of the island cracked, falling away, making the hole larger, ripping the island in two. Tears streamed down Whisper's face. "Mother! No!" she screamed.

A Selenthrax landed near her. "Pretty, pretty dragon. Don't cry. Soon Morthauron will embrace you and you will be his."

Anger engulfed Whisper. The Selenthrax snarled at her. "Do you wish to meet him by my hands or by your own?"

Whisper screamed and ran toward the Selenthrax. He repeated the action. He leaped at her. She took in a breath and fired at him. Freezing air slammed into the Selenthrax, wrapping him in ice. He landed with a thump. She turned and breathed again. Solid air slapped him, shattering him into a million pieces. She stood over him as the island fell to the ground. Explosions erupted around her as islands collided with the ground, sending mushroom clouds of dirt and death into the sky, turning the bright sky dark. As she fell to the ground, she swore she could see small red lights emerge from cave entrances.

Exalithor: The Distant Past

Exalithor laid across a flat rock, surrounded by flowers of beauty and plants that caused pain and death. Being the goddess of healing and disease, she was used to being around the dual nature of Wyrm. Animals hunted each other, plants fought back against potential predators of their fruit. Dragons caused pain to each other, pleading to her for assistance. She wished that Auroradraca had done a better job at making her creations more peaceful but it was what it was. Exalithor caught something in the corner of her eye: a small deer-like creature limped toward her. Blood dripped down its front. She sat up and reached her arm out, sending out a calming aroma from her plant patterned wings. The deer paused at seeing her.

"It's okay, little one. Come to me," she said, a pink mist coming from her mouth. The mist and aroma covered the deer, relaxing its body. It made a limping step toward her. "That's it, come here. I only wish to help you." The deer sniffed her talons, confirming to itself that she did not pose a threat. A disgusting gash colored its white chest. "Oh, you poor thing. You must be a strong one to have escaped whatever tried to eat you." She traced a green talon along the injury, muscle and skin sewing itself back together. She placed her hand on the injured leg, the bone snapping back together. "There you are, all better now." The deer bowed its head and took off.

"I am always amazed at the way you can handle my creations, even the little animals of this world," Auroradraca said as she faded into existence.

"It is the role given to me," Exalithor replied. "Healer, destroyer, depending on what needs to be done. Though, I much prefer the role of healer. Diseases can be so gross."

"But necessary," Auroradraca reminded.

"I know, sister. To what do I owe you the honor of your presence?"

"Futurarteon told me of events to come. I must use a piece of your essence to create a new clan of dragons to preserve Wyrm."

"Are there not others that you can ask? I would rather not be forgotten. I do enjoy your creations' devotion to me. It brings out more beauty to myself as they pray to me."

A scowl came across Auroradraca's face. "Sister, the future depends on my having your essence."

"And what is in it for me? I disappear, never to return, because Futurarteon is worried. Or is it that you are worried? Heaven forbid your creations believe in another deity besides yourself."

Auroradraca glared at her. "I will have your essence."

"No, you will not," Exalithor replied. "I will not willingly give it to you."

Auroradraca raised her hand. Tendrils sprung from the ground, wrapping themselves around Exalithor's limbs, forcing her to her knees. She struggled against the vines.

"What is this? You are not able to do this!"

"Oh, Sister," Auroradraca said as she placed her hand against Exalithor's face. "You are not the first god that I have spoken to. I will have what I want from you. By choice or by force." She dug her talons into the side of Exalithor's skull. She pulled back, ripping the flesh and muscle from her. Exalithor screamed in pain as Auroradraca warned, "I wish you had volunteered your essence to me. But now, you can truly represent your dual nature."

The piece in her hand glowed bright, changing into energy, and then absorbed by Auroradraca. Exalithor fought against the plants, sending a poison into them to weaken their grip on her. "I will have my revenge upon you! You hear me! Revenge will be mine! I hope that is the future you are so concerned with!"

"I am not worried about your threats, Sister. You will be on the other side, forgotten by my creations. You mean nothing to me." She faded out of existence.

The plants released their grip on Exalithor. She touched her face, skull and tendons exposed. She ran her talons across the injury but found that it would not heal. She screamed, a black mist erupting from her mouth like a volcano. The plant life began to wither and die as the land turned black and corrosive.

"I will leave my mark on this land before I leave, Auroradraca," she growled. "No life will grow here, only death to anything that tries to live here. I shall name it Mortem and it will be your end."

Chapter 21 Tilling the Soil

Mudball got off the tunnel raft with Steelheart following him and Florastryx buzzed around him. They had joined him and helped to push the raft down faster. As they left the tunnel, she turned around, swearing she heard something but ignored it, thinking it was just the water and echoes.

"Wez do goods," Thornseed asked. "Gets you heres fast?"

"Definitely," Mudball replied. "We'd only be halfway, probably, if you guys hadn't pushed us."

They made their way past the fighting circle and crop fields. Large stones hollowed out and carved by the Gaiajades provided homes for them. Gaiajades were going about their day. Some were practicing their fighting skills while others were tending to crops. He saw Gempath, who was talking with some elder Gaiajades. Mudball and his crew came up to her.

"Mudball, you have returned," Gempath said. "What have you learned?"

"Too much," Mudball replied. "I don't even know where to begin."

"Tuzu returned!" Thornseed and Petalspear said excitedly together.

Gempath looked at them, confused.

Mudball began to tell her about meeting Tuzu and Exalithor and how Stream met Futurarteon. Steelheart explained the Eclipsire and the other two clans.

"And Rageskin raced home because they were being attacked by someone, probably Eclipsire. I haven't heard anything yet from him."

"Forgotten gods, the Ferroliths. Auroradraca has a plan for us."

A rumble roared in the background. They turned to see where it could have come from. "I think that is the Inferoths' volcano. Erupting perhaps?" Gempath said. The volcano boomed in the background but felt like it was nearby.

"We need to gather everyone. Um, probably meet up by the fallen Zeyphrion island. Yeah, yeah," Mudball said, trying to reassure himself that it was a good idea.

Gempath addressed the four elder Gaiajades. "All of you. Get everyone together so we can leave as quickly as possible. Check the tunnels, make sure we don't take any that may have collapsed. Have the stronger fighters circle the clan when we move out." The Gaiajades shook their heads in agreement and left. Gempath looked at Mudball. "I know that you fell into leadership but you need to be decisive and quick thinking. The clan will look to you for answers on the go. You must be ready." Gempath turned and hurried away.

"Thats was means," Petalspear said.

"She's right though. I have to think quicker. Be like Rageskin or Stream. They are always fast to make a decision."

"But you're not them," Steelheart reminded him. "You need to be you."

"That's the problem. I'm not a leader. I'm not a fighter or anything useful. I'm just me and the last thing we need is me. Old Stone would know what to do." Mudball hung his head. He noticed the grass began to grow quickly under him. He thought maybe it was his magic. It happened sometimes without him thinking about it. The flowers began to move upward with tree branches reaching out of them in the shape of wings. Tuzu raised his head out of the ground, dirt and grass falling off.

"Tuzu!" The Florastryx yelled.

"Hello, little ones. I returns but onlys for briefests of moments."

"What's wrong?" Mudball asked.

"Auroradraca's upsets. Very upsets. I returns. Others returns. She's nots happies."

"She's like your sibling, right? Why would she be mad?"

Thunder boomed behind them, the volcano reminding them of its danger.

"Wez give hers our powers, to uses for her creations, to fights Morthaurons. She locks us ups. She fears wez want revenges."

"Do you?" Steelheart asked.

"Angrys, yes. Revenges, no. I sees what beauty yous have creates. Mudballs, yous has my powers in yous. Is whys you grows plants."

"That makes a lot of sense," Mudball said out loud. "Tuzu, do you know what's happening at the Inferoths?"

"Draegar returns. God of War and Afterlife. Very angries."

"Oh, well, we're doomed," Mudball joked, trying to reassure himself.

"Be strongs, youngs one. Lifes always finds ways to lives, even when deaths is alls arounds. You haves lifes withins yous. You wills finds lifes. Brings lifes where theres nones."

Mudball looked at him confused. "I have no idea what that means."

"I musts leaves nows, little ones," Tuzu said. "Auroradraca fumings." He laid onto the ground and disappeared, flowers and grass restored to their natural place.

"That was not helpful," Mudball said frankly.

"Whats does we do?" Petalspear asked.

"I, I, I don't know. Okay," Mudball said as he was trying to focus his mind. Too many thoughts scattered his brain. "Okay, we have dragons going into the caves. Petalspear, have some Florastryx join them and do that message thing you do if it's safe or not. Thornseed, have other Florastryx look for anyone who got missed and get them here." The Florastryx nodded their heads and took off. Mudball tried to take in everything happening around him. Gaiajades were going into the tunnels. Smoke loomed from the Inferoth's volcano. He could hear a strange humming coming from the sky.

"You hear that?" Steelheart asked. "Is that your breath?"

"No, it's coming from the sky, I think." They craned their necks to try and see if anything looked odd. Mudball saw small specks under the Zeyphrions' island. Suddenly, a beam of darkness ripped through the closest island. It began to drop immediately. Then another island was damaged. Then another. Soon most of the islands were dropping fast from the sky.

"That's not good," Steelheart said.

"We have to warn everyone. Now!" he exclaimed as he bolted into a run. Gaiajades were rounding up hatchlings and attempting to stay calm. As Mudball got to the tunnel entrances, he could hear screams. Gaiajades breath went off, lighting up deep in the tunnels. Everyone froze as the two tunnels grew quiet. The silence was broken by the crashing of the Zeyphrions' island. The ground shook from the crash landing. A yellowish smoke came out of the tunnel entrances. Everyone froze as red eyes lit up the darkness where the sun did not reach. A Florastryx crawled out of the darkness, gasping and coughing up blood. A black claw reached out and drug it back in. There was a quick scream and then nothing. A face emerged from the darkness.

"Thank you for the snack," Melthorn said, a pinkish drool escaping his jowl. "These dragons were a great warm up for what is about to happen. You are all lucky that the sun protects you from us."

The sky began to darken. Dark, dirt clouds crawled across the sky from the impact of the islands. Melthorn reached a black arm out. He pulled it back quickly. "Still stings but soon. Oh, so soon, you will be ours." A deep laugh came from the tunnels.

"What do we do," a Gaiajade asked Mudball.

"I don't know. That was our escape plan and now the tunnels are gone."

"We need a plan, now," the Gaiajade urged.

"I don't know," Mudball said, crying. "I don't know what to do."

"You need to decide something. Your clan needs you," Steelheart pleaded.

Darkness blanketed the land as the Eclipsire began to move out of the tunnels. Nearby Gaiajades tried to fire their breaths at them but were quickly outnumbered. Eclipsire began to rip out crystals Gaiajades, enjoying the blood flow. Mudball kept looking around. He saw Gaiajades being overwhelmed by Eclipsires. Florastryx buzzed around, spraying their acidic breath into the enemies' eyes. Many were swatted out of the air, making puffs of dust where they landed. An Eclipsire ran toward Mudball. The Gaiajade beside him fired a beam of pure light at the Eclispire, its head disappearing from the body.

"Mudball, we need an order. Fight or run?" he asked.

Mudball could not believe the violence he was watching. He had flashbacks to the Necrodrakes and what they would do to dragons. Everything seemed quiet as he watched in slow motion. Gaiajades and Florastryx were dying around him. He could see lips moving but couldn't hear what was being said. Beams of Gaiajade breath shot out in different directions, some connecting with Eclipsire, some with the ground.

Mudball shook his head. "I don't know, I don't know, I don't know." His breathing quickened. "Idontknow, idontknow, idontknow," he repeated as his back crystals began to glow a green light. His eyes glowed a bright green as energy crackled from them. The crystals hummed loudly. Eclipsires looked in his direction and began to cover their eyes from the light while some ran toward him. Mudball reached his head back and unleashed a beam of light from his mouth. It breached the cloudy sky, allowing sunlight in. Eclipsire began to retreat back into the tunnels. An energy ball erupted from Mudball's back crystals, moving in a half circle, its diameter growing in size. Thorny vines, some rock like, some plant like, grew rampant where the light circle passed. The vines reached out and searched for something to grab nearby. The Eclipsire that had not made it to the tunnels were caught and dragged against their will into the sunlight. The harder they fought, the tighter the vines got, impaling them with their sharp thorns. The Eclipsire smoked and sizzled in the sunlight, their screams quieting as their bodies cooked and turned to dust. The vines ignored the Gaiajades as if they were not there. Steelheart moved away from Mudball. She became wrapped in vines.

"Mudball, help!" she screamed as her body was mummified in green plants. The land became bright with Mudball's light. Then it stopped. The air was electrified with energy. The tunnel entrances were covered in stone vines. Mudball's crystals turned off, his eyes turned back to normal. The crystals had smoke coming off them. A couple of Gaiajades rushed over to help him.

"Mudball, what was that?" one asked.

"I-I-I," he stuttered. He felt like his brain was not working. He tried to put thoughts together. "I want everyone to go to the fallen island. Carry Steelheart." His eyes rolled to the back of his head and passed out.

Chapter 22 Boiling Rage

Stream raced through the travel tunnels, water rushed past him. So many thoughts raced through his head. He tried to decide where to go first. New tablet room? Dreamflow? There were too many decisions to make and not enough time to decide which answer was the best. Inferoths were under attack. Everyone else was potentially under attack as he swam to gather his clan. There was too much at stake for him to make a wrong choice or give bad advice to his friends. His magic helped but at the same time he had to interpret results. Aquanox were talking through the water quickly.

"Are we under attack?"

"Is it the Necrodrakes again? Did they escape?"

"Does the water seem warmer than usual this time of year?"

"Where is Stream off to? What does he know?"

He adjusted his back sail fins to change directions and to veer to the right. He had to find Dreamflow first. Where would he be right now? Usually the commons area. Everyone knew to meet there if they needed him or if there was a crisis. He turned his fins to turn left when he felt a tug in his head to go right. If his magic was pulling him to the right, then he should go. Maybe it was leading him to Dreamflow. A little bit of luck when things were turning bad for them. He was traveling fast when he realized where he was going: the tablet cave. He launched himself out of the water and landed on the cave floor. The magic pulled him toward the secret cave. He pressed the pressure plate, allowing the wall to split and grind against the floor. He slid in and saw Futurarteon waiting for him.

"You have returned," they said. Stream could not get used to seeing two heads on one body, let alone talking at the same time.

"Yes, things are getting bad out there. I suppose you have something to tell me. Maybe that Auroradraca is angry at all of you."

"We can see the future. There are dark times are ahead."

"I know, I know but I need information that is going to help us."

"Anything we give you may or may not happen. You have our gift. Knowledge is power, something stolen from us by Auroradraca."

"I'm sorry that she did that to you two but withholding information because of a grudge is not going to help. Please, tell me anything."

A rumble shook the cave. Water churned. "That was the Inferoth volcano exploding. Our brother has awakened."

"What? What do you mean? Which brother?"

"Draegar. God of war and underworld," they replied.

"Oh, that can't be good."

"His rage holds no bounds. Of all of us, he took his entrapment by Auroradraca the most personally. He will not rest until he finds her."

"And then what?"

The cave shook more. "Life versus war. Your clans are to be sacrificed for the impending battle. Auroradraca is trying to change the future so she remains in power."

"Sacrifice?" Stream said as he noticed the air becoming warmer. He looked to ask Futurarteon more questions but they were gone. He turned and left the cave. As he slid into the water, he noticed it was warmer than usual. Normally, the underground water was cool. Not freezing until one got deeper or maybe more to the north. But this water was unusually warm. He slid into the pool. Screams entered his ears. He raised his head above the water to silence them. He went back under. Aquanoxes were screaming in pain. Then stopped. Stream went further into the water and headed to the commons pool. The water seemed to be getting warmer. He ejected from the travel tunnel into the underground lake that took up the common area. He looked below and could see dead Aquanoxes. They were of a tribe that lived in the deeper waters. They looked like they were burned. He swam to the surface, trying to filter out the messages being sent.

"Oh, Auroradraca, save us!"

"The volcano exploded! Magma is rushing into the water!"

"They just died. The magma killed them!"

"What is going on up on the surface? Is it another attack?"

Stream tried to hurry over to Dreamflow. He found him on the bank. Dozens of Aquanox surrounded him, wanting answers.

Dreamflow said, "Relax, all of you. There is bound to be a reason for the volcano to have exploded. Stream, come, tell us what you have found out."

Stream swam his way to Dreamflow. He got beside him and turned to the Aquanox. He explained the Eclipsire and the returning gods. The crowd hung onto every word. They could not believe what was happening.

"We are meeting with the other clans, to unite once again to fight an enemy that wants to wipe us out. We need to meet at the lake that was made during the last war and we need to move now."

Everyone turned to Dreamflow. He nodded his head and they left.

"I was hoping for something better," he said.

"Sorry. You know me, Mr. Good News," Stream joked.

Dreamflow chuckled. "At least we have a warning, though I wish we had time to bury those who died from the magma. But we need to leave."

Booms came from the ceilings, dust coming down. They looked up. "That can't be good," Stream said. The lake began to vibrate and move. Crashing of rocks could be heard. Stream jumped into the lake and swam around. He could hear screams. Underwater entrances started to close with boulders. Some Aquanox had escaped barely as the rocks fell, others had not. He darted from entrance to entrance, trying to move rocks. The lake began to shake violently. He got to the surface as Aquanoxes were filling the pool.

"The tunnels are closing, we can't get out."

"Did anyone get out? Is it too late to escape?"

"Something is happening on the surface. What do we do?"

Dreamflow began to address and calm the Aquanoxes down when the support wall behind him exploded, trapping him and those around him under rumble. Stream was about to yell when he heard a loud pop. He looked up and the cave ceiling came crashing down on the lake. He took a deep breath and found a cave that had not closed yet. As he entered the transport tunnel, he heard the ceiling crash into the water, Aquanox screaming as their lives were lost. Magma poured into the common area. Water pressure shot Stream through the tunnel. He banged against the walls, unable to control his direction. Shockwaves rang in his ears from tunnels collapsing around him. He was not sure which way he was going but he was sure it went up to the surface. Behind him the tunnel walls began to collapse, the water forcing him to go faster. He gritted his teeth as his speed became uncontrollable. Scrapes and bruises tattooed his body as he slammed against the sides. The water became brighter as Stream reached the surface. He exited the tunnel and into the lake that had been created during the last war. Other Aquanoxes had beaten him to the lake. He tried to catch his breath but the scenario would not allow him to. Towards the Inferoths territory, he could see the eruption of the volcano. He saw the Zeyphrions' islands falling to the surface. The sky was darkening from the ash and dust in the air. An explosion happened to his right, originating from the Gaiajades' territory. His mind could not wrap around everything going on around him. The Aquanox around him were scared. They looked around, having the same problem as Stream. Many were crying as they realized loved ones did not make it out. A few turned to Stream.

"Any ideas?" she asked. "What should we do now?"

Stream paused. "I don't have an answer."

Chapter 23 Journeys of the Heart

Mudball woke up on the back of a large Gaiajade's back. The Gaiajade's crystals ran down in two rows in which Mudball was positioned between them. He tried to maneuver himself so that he could see better. What was left of the Gaiajades were migrating toward the lake. He could see Gemstone at the front of the group. The Gaiajade turned his head back to Mudball.

"You up, Mudball?" he said in a baritone voice.

"Yeah."

The Gaiajade stopped and laid on the ground. Mudball climbed down carefully. He landed on the ground. "How long have I been out?"

"Good part of the journey," the Gaiajade responded.

"I hope you didn't mind carrying me."

"Nah," he said as he stood up. "I knock down trees and drag them around. Don't call me Dirtspike the tree destroyer for nothin'," he said, laughing at his joke. "Compared to the trees, you weigh nothing. But the snoring was pretty loud."

"Sorry," Mudball said with embarrassment.

"Like I said, no biggie. You're the leader. Got to protect you."

"Everyone probably hates me right now."

"Why? You didn't attack us."

"Yeah but I made the order to go into the tunnels and, and."

"And what? Did you know there were blood sucking dragons in there? No, you did what was expected of you."

Mudball looked at him confused.

"You gave an order. Yeah, a number of us got killed. Some here will probably hate you for a little while for that but that's a part of being a leader. You make a decision based on what you think is best. Look, if you knew there were evil dragons in those tunnels, would you have sent us in there."

"Well, no I wouldn't."

"See. Good decision right there."

"How are you so optimistic?"

"Old Stone was my uncle. Got a lot of talks from him. Really, I should be mad at you. My mate was in the first tunnel when the attacks happened but I'll mourn her later. Right now, the clan comes first."

"I'm sorry."

"Thanks. Look what happened to you?"

"What do you mean?"

"Mudball, you exploded light and plants. Like sharp vines that held back the bad guys back. How'd you manage that?"

"I don't know." Mudball really did not know. He remembered being stressed and freaked out about what was happening around him. Tuzu had just visited him. Did he do something to him? He dids says his powers in Mudballs. "I even talk like them in my head."

"What's that?" Dirtspike asked.

"Nothing." A memory slammed into his head. "What happened to the Florastryx and Steelheart?"

"Steelheart was wrapped up in the vegetation that you spewed out. We tried to get her out but the vines were too thick to cut. Even tried with some of our sharper crystals but nothing. Got a couple of us hauling her somewhere around here. A couple of vines were loose so we are using them like ropes. The little dragons are good. Some are resting on our backs while we walk. Some are sad from their clan being attacked. I tell you, not a good day for anyone it seems like. The Inferoths' volcano exploded. The Zeyphrions' island came crashing down. The sky is still dark from all the smoke and stuff in the air but you managed to open it enough for some sun to peek through."

The violent memories came rushing back to Mudball. Of all the times to become leader, this had to be the worst time. Why could not he become leader when everyone was happy and the crops were ready for harvest? Easy stuff like that. He did not even want to be leader. Maybe later when he was older. How did Rageskin do it? He was not much older than Mudball. All these thoughts ran through Mudball.

"What's the plan, Mudball?" Dirtspike asked.

"What?" Mudball said, coming back from deep thought.

"What do we do next?"

Mudball thought for a moment. "I think we should continue to the lake and hopefully meet up with the other clans. Our clan took a hit but hopefully they can reinforce us. We attack the bad guys and then." He paused. "And then, I don't know. Seems like going back to the way things were seems pointless. We did that and now here we are."

"Sounds like a plan to me. I'm going to relay the message to Gempath. She wanted to know when you woke up." Dirtspike took off, moving faster than a normal Gaiajade.

"How does someone that big move so quickly? Scary," Mudball thought to himself. He scanned his clan. Most of the Gaiajades were moving just fine. A few looked injured but nothing terrible. Scratches. Couple of broken crystals. Gaiajades were a hearty group and could take punishment but attacks from blood sucking dragons was a different thing. He started to count the dragons. He guessed not even half the clan was here. Did they really lose that many Gaiajades under his leadership? Was he that terrible? Sadness took over. He wanted to cry but he knew others would be looking at him. He had to be strong for the others. He had to make a plan. Rageskin, Stream, and Whisper would meet him at the lake and they would tell each other a plan and they would defeat the bad guys. Then what? Forgotten gods are returning. How many were there that no one remembers? Were they all nice like Tuzu? Exalithor wasn't bad. Little anti-social. Having a skull face would do that.

Mudball was lost in his thoughts when he realized they had reached the lake. He remembered when the lake was made, how he flew through the air on a rock; then crashed. Gaiajades laid down to rest near the lake while others got drinks. Everyone just looked exhausted to Mudball. He could see the destruction of the Zeyphrion's islands in the distance. The one from the last war was a grim reminder of what happened. He thought maybe Whisper and her clan would be here already since they were not too far. Dust hung in the air. Mudball heard a thump behind him. Steelheart, mummified in vines, was sat down. He went to inspect her. The vines were tight like a cocoon. He could feel a pulling in his legs, like his magic was trying to force him to touch her. He slowly raised his claw when he heard a voice yelling.

"Help!"

He turned around and saw a dragon he had never seen before. He was yellow and red with shoulder wings. Dirtspike got between him and the dragon. "Hold it right there!" he demanded. The dragon halted.

"I mean no harm! Please, I only want help and to pass word," he begged.

Mudball went to Dirtspike who had taken an aggressive stance. "Who are you? What do you want to say?" Mudball asked. Other Gaiajades began to move forward, in case something happened.

The dragon tried to catch his breath. "My name is Brightray. My clan is called the Solari. Our leader, Skyblaze, has gone crazy. He threatened the Inferoths. Are you friends of theirs?"

"Yeah. That was probably not a good idea on your part," Mudball remarked.

"Something awakened in the volcano. A god that was not Auroradraca. We escaped and once we were out of range of the volcano, I tried to reason with Skyblaze, tried to make him see that Auroradraca was not the only god. I don't agree with his singular thought. I was," he paused. "I was excommunicated from the clan. Skyblaze is looking to take out anyone who doesn't agree with him on Auroradraca. And there's another dark clan that follows Morthauron."

"We've met," Mudball said. "Got attacked by the Eclipsire."

"Please, let me help. I'm clanless. I have nothing to lose."

Mudball looked from Brightstar to Dirtspike. "What do you think?"

The giant Gaiajade walked up to Brightstar. He looked up to Dirtspike, fear in his eyes. "You do one thing, anything, to harm our clan, I will bury you so deep in the ground that even Auroradraca can't find you. Understood?"

Brightstar shook his head in agreement. "I only want to stop what is coming to our world. I swear."

"He's good, Mudball," Dirtspike said as he turned. "He's fertilizer otherwise."

Mudball was happy that Dirtspike was on his side. Behind him, a pair of flowery eyes watched.

WHISPER LANDED ON THE ground. The island had crashed into the ground, throwing dirt and smoke into the sky, darkening it. She wanted to cry but the dust prevented her. A few Zeyphrions appeared and limped toward her. The ground was uneven from the impact. Ash snowed down on them, making the landscape gray. Exhaustion threatened to put her to sleep. Several Zeyphrion wrapped their arms around her and cried. More Zeyphrions came into view as they moved closer to her. Shinestar tried to move close to her.

"I am so sorry. I didn't think she would do it," she apologized.

Rage overcame Whisper. "You didn't think she would do it! You didn't think so? You knew that she was crazy but waited until the last minute to warn us!" Whisper started stalking over to Shinestar, her claws curled up. "My clan has been murdered by yours and the best you can do is say sorry!" Her purple eyes were focused on the young Selenthrax. Shinestar did nothing to protect herself.

"You're right. I waited too long. Whatever your punishment is, I deserve it." Shinestar lowered her head and waited. Whisper stopped in front of her. She put a talon under Shinestar's jaw and raised her head up. She stared into Shinestar's eyes, tears forming.

"Whatever punishment?"

"Yes. I was put on this path for a reason by Morthauron. If it's death by your claws for failure, then it has been determined before I took action." She closed her eyes, waiting for a talon to pierce her brain. She felt the talon leave her skin.

"If I let you live, will you return to your clan?" Whisper asked.

"No. I would be seen as a traitor and killed on site. They would never take me back."

"Then you will join my clan. You will earn your life by redeeming the lives that have been taken. You will fight and die in my name. Do you accept your punishment?"

Shinestar could not believe what she was hearing. A leader that gave failures a second chance? Impossible. But here she was, giving her a spot in her clan. "Yes."

Whisper turned to the Zeyphrions. "Everyone! Find any survivors. Help the injured. Bury the dead. We will leave for the lake soon. We can only hope everyone else has made it there without incident. And keep an eye out for Selenthraxs. No prisoners."

Nearby in a dust cloud, a skeletal face watched the Zeyphrions.

STREAM HAD HIS CLAN hide deep in the lake. It seemed like the best option in case any enemy clans found them. Small caves that had been dug out over time allowed them to hide while others swam around near the surface to keep an eye out.

"It's gone," Stream thought to himself. "Everyone's gone. No way did they survive. I don't even know how many were crushed by collapsing tunnels. We were trapped by our own home. And the magma. Why did the Inferoths' volcano explode? Eclipsire maybe? The explosion didn't seem natural. And then there's the forgotten gods returning. It's just too much. And what happened to the Zeyphrions? Their islands just don't fall. Well, that one time but still they just don't. There is just a lot happening all at once. I just hope the others still have their clans intact."

He unwound himself from the cave and swam out. He could hear Aquanox sending their thoughts through the water.

"They were crushed. Why would Auroradraca allow this to happen?"

"I don't think the deep Aquanox made it. I haven't seen any."

"I saw my family get crushed in the tunnel. Why did I only survive?"

"Dreamwave, he was killed by our home."

Sadness filled his eyes. Stream tried to shut his mind from the water messages but there were so many. He swam to the surface and slowly raised his head above the water. The sky was still dark from the volcano and islands. He heard voices. He swam over to some lilypads and moss that were growing in the lake. He raised his green head from under the vegetation. He saw Gaiajades coming to the lake's edge to get water and clean themselves. He waited, making sure they were friendly. "Knowing my luck they are probably possessed or something."

He swam down to send a message to the remaining Aquanox. "Gaiajades are here. Wait so that we know they are still friendly. Be ready."

Stream went back up to the surface. He tried to listen to any conversations that were being had. Many were sad as they seemed to have suffered the same fate as the Aquanox. Then he heard something interesting.

"I only want to stop what is coming to our world. I swear."

"He's good, Mudball. He's fertilizer otherwise."

He watched as Mudball walked over the lake dam's top and slowly made his way down the embankment. Mudball got to the edge and said, "That was nuts. Could anything else happen today?"

Stream ducked below the surface and swam. Behind him a pair of eyes watched. Stream could see Mudball drinking from the lake. He rushed to the surface and broke it.

"Hiya, Mudball!" Stream said.

Mudball screamed and tried to run backward. The ground was muddy and did not let him get traction. Dirtspike came from over the edge, his crystals charging up. "Mudball, you okay?" he shouted.

"I'm good, I'm good. Stupid Aquanox and his stupid head scaring me. Don't do that ever again!" Mudball said, trying to put his thoughts together.

"I'm sorry, Mudball. I thought you were used to me doing that."

"I will never be used to you doing that. Especially after today's mess."

"I'm sorry. I really did mean it as a joke. Magic of knowledge and I can still not think things through."

"It's okay. Just not again, okay, Stream?"

"Want me to blast him?" Dirtspike asked. "Got a clean shot."

Stream had a worried look on his face.

"It's all good, Dirtspike. Just a prank gone wrong."

"I could still get him."

"It's okay. Just let everyone else know the Aquanox are here." Mudball looked at Stream. "There are other Aquanox here, right?"

"Yeah. Our tunnels collapsed. Many didn't make it out."

"Sorry, we had a similar issue. The Eclipsire attacked us in our tunnels and then out in the open when the Zeyphrions' islands fell and covered the sun. But then my magic went nuts and my breath made the clouds scatter and sun rays killed some of the Eclipsire. I guess sunlight hurts them."

"Sorry. How are the Florastryx?"

"Just like us. Scared and tired. Don't know what's going to happen next."

"At least they are helping us. I'm going to go underwater and let everyone know about you guys. We can start helping each other." He dove under and sent out a message in the water. Aquanox began to stir and come to the surface. He came back up and out of the water. He went over to Mudball who had Thornroot and Lilypetal on his crystals.

"Have you seen anyone else? Rageskin or Whisper?" he asked.

"Nothing yet. I'm worried. Thornroot, could you send some Florastryx to them and get an update?" Mudball asked.

"Oh, yes, already dones," he replied. "I knews new friends mights be in troubles."

An aftershock rattled the ground. Everyone looked around, trying to find the source. "Probably from the volcano erupting," Stream said, looking off in the distance. Plumes of black smoke continued to spew out the volcano.

"I still can't believe everything that has happened," Mudball said. "Three homes destroyed. New gods. So many dead." A tear went down his face. "Why would she let this happen?"

"Who?"

"Auroradraca. After what we did, why is all this happening again?"

"I might've been able to find answers in my new tablet room. Now, I'm not even sure that I can get to it or if it is destroyed."

"Come help! Quick!" someone shouted.

Stream and Mudball turned their attention to where everyone was headed. They ran over to the crowd. The Zeyphrions had arrived, covered in dust. Exhausted Zeyphrions were loaded onto the backs of Gaiajades and taken to the lake to be cleaned off. Stream and Mudball looked around for Whisper.

"There are so few of them," Mudball noted. "Hey, Whisper! Over here!"

Whisper looked up and tried to smile. She had an arm draped over Shinestar for support. They ran over to her. "Hey, guys," she said.

"Are you okay? What happened?" Mudball asked. He looked at Shinestar. "Who's that?"

Shinestar lowered her head, as if she was trying to hide herself by not looking at them. "The Selenthrax attacked us. They are in league with the Eclipsire. Shinestar, here, is one of them but tried to help us. She's on our side."

"There are some flat rocks over there. Let's sit down and rest while we can," Stream suggested. The four dragons made their way to the rock formation. The rocks were pieces of the fallen island that had landed near the lake. The Gaiajades had moved the boulders around so it could be used as a lounge area. Whisper sat down, wincing in pain.

"Is your magic working? You could heal yourself," Mudball said.

"It is but I haven't had a moment to use it." She grew quiet. "My mom's dead. The Selenthrax breath vaporized her as..." she paused as tears went down her face, making muddy trails. "As she was carrying an egg to safety."

Stream and Mudball did not know what to say. "I'm sorry," Mudball said.

"She had just made me leader and they all died," Whisper cried out. Shinestar lowered herself to the ground, feeling ashamed of her clan's actions.

Mudball teared up as well. "I understand what you are going through."

"Do you?" she snapped. "Were you just made leader and everyone died around you?"

"Yeah, actually. I had to make a decision and it was wrong and a lot of Gaiajades died from the Eclipsire hiding in the tunnels. So yeah, I do."

"That was wrong of me," Whisper apologized. "It's just, so many bad things happened at once. I didn't mean to snap at you."

"It's okay," Mudball reassured. "It happens. We are here and alive. Now, we need to recover and get everyone organized."

Shinestar perked her head up. She sniffed the air and ran off.

"She does that alot?" Stream asked.

"She's been pretty tame. I have no idea," Whisper replied. "We better go after her."

"You stay," Stream said. "Rest up. We can handle it."

Whisper showed a look of relief. Her muscles ached and she felt like she could not move an inch. The two dragons chased after Shinestar. Shinestar sprinted in a straight line, focused on someone: Brightray. She hissed at him and tackled him.

"Scum!" she shrieked at him as they tumbled to the ground. She tried to bite him but he dodged at the last second.

"Heretic!" Brightray responded as he kicked her in the gut.

The two dragons ripped into each other's skin with talons. They gnashed their teeth, trying to connect with the flesh of the other. They rolled around on the ground. Dragons started to run over to stop them. Dirtspike swung his tail, smooth crystals like a club on the end, and connected with Brightray as he was starting to open his mouth to breathe fire. He went hard into the ground, fire leaving his mouth in a puff. Shinestar tried to roll and get on her feet. She opened her mouth to release. Dirtspike gave her a look. She thought twice and closed her mouth but glared at Brightray. He got up and thought about running toward her when received the same look from Dirtspike. He decided to stay in place.

"Knock it off, both of you!" Dirtspike demanded. "Do that again and I will not hold back!"

Mudball and Stream caught up to the group. "What happened?" Mudball asked.

"There is a follower of Morthauron among us. She must be destroyed," Brightray growled.

"Weak minded idiot," Shinestar retorted. "Blindly following Auroraradraca who doesn't even have the decency to help you."

"Enough!" Stream shouted. The two dragons looked at him. "Both of you don't have clans anymore, right? You left yours willingly. You got kicked out. We took you both in. I'm not going to ask either of you to like each other but you will tolerate each other until this is over. Do I make myself clear or does that Gaiajade get to finish this conversation?" Dirtspike smiled at the possibility of roughing the two dragons up some more.

"To honor the life I was given by Whisper, I will tolerate the Solari welp."

"I will support Mudball in his decisions, so I will ignore that Selenthrax monster."

The two rivals went in opposite directions to help the Zeyphrions. "Well, that was intense," Mudball noted.

"Little bit," Stream agreed. "Now, we need to check on-." A rumbling came from the direction of the volcano. "Now what?"

The dragons gathered together to see what was happening. Stream could make out the outlines of dragons flying toward them from a distance but were flying swiftly.

"Rageskin?" Mudball asked.

"I think so but," Stream answered, lost in thought. He swore he saw the outline of a giant dragon behind them, carrying a large two headed ax. As he tried to focus more on it, the outline slowly disappeared.

"But what?" Mudball asked.

"I thought there was something large behind them but it must be all the dust in the air, messing with my vision."

Whisper walked over to them, with Thornseed and Petalspear helping her in case she fell. She kept shooing the little dragons away.

"Wez just wants to helps," Petalspear pleaded.

"I'm fine. I used my magic to heal myself. I can walk on my own."

The Florastryx gave up trying to help her and flew over to Mudball, landing on his crystals. Stream looked at the Inferoths with a scrutiny in his eyes.

"What is it?" Whisper asked.

"I've studied how the Inferoths fight, hoping to see what they do could translate to my clan. They are in a battle formation. We should be ready for anything."

RAGESKIN FLEW WITH his Inferoths. A new fire burned in him, a violent passion that he had not felt before. The sneak attack by the Eclipsire would not go unpunished. They would feel Inferoth rage before it was all said and done. He noticed the Zeyphrion islands had fallen.

"*They were frail,*" Draegar said in Rageskin's head.

"They are not, not anymore. I've trained them."

"*You trained the false queen.*"

"She is my queen."

"*She is not of your clan. She does not embrace war like you do.*"

"She passed the tests. Whisper deserves to be."

"*Then you are soft. Ineffectual kings lead weak clans. No wonder you were caught off guard.*"

Anger filled Rageskin's chest. "Who are you to tell me what is weak or strong? You were trapped in a volcano."

"*Listen, little creation, I am the one that your ancestors once prayed to. I will not tolerate your insolence. I am the god of war and afterlife. I am battle incarnate. Your enemies will submit once they know I am with you."*

"I will wipe out the Eclipsire for what they did. They will not be allowed to continue to live."

"And I will not be disrespected by a creature that will expire."

"And if you are in my head then you will listen to me. I freed you from your prison to help us wipe out our enemies. Auroradraca has not been of any help with this new enemy like she had in the past."

"She is pathetic. Her love for Morthrauron blinds her ego. She only thinks for herself and how she will benefit."

"How was she able to trap you if she is so feeble?"

There was a pause. *"Early in your kinds' creation, Auroradraca wanted to bind magic to her followers. To be able to protect themselves. I lent my leadership to her for what is a battle without leaders and direction. Violence just to be violent serves no purpose. In a moment of weakness from loaning my power, she trapped all of us, wiping out any memory of us from her creations in an instant. I've bided my time, secretly influencing you Inferoths."*

"What do you mean?" Rageskin questioned.

"The armor binding. Natural fighting abilities. The onyx armor you wear. All me."

"Auroradraca built me this armor, to save my life."

Draegor chuckled. *"Is that what you think or what she told you?"*

Rageskin thought about it.

"You were near death. But she tapped into my magic, that she stole, that is in you to bring you back, creating the armor. She stole my ideas."

"Is she just using us? For what purpose?"

Draegar waited a moment. *"Look around, Rageskin. I can feel the ash of the dragons that have died today leave this mortal world. Now that I am free, the afterlife will be more of a reward for you."*

Rageskin thought about it. "The Eclipsire said the otherside was dark and directionless."

"That is true. Without me, it simply didn't exist. She is building up her power, using the ash of those who have fallen to make her stronger."

"She uses our ash? To be stronger for what?"

"To put me and my siblings back in our place. She doesn't like competition."

"So we defeat the Eclipsire. Take care of the Solari. Then what?"

"There is always a need for war. It never ends."

Rageskin thought about his words. He saw the clans up ahead. He hoped they had good news.

Chapter 24 Balance of Hate and Love

Rageskin arrived with his clan at the lake. He saw his friends talking. He could tell their journey here was rough. Whisper looked up at him, smiling. His heart felt nothing, his mind cold and uncaring. "This isn't normal," he thought to himself. "I should be happy to see her."

"*It's the price for worshiping me,*" Draegar said. "*She makes you lesser.*"

"No she doesn't," Rageskin said, anger in his thoughts. "She makes me better."

"*Weaker.*"

Rageskin landed on the ground by his friends. They told him about what happened to their clans. He could feel the anger and need for revenge grow within him. Draegar whispered to him after each tale.

"We will wipe out the Eclipsire," Rageskin said. "They are a danger to all."

"Is genocide really the best option?" Stream responded. "There may be some who don't want to live by the choices being made now. We have two dragons from other clans who defected."

"Yeah, one clan threatened mine and the other destroyed Whisper's islands. They should be made examples of."

"Rageskin, do you hear yourself?" Whisper asked. "You would never condone these decisions if your father was making them."

He glared at her. "Maybe my father had a point. These new clans have been nothing but a thorn in our side."

"The Florastryx have been friendly and helpful," Mudball chimed in.

"Only for their own protection. Look at them. They are small and frail. They need dragons like us to protect them. They ran from the enemies that we are now dealing with."

"And they have also been helping us when the dangers occurred," Mudball defended. "You are just angry and upset and taking it out on us."

"Your home was the only one not destroyed by an enemy's attack."

"I lost members of my clan, you red-skinned idiot!" Mudball snapped. "Maybe if you weren't going around acting all moody you would've listened better. We all lost dragons today. It used to be really crowded when our clans came together for trade and stuff. Now, look at us." Mudball gestured his head. "We are hurt, low in number while these bad guys are just waiting."

"He's jealous of your leadership," Draegar whispered.

"At least my clan was able to fight back while I was busy doing other things. They can carry on without depending on my leadership."

A tear went down Mudball's face. "Take that back."

Whisper was concerned. "Rageskin, what is wrong with you? Why are you being such a jerk?"

"We were attacked by dragons that want our blood, another clan threatening our death because we don't see eye to eye about Auroradraca, and now you have one of them working for you. How do you know he or the other one won't betray us?"

"They pledged loyalty," Stream said.

"Oh, so we are to just take their word that they won't join their clan at the last minute or simply leave to bring them here?" Rageskin snapped.

Whisper responded, "I don't know what has gotten into you but you need to be more supportive of everyone. We are tired and sad from seeing our loved ones die. At this point, the four of us are the clan leaders and we need to show unity."

Rageskin waited to respond. "We will fight. Then after the battle we will discuss our arrangement as king and queen further." His words were cold as ice. He walked off to order his Inferoths while supporting the others. Whisper tried to keep her emotions inside.

Stream commented, "Did I miss something? Why is Rageskin acting this way?"

"He's a jerk," Mudball said, trying not to sound like he wanted to cry. "A big armored bully."

Stream thought for a moment. "You know, we have each received a gift from a god and met one. Maybe Rageskin met one and is being manipulated?"

Before they could discuss anything, Dirtspike yelled, "Mudball, you need to check this out! Now!"

The three dragons headed over to Dirtspike who was standing by the entangled Steelheart.

"What is it?" Mudball asked.

"I was just checking her out, right. Seeing if we could unwrap her or something. When I moved her, she was a lot heavier than before. I thought I heard her say something but she ain't been moving. Thought I saw her wiggle but it might have been a trick of my eyes."

Stream slid over to inspect. He took note of the vines that covered her. "This happened when your magic went nuts?"

"Yeah."

"Curious," Stream said as he looked over the dragon-shaped plant statue. "Were these vines like the others that attacked the Eclipsire?"

"I'm not sure. Those vines had thorns on them. Why?"

"These plants, I've seen it somewhere before. No thorns. Wait, it's a healing vine. We have something like this back home." He paused, sadness tugging at his heart. "We used these whenever someone was hurt with a major injury like a broken bone. Wrapped it around until the bone was healed. It has a substance in it that helps."

Thornseed and Petalspear came out from behind Mudball's crystals. "Wez know thoses," Thornseed said. "Those differents froms Mudball's attacks. Theys healings vines. Yuppers."

Mudball jumped. "I totally forgot you guys were there."

"Sorrys," Petalspear apologized. "Wez good at beings quiets."

"Any idea what is happening to her?" Mudball asked.

"Not offhand," Stream remarked. He continued to look her over. "It's almost like a cocoon."

The sky above them opened up, allowing sunlight to cover the land. A circle of blue sky opened above them. A being of light came through the circle and flew down. Her wings were long and wide, pure whiteness reflecting the sun, giving her more radiance. Her white scales covered her in an ethereal light. She stopped on the ground amongst the dragons. Her white eyes surveyed the landscape.

"My children," she spoke with happiness in her voice. "I have returned in your hour of need."

"Auroradraca," Brightray muttered. "In all her glory. I am not worthy of seeing her, of being in her presence."

"Suck up," Shinestar said as she walked by him.

"Morthauron has once again created an abomination, a threat, to my world. You must defeat his creatures and restore Wyrm to its rightful state."

"Why did you let us die?" Rageskin demanded.

Auroradraca looked at him. "It is a part of life, Inferoth."

"No, last time you came to help us before, you let everyone start dying. I understand death being a part of life but not your ignorance."

Auroradraca squinted her eyes. "Do not talk to your creator with such a tone, Inferoth."

"You keep not telling us things that would be helpful or showing up whenever it's convenient for you, so, no, I will keep talking to you like this. And my name is Rageskin."

"I will tolerate your misplaced anger, Inferoth, as long as you fight in my name."

Rageskin tried not to laugh. "Seriously? Seriously? You made us forget that other gods existed beyond you and Morthauron. They could have been useful in past battles."

"Do not speak of other gods."

"Or what, exactly? You won't kill me, Goddess of life, not death."

"Do not try my patience, Inferoth. I am upset that you have allowed other gods to escape but I will look the other way so long as you pray to me."

The other dragons looked at Rageskin. They could not believe what he was saying. They agreed with him but they did not want to anger her further.

"You know, I had some interesting information given to me. Would you like to know?" Rageskin asked.

"Humor me, Inferoth."

"I was told that the only reason that you haven't helped us is because as our clans died, you gained power from their ash. That the forgotten gods being remembered has weakened you."

"Mind your tongue, Inferoth."

"They are angry with you for what you did, Auroradraca! You used them to make us and then hid them away so that you were the only god to pray to! We're tired of the lies and the manipulation!"

"Inferoth, you-"

Rageskin interrupted, "Rageskin. My name is Rageskin."

"Inferoth, you will need to-" Auroradraca paused. "What is happening? There." She pointed to Steelheart. The vines began to crack and peel off. There was a roar as the vines began to snap apart. Triangular plates exploded through the vines from her spine. Steelheart stood on her back, muscular legs. Vine dripped off her, revealing the change to her body. She was tall like an Inferoth but without the wings. Two long horns curved forward on her head, showing a hollow tip. Her scales on her back were an ash gray, transitioning to a dirty white on her belly, shimmering in the light. Her tail whipped back and forth, showing the threat of three spikes on the end. Steelheart flexed her claws, clear and sharp. Her eyes were silver with a black vertical slit.

"Steelheart? Is that you?" Mudball asked. "Please still be you."

"Mudball, what did you do?" she asked. The metallic echo Mudball was used to hearing from her was gone. "I feel." She paused. "I can feel it." She dug her claws into the ground and brought up a clump of dirt. "It's dry and warm. I can feel the scratchiness, the, the everything!" she screamed with excitement in her voice.

Auroradraca glared at Mudball. "What have you done?"

Mudball's eyes widened with fear. "Um, I kinda, well, you see," he stumbled, trying to find words. "I really don't know what I did."

"You have created life," Auroradraca growled. "You commit a sin in front of me."

Mudball shook with fear. "I didn't mean to, I really didn't. I don't even know what I did. I like-."

"Enough!" Auroradraca screamed. "All of you have erred before me. You allowed Morthauron to gain power. You allowed him to create life with the Eclipsire. You allowed other gods to reappear. I am angry with you. I turn my back to you. You are on your own with the oncoming battle." In a flash of light, she was gone. The dragons stood in confusion with everything that transpired.

"Abomination!" Brightray screamed as he released his breath at Steelheart. Steelheart released smoke from her head horns, obscuring her. The Solari fire passed through her like she was a ghost. "Die, foul creature!" Brightray yelled when Dirtspike headbutted him. Brightray stumbled, then fell to the ground, unconscious.

"Idjit," Dirtspike said.

Mudball walked up to Steelheart. The smoke from her horns dissipated, making her go from transparent to solid. Stream and the others followed him. Mudball admired her new look.

Whisper asked, "Stream, do you have any thoughts?"

Stream looked her over. "Did you look anything like this when you were a Ferrolith?"

"No, not even close. I mean, I'm still female so that's nice."

"Hmmm. My guess it would have something to do with Mudball's magic. Thornseed, you said Tuzu worked closely with Auroradraca, right?" Thornseed shook his head. "If Mudball's magic came from him, a plant god, who worked with the goddess of life." He paused in his thinking. "You said you exploded without thinking about what you were doing, Mudball. So somehow, subconsciously, the magic in you brought Steelheart back to life with a new body. I've never seen a dragon like you before but we've met three other clans so it's possible you made her like another dragon that exists in our world somewhere."

"A name is in my head," Steelheart revealed. "Mistralyx."

"Could be the name of the clan you represent," Stream noted. "And your breath is intriguing. It made you like a shadow or fog. There but not there. I wish I had more time to study it."

"We need to get everyone ready for war," Rageskin said. "It will be nightfall soon. We bought some time with the sunlight coming out from Auroradraca but it will still set."

"We need a plan," Whisper said. She tried to hold Rageskin's hand but wasn't met with the same action. She brought it back to herself.

Stream began. "Right, Whisper, you should use your magic to heal everyone who needs it. Rageskin, get everyone in strategic positions. Mudball, have the Gaiajades form a defensive circle. You guys are best with long range if we can see the enemy. I'll figure out what we have in numbers and abilities. Having these new clans might give us an advantage."

"Wez help?" Petalspear asked.

"If you can, send out your clan, see if we can find the enemy before they find us." Petalspear and Thornseed took off.

"What do you think?" Whisper asked.

"Of what?" Stream replied.

"Our chances of winning this battle?"

"Three clans looking to end us. Small army for us. No Auroradraca support. New deities influencing everything. I'd say our chances are low."

Part III Battle lines are drawn

Chapter 25 Calm Before the Storm

The sun began to set on the horizon. Inferoths patrolled the sky, keeping an eye out for the Eclipsire. Gaiajades spread out around the perimeter, their crystals glowing to provide light as the land darkened. Zeyphrions perched themselves on the fallen island, able to see in all directions. Aquanoxes moved about, seeing if any of the other clans needed water or food with Florastryx assisting. Rageskin stood watch, concentrating on his Inferoths, and determining if they needed to change pattern.

"*They are well trained,*" Draegar complimented. "*They will kill many enemies tonight.*"

Rageskin grunted. "Having your support helps."

"*I am empowered by the anticipation of blood and glory.*"

"Figured so."

"Who are you talking to," Whisper asked as she flew down and rested on a flat rock.

"No one. Just talking out loud to myself," Rageskin lied.

"Are you okay?"

"Yeah, why?"

"*He lies,*" Exalithor whispered to her. "*Draegar poisons his mind.*" The sudden voice caught Whisper off guard. "*Tell him the truth, how you feel.*"

"Ever since you left for your clan, you've been acting differently. More aggressive."

"Part of being the leader of the Inferoths, I suppose."

"*He only wants the glory of war, in Draegar's name,*" Exalithor suggested.

"More than that. You aren't the same Rageskin that I have started to fall in lo-." She paused. "I want to continue being Inferoth queen but I need you to talk to me. What's going on in your head?"

"The stress of war. Once again, I am watching my clan be attacked by Morthauron's creations. That will change a dragon."

"My islands have been destroyed and I watched my mother die by the Selenthrax. Most of my clan was wiped out by the destruction or attacked by our enemies but you don't see me acting like a jerk to everyone."

"I'm only doing what is necessary to win."

"Including closing your heart to me?" Whisper asked.

"*She makes you weak,*" Draegar whispered. "*Don't let her make you weaker.*"

"I'm doing what is necessary to survive. The sun will set soon. We will need to be ready," Rageskin growled.

"You asked me to be your queen, to stand beside you. Do you still want that? Or was I just a power play?" Whisper asked, holding back tears.

"*Love will heal him,*" Exalithor promised.

"Say something. Please," Whisper asked.

Rageskin turned his back to her. Whisper flew off, crying.

"*You made a smart decision,*" Draegar said.

Rageskin stared off in the distance, the light from the sun slowly disappearing.

MUDBALL KEPT INSPECTING Steelheart. He tried to take in all the details of the Mistralyx: the backspikes, the horns, and the lack of wings.

"Am I what you expected when you put the vines around me?" Steelheart asked.

"I don't even know how I did it. I mean, you were just ash in a metal body. Now, you're, you're . . ." he tried to speak but could not find the words.

"A brand new dragon? Beautiful? Alive?" she said flirtatiously.

Mudball gulped. "Um, yeah, all that. Especially the beautiful, I mean, alive part." He could not believe how embarrassed he felt. "What is wrong with me?" he thought to himself. "So, um, do you miss being a dragon? I mean a Ferrolith."

"I mean, yes, but really this body is much better. I feel lighter and can move so much easier. Wish I had wings but you know, some of the best dragons don't need wings," Steelheart said with a smile on her face.

"Oh my," Mudball thought. "So, um, are you, are you keeping your name?"

"Probably, I mean, there's no reason not to. I think the Eclipsire kept their names or the ones they stole when . . ." She paused. "When they stole other dragon's bodies and identities."

"Yeah, that's true. I'm still getting used to seeing you like this; let alone calling you something else."

They paused at the awkwardness between them. "So, your breath, with the, uh, horns," Mudball tried to say.

"I know, right? I mean, it's not as impressive as your crystals but yeah, I can go intangible so that's handy. Better than the poison breath of the Eclipsire."

"So, do you think you can make other dragons go misty or just you?"

"I haven't tried it out yet. Maybe you and I can, y'know, try it sometime."

"Oh my, oh my, oh my, oh my," Mudball thought as his heart started beating faster. Out of the corner of his mind, he could see a group of flowers moving. They started to take the shape of Tuzu.

"Hellos, my littles ones," Tuzu said, petals falling from his mouth. "How ares yous?" He looked at Steelheart. "Whos are yous? I feels likes I haves seens you befores."

"I'm Steelheart. I was the Ferrolith in a metal shell. Then I got covered in vines."

"Oh, yesses, I remembers nows. Yous a Mistralyx now. Verys interestings, indeed."

"You knows what I ams?" Steelheart said, realizing she started to talk like him.

"Annoying, isn't it? Talking like him," Mudball joked. Steelheart gave him a look.

"Oh, yesses. I remembers helping Auroradracas when she came to this world. I follows hers to Wyrms, she started to makes all sorts of dragons. Bigs ones, small ones, giants. Places them all over the worlds. I mades the plants for her creations. Mades the Florastryx." The leaves on the fake body wilted a little, showing his sadness.

"What did she do?" Steelheart asked.

"She was happy, mades my creations lives. Tooks some of my powers for Gaiajades when firsts mades. Then sealeds me aways like the others."

"She was mad at me for making Steelheart her new body," Mudball said.

"Yous makes Steelheart news?" Tuzu asked.

"Not on purpose but yeah. The magic, I guess your magic technically, changed her somehow. I didn't mean to, it just happened."

"No worries," Tuzu replied. "I don'ts minds you dids this. Meant to bez."

"Thanks," Mudball said. "Auroradraca is really mad at us. She said she won't help us in the upcoming war. Can you help us?"

"I can'ts. I musts waits for my parts in whats to comes."

"And what's that?" Steelheart asked. The plants that made up Tuzu came apart and fell to the ground. A wind swept through, moving the flowers and leaves about. "Think that's a good thing?"

"Not really. No, it can't be good," Mudball said, watching as the sun went down.

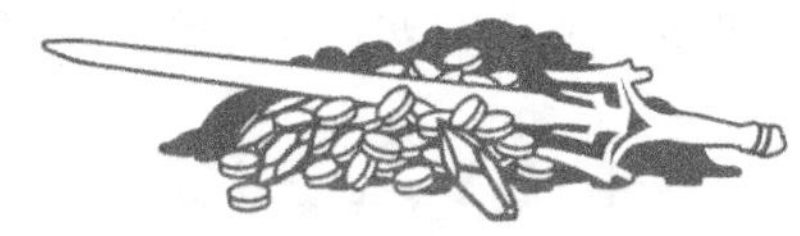

STREAM RESTED ON THE lake shore. His clan had been healed by Whisper and were preparing themselves for war. He tried to think of a way to avoid a battle. Maybe the Selenthrax and Solari could be reasoned with. The Eclipsire were once noble dragons, based on Ironfire and his behavior but were they too far gone? They are far too willing to kill and drink the blood of dragons, almost as if they enjoyed it. Stream wondered if the clans could survive the upcoming battle after having suffering heavy losses.

"Wish Dreamflow was still around," Stream thought to himself. He wanted to cry as he realized he had not had a moment to mourn Dreamflow's death. Lilypetal and Thornroot floated on the water's surface, their pink wings laying flat.

"Whats is wrongs, Streams," Lilypetal asked.

"I just. I just haven't had a moment to mourn my clan leader. It just sort've hit me."

"Wez sorry for loss," Thornroot said. "Many dragons has dieds suddenlies. Wez sad for ours fallen as well."

"Oh, I didn't even think about you guys," Stream apologized. "You just got lumped into our war without even complaining."

"Is goods," Thornroot replied. "Our deaths allows news flowers to blooms. Its whats we can asks fors when we dies."

"That's an upbeat way of looking at death."

"Is parts of lifes," Lilypetal said. "Is hards to lives if you onlys worries about dyings."

Stream watched as the sun slowly set. "I hope our preparations are enough to thwart off the Eclipsire and Selenthrax."

"What ofs the Solari?" Lilypetal asked.

"They are wild cards in this battle. I assume they would side with us but Rageskin may not be too happy with that or unwilling to accept their help."

Beneath the water's surface, a gold and blue light shimmered. The Florastryx paddled over to Stream and hid behind him. Two twin dragon heads rose out of the water as their feathery wings spread open.

"Futurarteon, you're here," Stream said.

"We bring news to you, Stream," they said together.

Stream looked around and realized no one was reacting to them. "Can anyone else see you?"

"We can allow ourselves to be seen as we choose. The future cannot always be seen or known."

Stream thought about what they said, making sense of it. "So, what news do you bring me?"

"We can tell you what we are allowed to, too much information may not bring the future that we want. Decisions made today will determine the fate of Wyrm. Friends will become enemies or lovers. New alliances will be made. Auroradraca will pay for her past actions."

"How will she pay?"

Futurarteon paused. "It will be determined by the outcome of the battle ahead."

Stream was frustrated. "That doesn't really help me. Can you tell me if our plan will work? Will we succeed? Or are we going to be wiped out?"

They did not answer quickly. "We cannot tell. To give the outcome will create a future that is not meant to exist."

"Yeah, kinda figured that. Can you at least help us? Is that something you can do?"

"Pray to us. Believe in us. Accept us."

"Then you'll help?" Stream asked. Futurarteon kept neutral faces, as they slowly faded away. Stream stared into the lake behind them.

Lilypetal asked, "Whats dos you thinks?"

"I think." He paused to gather his thoughts. "I think we might be in trouble." Darkness began to paint the land

DIRTSPIKE WALKED BETWEEN Shinestar and Brightray. The two dragons snarled at each other.

"Night demon!"

"Day monger!"

"Knock it off, you two, or you will get a wing whooping like you have never seen before."

"I sincerely doubt it," Shinestar retorted. "You haven't been around my clan leader."

"No, I haven't but she ain't here and I don't care."

"You will when she's here."

Dirtspike stopped and glared at her. "Listen here, little dragon. I don't care what kind of deal you have with Whisper but you don't have it with Mudball. Step out of line, say something I don't like, stare at me with that creepy look on your face, you'll find out what Gaiajade breath is like up close." He turned to Shinestar. "Same goes with you. We have enough to deal with without worrying about you two."

"I pledged to help and I will do so. I cannot follow what Skyblaze says anymore," Shinestar said. "He's twisted our beliefs into fanaticism."

A yellow winged Florastryx landed by Dirtspike. "I gots orders for Dirtspikes. Yous are neededses with outer circles. Goes nows." The little dragon flapped his wings and took off. Dirtspike smiled.

"Looks like I'm wanted. You two stay here and work out your differences. Come nightfall, we will see where your loyalties really lie." Dirtspike took off in a run, the two dragons left staring at each other. Shinestar took a few steps away from him and laid down. Brightray laid on his stomach. The two stared at each other. The silence held an awkward charge in the air. Brightray looked around, seeing other dragons preparing for the upcoming battle.

Brightray broke the silence. "Your leader cannot be as bad as mine."

Shinestar tilted her head. "Mine is the absolute worst. One time, someone spoke out of turn and she got angry. She blinded him with her breath, forcing him fly low to the ground." She paused. "She commanded him to fly at top speed. He broke his neck running into the side of a rock structure."

Brightray was taken back from the admission. "Mine once coated a dragon in fat from a kill, then lit the fat on fire with his breath. I can still hear his screams as the fire consumed him."

"What did he do?"

"Disagreed with an order from Skyblaze."

Shinestar took it in. "One time my sister told Lunawind that her plan wouldn't work. Lunawind used her breath to wrap her in darkness. While my sister was trying to find her way out, Lunawind bit her wings off. Right at the keel." She lowered her head. "She bled to death in the darkness."

"I'm sorry. That is not an honorable way to die. She did not deserve that."

"What about your rebellious one? Who was he to you?"

"A friend."

They sat in silence for a minute, sadness hanging in the air. "So, you believe in Morthauron?"

"You really hate silence, don't you?" Shinestar replied.

"You get used to having someone yell at you all the time, noise was a constant I didn't realize I had until now."

"Understandable. But yeah, I do."

"Why Morthauron? He's evil."

"Depends on your perspective, I suppose. He loved Auroradraca, tried to win her over. In some stories, he did everything to please her but she still rejected him. The dark can be loving, holding you while you sleep, relieving you from the heat of the day. Yes, he's the god of death but everything dies. He has a job I'm sure nobody would willingly take. Plus the chance at living forever with him does have an appeal. I don't want to die. There's so much to see in this world."

Brightray thought about what she said. "I suppose you could think the same of Auroradraca. We believe in her because she gave us life. She is like a loving mother but when I overhear the others talk, they speak of our goddess in a negative light, like she is the evil one."

"All about perspective," Shinestar replied. "Maybe both of the gods are just jerks." Brightray nodded his head in agreement.

"I've always been told that if a dragon didn't believe in Auroradraca, then they should be killed on sight. That they were not worthy of her love. I'm beginning to think that Skyblaze's line of thinking isn't worthy of Auroradraca, that it's too extreme."

Shinestar looked at him. "Same with Lunawind. She's gone crazy but everyone is too afraid to do anything about it. Or they just like the frenzy she stirs up in them. Gives them a reason to be evil. Look at the poor Zeyphrions. We crashed their homes. They did nothing to us and Lunawind just had their lives snuffed out of convenience or spite."

"We wanted to take out the Inferoths because they insulted Auroradraca."

"Ouch."

"Yeah, come time for battle, I hope my clan doesn't get wiped out by friendly fire."

They laid in silence. "Does your leader have a weird way of speaking?" Shinestar asked.

"Thought you liked the silence?"

"Your stupid Solari habits are rubbing off on me. But does he?"

Brightray thought about it. "No, not really. He is kinda harsh with his words but no. Why?"

Shinestar looked at him with a brightness in her eyes. "She says yes yes and no no all the time when she talks. 'Shinestar, did you clean your kill's bones, yes, yes.' 'Did you sharpen your nails, no, no?'" She giggled. "It's so annoying."

"Kinda creepy sounding too."

"Yeah, a little but you get used to it."

Their shadows grew longer as the sun set. Brightray looked at her. "On the battlefield, I promise to fight alongside you, to watch your back."

Shinestar had a look of surprise on her face. "Really. Even though long live Morthauron and all that?"

"If you can look past all praise Auroradraca and all that, yes. I would consider you an ally."

Shinestar looked at him. "Done."

The night sky took over. The outer circle of Gaiajades lit up the border with their crystals. Their encampment glowed under their light. Tension filled the air as all the dragons kept an eye for any movement from the shadows. Shinestar and Brightray got up and made their way to the other dragons. Shinestar sniffed the air.

"What is it?" Brightray asked.

"She's here," Shinestar replied with fear in her voice. "They are all here."

Chapter 26 The Calm Before

As night gathered, the four dragons met again, each wearing a look of concern on their faces.

"Any news, guys?" Mudball asked.

"I've not heard anything from my clan," Whisper stated.

"No sign of the Eclipsire or Selenthrax," Rageskin said.

"Nothing for me. Everyone seems to be ready but also on edge. These dragons aren't like the Necrodrakes, they announced themselves so you could find them in Mortem. These dragons are more . . . predatory," Stream said.

They stood in silence, waiting for something to grab their attention. Mudball broke the silence. "Remember that one time, we were playing in the western forest. Rageskin was hiding behind that green tree and got covered in pollen."

Rageskin tried not to smile. "I was sneezing for weeks."

Whisper started to giggle. "You have the funniest sneeze. Wha-choo!"

The group started to laugh with her. "I do not," Rageskin protested.

"No, you do," Stream reiterated. "Wha-choo, Wha-choo, wha-choo. Three times, everytime."

Rageskin pursed his lips. "I do not. I also couldn't get that stuff off me. It got everywhere. It was all over the volcano, every crease and crevice had that junk."

"I can see it now," Mudball started and changed his voice so it sounded like Sharpfang. "Rageskin, that is not how an Inferoth sneezes. It is not tough enough. Watch how a real Inferoth does it."

Rageskin's chest bounced from him trying to hold back his laughter. "What's sad is that is basically what he said. If it was possible, I would've burned the place down just to be rid of the pollen."

"*Stop being weak,*" Draegar whispered.

"I'm glad to see you back to your usual self," Whisper said, reaching for his hand. He shied it away. She felt slightly hurt from the gesture.

"*We need to remain focused on the battle and our plans,*" Rageskin spoke.

"Are you feeling alright?" Stream asked. "You've been acting odd."

"*Don't be weak.*"

"I'm fine. Little hard to be so jolly knowing that some of us won't live through the night."

Everyone stopped smiling. "Well, that killed the mood," Mudball said.

"*He's soft. He's not worthy of being leader of his clan.*"

"Stop it," Rageskin mumbled.

"Stop what?" Mudball asked. "It's nice to just be together for once, even if the reason sucks."

"*So pathetic. We will lose this war because of him.*"

"No, we won't," Rageskin argued.

"Are you sure you're okay?" Stream asked. "Seriously, if you need anything, just tell us."

"*The impromptu leader. He will die at the start.*"

Whisper said, "What is going on with you?"

"*The wannabe Inferoth. She will be your downfall, spilling your blood.*"

"Enough!" Rageskin screamed. "That is enough! If I want your opinion, Draegar, I'll ask for it. Just be there for the fight!"

The three dragons looked at him with worried faces. "I have to go. I don't like that there's nothing happening with it so dark." Rageskin flapped his wings and took off.

"You guys heard him arguing with himself, right?" Mudball asked.

"Who is Draegar?" Whisper asked.

"*The god of war and the afterlife,*" Futurarteon said into Stream's head. It made him jump.

"You good?" Whisper asked.

"Yeah," Stream lied. "He's the god of war and the afterlife."

"Read that somewhere in your tablet room?" Mudball wondered.

Stream paused. "Have you guys been visited by forgotten gods?"

"Tuzu, god of plants," Mudball said.

"Exalithor, goddess of healing and poison," Whisper said.

"And I had Futurarteon visit me. Goddess of knowledge and the future. She told me about Draegar just now. In my head."

They looked at each other with concern. "Should we be afraid?" Mudball asked.

"Of these forgotten gods? Maybe. At least our three seem to have our best interests at heart. They want to be worshiped again. Draegar has me the most worried. He seems to be influencing Rageskin in a negative way," Whisper said.

"He changed after the Eclipsire attacked his volcano. That must be when Draegar showed up."

"We all got attacked at once, right?" Stream said, thinking out loud. "Mudball, with the Eclipsire, you with the Selenthrax, Rageskin the Solari. I received the after effects of the attacks with the volcano exploding and the islands falling. It can't just be coincidence with the forgotten gods showing up as well. Something is just not adding up."

"Auroradraca? She tends to hold a grudge," Mudball suggested.

"No, she really didn't like the other gods showing up so that can't be it," Stream reasoned.

"Morthauron then?" Whisper said. "He seems to have it out for Auroradraca."

"*There are more players in this world than what you know,*" Futurarteon whispered in Stream's head.

"What do you mean?" Stream said out loud.

"Who are you talking to?" Mudball asked.

"*We are not the only gods that Auroradraca has angered. We are simply the first to get our revenge.*"

"There are more gods? Who are they?" Stream asked.

Silence.

"What was that about?" Whisper asked.

"Futurarteon was telling me that there are more gods acting in the background than we know."

"Could things get any worse?" Mudball commented.

Petalspear and Thornseed flew in and landed on Mudball's crystals. "Wez bring informations," Thornseed said, trying to catch his breath. "Scouts saw darkness rollings on the lands. Likes nightskies movings durings the days."

"Probably the Selenthrax using their breath," Stream concluded. "Helping the Eclipsire move during the day. They may not be able to use the tunnels with all the damage that's been done. What direction are they coming from?"

"Alls," Petalspear said with fear in her voice. "Alls around us."

The three dragons looked at each other with concern. Shinestar and Brightray ran up to them. "She's here," Shinestar said with fear in her eyes. "Lunawind is here. I can smell her."

"We need to get the word out to Rageskin," Stream said.

"Wez go," Thornseed said. Stream nodded his head and the Florastryx took off.

"We need to get everyone ready for battle," Stream ordered. Mudball took off as Whisper flew into the air and headed toward the fallen island. He looked around, trying to decide what the next plan of action should be. He could see the glow of the Gaiajades from the perimeter. They were not in a perfect circle but enough to look like one. He saw one that was further out than the others. "Probably should have the farthest Gaiajades out come in closer," he thought to himself. As he watched the far Gaiajade, the glow from the crystals started to blink. The glow turned on and off. A scream saying "Help me!" pierced the night. Then silence.

"It's Lunawind. She was playing with her food," Shinestar said flatly.

"What do you mean 'playing with her food'?" Brightray asked.

Shinestar looked at him. "She's a cannibal."

Chapter 27 Choices

Tension filled the air as the Inferoths continued to circle the sky, looking for an enemy that seemed to have turned invisible. Rageskin landed on the ground, meeting with the three young leaders along with Shinestar, Brightray and Steelheart. He wore a scowl across his face.

"The Eclipsire are using the darkness to their advantage. We can see shadows move but when we inspect them there's nothing there." He growled in frustration.

"It's the Selenthrax," Shinestar suggested. "Our breath is a solid darkness that we can manipulate to what we need it to be. It's like a solid shadow."

"So what, you just hide in the dark," Rageskin said snarky.

"A way to mess with her prey. Lunawind is big into mind games. She likes to create false images for enemies and prey to attack. Probably what happened to that sentry that just disappeared."

"*She is the enemy. Most likely a spy,*" Draegar whispered.

"This is information we could have used earlier, you useless moon dragon!" Rageskin yelled.

Whisper said, "Rageskin, that's enough. We have enough going on without you getting angry at every little thing."

"*She aids the false ally instead of you.*"

"You said that thing pledged itself to you. And you just took her word for it?" Rageskin accused.

"Yes, I do believe her. She has had opportunities to be disloyal and she hasn't. She's even made amends with the Solari," Whisper retorted. "These two hate each other but have put aside their differences to aid us."

"*Lies. Lies to confuse you.*"

"Enough!" Rageskin shouted.

"Enough of what, exactly?" Steelheart retorted. "I know I'm new here and technically part of the enemy too, but what is your deal? I barely know you and I don't want to work with you. Mudball has been kind and sweet to me and you have been nothing short of a jerk to everyone."

"*False dragon. Wears the skin of another clan but claims to be one with you.*"

"Rageskin," Whisper started, "If Draegar is too much, you should renounce him and-."

"No!" Rageskin interrupted. "He has helped me to prepare the Inferoths for war. Helped me be the true leader that we need. It's all of you that aren't willing to do what is needed to end this."

"And what's that?" Mudball asked. "We fought against the Necrodrakes. We can fight."

"Battling the mindless undead puppets isn't the same as a living, breathing, thinking dragon," Rageskin said cruelly. "It's easy to kick a corpse that can't strategize."

"We need to remain unified," Stream interjected. "Fighting amongst ourselves isn't going to help."

"We are unified," Rageskin said. "I don't know about afterwards but for now, yes, we are."

"Draegar is hurting you, changing you," Stream said, trying to sound convincing. "You can't see it because he's in your head."

"He will be the reason that we win this battle! Maybe if you accepted your new gods we would have won already, instead of waiting around for the enemy to attack," Rageskin snapped back.

Lightning broke across the sky, illuminating the landscape. An outline of Morthauron emerged from the clouds that had moved in as the sun had set. Lightning cracked against the outline of the death god. On the small hill where the Gaiajade had disappeared Melthorn and Lunawind emerged. She held the bloodied stump of the Gaiajade's crystal. She licked it with a smile.

"Dragons of Wyrm," Melthorn addressed, his voice booming deep. "I offer you a chance to end this war without a loss of life. Simply submit to us as your masters, giving a daily blood gift to quench our thirst."

"You ask us to be your slaves? To be a blood source for your own needs? What do we receive in exchange for this?" Rageskin mockingly asked.

Melthorn looked down with him, arrogance in his eyes. "What do you receive? You simply get to live out your pathetic lives, thanking us for allowing you the right to live. We will be living, undying gods to you."

Rageskin glanced at the three dragons. "Give us a minute." He turned his back to Melthorn.

"You aren't really considering this, are you?" Mudball asked. "I really don't want to have someone drinking me every day."

"Of course not but this meeting gives our troops a moment to get themselves ready for the war that's about to happen."

"The leaders are there but where are the other Eclipsire and Selenthrax?" Stream asked.

"I'm going with the fact that they have surrounded us on all sides. It's what I would do if I was him," Rageskin suggested.

"Hurry up, yes, yes," Lunawind said as she stroked the crystal like a pet. "We grow impatient and hungry, no, no." Blood stained her mouth.

"She is so creepy," Whisper said as a shiver went down her back.

"Agreed," Mudball said. "So what do we decide? Fight or slavery?"

"Fight."

"Fight."

"Mostly definitely fight," Rageskin said.

Mudball let out a sigh of disappointment. "Fight."

Rageskin turned to address Melthorn. "Sorry, we must reject your offer."

"Disappointing," Melthorn said. "I could have saved you from so much pain. So be it."

Lightning once again broke the sky into pieces. Thunder from the dark god's outline boomed into laughter. Boom. Boom. Boom. Rain began to pour down. Steam rose from the Inferoths as raindrops hit their burning skin. The dragons steeled themselves ready as the sound of rain blanketed the landscape. Melthorn's three tails shook and pointed toward the four dragon leaders.

"Attack!" Melthorn screamed. Lunawind hissed with laughter. Eclipsire and Selenthrax appeared from the darkness, attacking at all angles. Dragons roared as the battle started.

"Attack!" Rageskin yelled, flying into the air, his onyx sword thrusted forward.

"I hope we live through this," Mudball whimpered as fear crept into him.

"You're not the only one," Whisper said.

Chapter 28 Temptation Amongst Ruin

Roars and screams pierced the air. The Eclipsire emerged from moving black fog provided by the Selenthrax. Gaiajades along the perimeter charged their crystals, sending their breaths into the incoming army. Some Eclipsire dodged the incoming beams while others saw pieces of their bodies disintegrated but continued on. The Inferoths battled airborne enemies, dodging tendrils and snapping maws. Molten fire from the Inferoths brought light to the ground. Zeyphrions used their solid air breaths to knock enemies from the sky as well as pushing Eclipsire from their island base. Aquanox slithered about the ground, aiding fallen allies and firing their water breaths into foes. Dust was kicked up into the air, mixing with a bloody mist.

Mudball charged forward with Steelheart by his side. An Eclipsire lunged at Mudball; Steelheart intercepted him, driving her back plates into him. He screamed with pain as he reared his claws back to strike. Steelheart poured breath from her horns. The Eclipsire brought his claws down only to strike through her and tore into his own flesh. As he was trying to figure out what had happened, Mudball fired his breath into the creature. He went flying back, landing on the ground. The two dragons smiled at each other about their teamwork. A second Eclipsire lunged at Steelheart, passing through her like she was air. Mudball ran up to the dragon and headbutted him. The Eclipsire stumbled backward and fell to the ground. A Selenthrax arrived and breathed a solid mass of black at them. Mudball fired a beam of white at it, hitting the Eclipsire in the leg. Steelheart leaped into the air and slashed at the dragon's eyes. It screamed in pain and ran off.

"Thank you for this new body," Steelheart said. "It's really good for fighting."

"Um, you're welcome," Mudball said as he fired another shot at an Eclipsire. It spun in the air and fell on its side. The tendrils rose up and shot at Mudball. Steelheart shot her breath at Mudball. The smoke contacted the tendrils. Mudball screamed as the spike went into him.

"I'm hit, I'm hit!" he yelled. He backed up and looked for blood but there was no pain. No blood leaked to the ground. The tendrils snapped at him, fading in and out. "I'm not hit" he said as he realized the tendrils were phasing through him. Steelheart looked at him. "Told you. Great for fighting." As the Eclipsire started to get up, she fired again at it, the smoke covering the ground below. The Eclipsire snarled as he sank into the ground. She blew again, solidifying the rock. There was a crunching sound as the Eclipsire slumped over.

Mudball stood horrified by what he just witnessed. "Remind me never to make you angry."

Steelheart just grinned at him. "Be a loyal mate and you'll be fine." She leapt into a group of dragons that were attacking some Zeyphrions.

"Mate? I have a girlfriend? When did that happen?"

"*Tuzu do nots knows*," he said in Mudball's head.

Mudball screamed. "Who said that? Where are you?"

"*I in yours heads.*"

"What do you want? Now's not really the time to be scaring me."

"*I wishes to helps.*"

"Okay, so do it. My clan is being torn apart and I can only do so much."

"*Believes in mes. Accepts mes.*"

Mudball looked around, trying to find Tuzu's flower body but to no avail. "Okay. I believes in yous."

"YOU GO HELP THE INFEROTHS! You guys, there's a group of Gaiajades that are hurt! Get them and bring them back here!" Stream ordered various dragons who were nearby. They listened to him and tried to avoid the enemy. Stream looked around, trying to take everything in. Dragons were fighting in every direction.

"There's no rhyme or reason to their tactics," he said to himself. "It's like they are just animals." His eyes tracked the movements around him but he simply could not keep up. He tried to tap into his magic but he simply could not focus while he was trying to strategize. "Inferoths in the air, Gaiajades protecting our border. Maybe we need to shrink our circle?" he thought out loud. "I got the Aquanoxes helping everyone. Zeyphrions are fighting around the fallen island. We are just too scattered."

An Eclipsire landed near Stream, a piece of Aquanox backfin in his bloody claws. "You water dragons taste so fishy and muddy," it teased. "Your flesh is so disgusting. Blood ain't too bad." A tendril shot out at Stream. He dodged it, bit into the body, slid his long body under himself, and used the momentum to fling the Eclipsire. Stream felt sick from the taste. He vomited up some water to cleanse his mouth. "Like rotten iron fish." He could feel his stomach wanting to throw up more but he calmed himself. The enemy dragon regained its footing and glared at Stream. It took in a deep breath and released an olive colored fog from its maul. It swiftly moved toward Stream. He tried to slide backward but fear started to creep up into him. As the mist crept closer, Stream felt like he could not move. The smell of the fog was sulfuric with traces of old blood mixed in. His muscles began to tighten as more fog made its way into his nostrils. He tried to cough it out but it only made it worse. The Eclipsire stalked toward Stream, an evil smile stretched across its face.

"Aquanox blood is not yummy but you'll do in a pinch," it growled, red drool trailing from its mouth. Stream felt his body tighten. As the Eclipsire got closer, a pack of a dozen Florastryx swooped in, blowing the paralyzing fog away from Stream. The Eclipsire slashed at the little dragons but kept missing. "Stupid pests," it remarked. "Get away from my prey." The Florastryx dive bombed the Eclipsire, spitting their acid breath into its eyes with each fly by. Stream could feel his muscles relax and could move them freely again. He coughed up a yellowish liquid, spitting it to the ground. The Eclipsire kept swiping at the Florastryx, hitting a random one every other swing. "Stupid pests!" He opened his mouth wide to breathe in. As he did so, Stream released his breath, sending gallons of water into the Eclipsire. It choked for a moment, trying to spew the water back out. Stream quickly slithered up to it, wrapping himself around the Eclipsire. Florastryx ganged up on the tendrils, trying to pin them to the ground. Stream wrapped his body around the neck and forced the dragon's head up. Stream got his head above the other dragon's head. When it opened its mouth again, Stream released his breath into the Eclipsire. Water poured into the Eclipsire. The dragon tried to fight back but could, its body going limp. Stream stopped and released the Eclipsire, the body thumping onto the ground. The Florastryx looked at Stream as they released the tendrils. Stream tried to catch his breath and looked at the little dragons.

"Thanks for the save, guys," Stream said. "I wondered what their breath was. Not the way I wanted to find out." The Florastryx nodded their heads, took off, looking to see who else they could help. He watched as they flew off. The fighting continued around him. "Now what?" he pondered.

"*Believe in us. Worship us,*" Futurarteon whispered. "*Accept our power.*"

Stream was caught off guard by the sudden voice. "What happens if I do?"

"*We are the goddess of the future. Believe in us and find out.*"

Stream pondered it for a moment as he watched dragons fight above and around him. He saw fallen friends on the ground and others with Eclipsires drinking blood from them.

"Okay."

BRIGHTRAY BLEW FIRE in the faces of several Eclipsires. They screamed in pain and ran back. "It's so hard to see in the dark," he complained. "Even my breath cannot light up the land."

"It's my clan," Shinestar said, spitting out tendrils. "They are making it darker for the Eclipsire. Sunlight seems to hurt them."

"We are hours from sunrise. I'm not sure if we can survive until then."

"Poor little, sun dragon," Shinestar teased. "Afraid of the dark?"

Brightray huffed. "No, I just don't have the greatest night vision."

A glow came from behind them. The Gaiajades that were there had left to help out other dragons. "You see that?" Shinestar asked.

"Yeah," Brightray replied with worry in his voice.

"Thoughts as to what it is?"

"I think it's my clan. I don't know if it's a good thing or not."

Several Eclipsire jumped onto the raised rocks that were near them. They started to release their breath when a wall of fire engulfed them. The deadly fog burned away as the dragons fell to the ground. Skyblaze stood on top of the rocks, spreading his wings wide like half a sun.

"What horror have you found yourself in, Brightray?" he asked with his deep voice. "And why is that Morthauron believer still standing? You must rid our land of her kind."

"She defected from her clan. We fight together, along with the other clans, to end the threat of the Eclipsire and the Selenthrax."

Skyblaze looked down on them. "Has she renounced Morthauron?"

"Hasn't really come up. Not a big concern compared to the threat going on behind us."

"Have you renounced Morthauron and reclaimed Auroradraca as your savior?"

"Not yet. Weighing my options right now," Shinestar sarcastically replied.

"Skyblaze, help us with the fight. We can use the power of the Solari," Shinestar pleaded.

Skyblaze lowered his eyes at Shinestar. "No."

"No? No? You really will let everyone suffer and die rather than help?" Brightray replied. "These dragons could take over Wyrm and you just say no?"

"Correct. These heathens don't have the light of Auroradraca protecting them. They are not worthy of our help," Skyblaze said as he began to turn around. The other Solari began to follow his lead. "You align yourself with these nonbelievers. It was good that I kicked you out of the Solari."

"You're a coward!" Shinestar shouted. "Nothing but a loud, obnoxious coward."

Skyblaze turned back. "I am no coward. Just don't want to waste my time with the unworthy."

"Oh, bright golden dragon, am I worthy of your attention, yes, yes?" Lunawind hissed. The Selenthrax leader walked in behind the two teen dragons. They froze in fear from her sudden appearance. "Oh, little Shinestar, we will talk when I am through with this dragon, yes, yes." Ice ran down Shinestar's back. They watched as she slinked her way toward Skyblaze.

"Who are you?" Skyblaze asked.

"Morthauron's priestess on Wyrm, the seductress of the night, yes, yes. The eater of life believers."

"Demon," Skyblaze growled. "I will rid Wyrm of your foul stench." He raised his head back and released his breath, fire raining down on her. Lunawind sidestepped and rolled away.

"Hmmm, pretty fire, no, no. Does it allow me to cook your flesh, yes, yes?" She fired a solid mass of darkness at him. The ground below him cracked, forcing him to slide down. She ran at him, reaching her claws out. He swung his tail as he came down, connecting with her ribs. Talons scratched down his wing. Both grunted from the sudden pain. The dragons snarled at each other and ran to each other. They clawed and bit each other. Skyblaze bit down on her wing and breathed fire onto her back. She screamed in pain. She breathed out, forming her darkness into long spikes, piercing his hide. He growled as he leaped off of her. Both stared at each other, blood dripping to the ground. Lunawind still had fire on her back as the spikes disappeared from Skyblaze's flesh, holes being left behind. A rage overcame the both of them and they released their breath at the same time. Fire and darkness slammed together between them, missing together. The two leaders took steps toward each other as their breaths combined together to form a tar that splattered on them. Both refused to quit as hot tar landed on their scales. They increased their power, both dragons not giving up an inch. The two breaths exploded as each took a step closer. Hot tar covered the two dragons' heads. They tried to scream but each found the sticky substance covered their nostrils and sealed their mouths shut. They tried to step closer to each other but collapsed to the ground.

Shinestar and Brightray could not believe what they just witnessed. The other Solari looked at each other in surprise. Shinestar walked up to Lunawind. She tapped Lunawind on the tail. No movement. She went over to Skyblaze, repeated her check. No movement.

"Both dead," she said. "Brightray, you're up."

His eyes widened. "What?" She swung her head toward the Solari. He figured out what she meant and stepped toward his former clan.

"Solari, I will give you two choices: join in the battle behind us, to redeem yourselves for past actions or leave and take your chances hiding from the enemy without your clan's support."

The Solari talked amongst themselves. Half of the clan left, disappearing into the night. The remaining Solari turned to Brightray with one asking, "What are your orders?"

RAGESKIN SWUNG HIS sword at two Eclipsire, beheading both of them. Behind him, Whisper was swatting dragons with her bo staff toward Rageskin. They kept back to back, moving as one body. Rageskin blew his breath onto moving darkness, lighting up any dragons that tried to use Selenthrax breath as cover. The napalm fire splattered on its targets. Whisper forced dragons back with her breath, punching their bodies with invisible force.

"Are we making any progress?" Whisper asked as she slashed the face of Eclipsire. "They just seem never ending."

"Don't know, don't care," Rageskin replied. "The thrill of battle is intoxicating right now."

She gave a sideways glance. "Is that you or Draegar speaking?"

"*She is too weak to survive this battle. End her now so you can focus,*" Draegar whispered.

Rageskin paused. "It's me. My thoughts."

Whisper felt like he was lying. "*He is,*" Exalithor whispered. "*Draegar has dug his claws into him deep. Poisons his mind. I can heal him if you believe in me.*"

As Whisper was distracted by Exalithor, the Selenthrax and Eclipsire stopped fighting and took off. In the distance, Whisper could see Solari joining in the fight. The rain continued to come down. Rageskin cocked his head, looking like he was listening.

"What is it?" Whisper asked.

"Someone is coming toward us. Two of them. Be ready. I can't tell from where with all the fighting and rain." They stood back to back, trying to scan for the enemy. An Eclipsire tendril speared out of the darkness, wrapped tightly around Whisper's bo staff, and ripped it from her claws. Whisper could make out two dragons being outlined with rain. A male and female Eclipsire walked toward them.

"Oh my, how the Inferoth have fallen since you have taken over," the male one said. "Death and destruction, loss of clan members. Relying on others for help. You would make your father and brother ashamed."

"*It's him*," Dragegar whispered. "*The betrayer.*"

"Blackwing," Rageskin growled.

"Oh, you recognized me," Blackwing said with arrogance. "I wasn't sure if you would, seeing as I was upgraded by Morthauron. I have to admit, pretending to be Blackwing was really hard. Having to scour his mind for all things Inferoth. Being your advisor. It was as if you couldn't think for yourself."

The female Eclipsire stepped forward. "Oh, pretty birdie, you are still alive? I'm surprised another female didn't step up and off you while I was away." She held the bo staff, tapping it on one black hand.

"Darkheart," Whisper said.

"Well, maybe just in name. Took a little bit to control her body but I must say her hatred for you seemed genuine. Really easy to use that to fight you."

"If memory serves me right, you lost," Whisper retorted.

"I was still getting used to her body but now," Darkheart said as her wings spread out, displaying her five tendrils, blood dripping from their ends, "Now I get to kill you with my own hands." She hissed and leaped toward Whisper. She landed on top of Whisper, amazing the Zeyphrion with her speed. Blackwing sent his tendrils at Rageskin. He swatted them away with his sword and breathed his fire at Blackwing.

He dodged and leaped at Rageskin, his weight crashing into Rageskin's chest, pushing him down. He clawed at Rageskin's head, talons leaving scratches in the black armor. Rageskin felt the tendrils wrap around his limbs. Whisper found herself trapped as well, as she tried to grab the ground for footing but sliding from the mud.

"Truly accept me. Truly believe in me and we will defeat these creatures," Draegar demanded.

"Any last words, Rageskin?" Blackwing said as he forced Rageskin's neck to be exposed. Long black fangs extended as he opened his mouth, bloody saliva leaking down.

"I do," Rageskin replied to Draegar.

Blackwing paused for a moment, confused by the statement. Rageskin's scales began to glow, transforming rain into steam before hitting him. Blackwing's scale began to glow from where he gripped Rageskin. He released Rageskin and jumped off him, trying to cool off his body with rain water from the ground. Darkheart saw what was happening but refused to release Whisper. Rageskin's eyes glowed a bright red. Yellow energy shimmered off him, lighting up the area. Blackwing was afraid.

"Inferoths can't do that. What are you doing?" he said, confused.

"Ending this," Rageskin said with Draegar speaking at the same time. He took a breath in and released his molten fire. Blackwing moved to the side but found himself in the clutches of Rageskin, not seeing the Inferoth move. Tendrils went to stab Rageskin but bounced off his armor. With one hand on Blackwing's throat, his free hand used his sword to cut off the tendrils. Each time Blackwing tried to scream, Rageskin tightened his grip around his throat. When the last tendril was cut off, he raised Blackwing into the air, cut open his chest and sprayed his breath into the exposed torso. Blackwing flayed for a moment, then stopped moving. Rageskin dropped him to the ground.

Darkheart hissed at him and tried to sink her fangs into Whisper. In a movement between the blink of an eye, Rageskin stabbed

Darkheart in the back. He repeated the action several times until she stopped moving. Darkheart collapsed on top of Whisper. She pushed the Eclipsire off and grunted in pain. Her body wore mirrored injuries as her opponent, blood pouring out of her. She was shocked to see her injuries.

"Rageskin, what did you do?" she asked, hurt in her voice.

"*As I said, pathetic. A true Inferoth queen would embrace you, enjoying the blood on your hands,*" Draegar said. "*She deserves her death.*"

Rageskin stared at her. In his mind he was screaming at what he had done but Draegar seemed to control his body.

"*Accept me. Believe in me,*" Exalithor whispered. "*I will heal you and together we will heal Rageskin.*"

Whisper winced in pain. She raised her hands to her face, blood gloves on her talons. "I do." Golden light began to glow from her wounds as they began to heal.

Chapter 29 Divine Intervention

Whisper stood up and looked over her scales. She had faint scars from where she had been stabbed. She could feel a new awareness of the world around her. Dragons had different colored auras to them, based on if they were injured, dead, or not hurt. Her eyes glowed a bright gold and white. She felt a shield about her, protecting her from the rain. She glared over to Rageskin, a bright red and black energy pulsating off him. She could see the outline of Draegar standing behind him like a shadow.

"See how Draegar aligns himself with Rageskin's ash?" Exalithor noted. *"They are one as are we. As are the others."*

"Others?" Whisper thought. "Mudball and Stream?"

"They too have a forgotten god within them. But Draegar is a poison that we need to cure or at the least help Rageskin to control."

Rageskin glared at Whisper. "I see you have a god within you as well." Draegar's voice echoed as he talked.

"Yes, but unlike you, I am at peace with mine."

"I am at peace. I accepted Draegar, to help me win this war."

Lightning cracked against the night sky.

"He's using you. You think you're in control but really he is."

"You lie. Your god speaks lies to you."

"She doesn't. Think about your actions. The Rageskin I know would find a solution that wouldn't end in the life of dragons that he knows."

"This is war. Casualties happen. I am an Inferoth. We are bred for fighting." He began to breathe heavier, anger taking over.

"You aren't the same dragon that asked me to become his queen. To go through Inferoth trials to prove my worth to rule by your side." She paused. With tears in her eyes, she said, "You're not the same dragon that trained me. That asked me for help. You're not the same Inferoth that I fell in love with."

Rageskin tried not to open his mouth but Draegar forced him to say, "Love is for the weak."

Whisper began to cry. "For the weak? Is that why you stabbed me while I was on the ground? You killed Darkheart but made no effort not to hurt me. Rageskin would never do that. He would hesitate before even thinking of driving his sword into an enemy where I would be harmed."

Rageskin's face changed to pure hatred. Draegar was the sole voice as he said, "His love for you will only end in his death. You are making him less. You must not be allowed to weaken his mind." With a scream, he ran toward Whisper, sword first. She sidestepped, pushing the sword to the side. She drove an elbow into his ribs. Nerves went numb when she caught a piece of skin protected by armor. She took a few steps over to Darkheart's body and retrieved her staff. As she turned around, liquid fire came flying at her. She rolled, firing her breath like an uppercut to his jaw. He stumbled back a few steps, regaining his balance.

"Rageskin, this isn't you!" she screamed.

"*You must heal the poison of Draegar,*" Exalithor whispered. "*Touch him so my magic may flow to him.*"

Whisper groaned in frustration. She knew a one-on-one fight with Rageskin was difficult enough but Draegar would not hold back. She knew the god would kill her. Rageskin released his breath again. Whisper took in a breath and released her ice weapon. The two dragon breathes met between them, violent steam hissing. She took to the sky, using the steam as cover. She came down on top of him, her staff smacking him on top of his armor. He stumbled back, swiping at the air. Whisper blew ice at him, his legs becoming stuck to the ground. She fired again, his arms covered in ice and attached to the ground. Rageskin snarled.

"What are you doing?" Draegar growled.

"Brother, you are too unbalanced with your hunger for battle," Exalithor spoke through Whisper, eyes glowing gold. "Let me heal you."

"Never! Don't!" Draegar yelled as fire began to leak out of Rageskin's mouth. Exalithor clasped his maw shut, liquid fire drooling out. Whisper tried not to scream as the fire leaked over her fingers. A yellow glow of energy spread from her to Rageskin who was violently throwing his head side to side, trying to get Whisper to release her grip. The energy climbed over him. Lightning lit up the sky, Exalithor standing behind Whisper and Draegar holding onto Rageskin. The energy coated Rageskin and became a shadow on Draegar. The ground glowed with light. Rageskin's breathing slowed down, a calmness coming over him. Whisper felt his body relax and removed her hands from his mouth.

"Rageskin, are you with me?" she asked, trying not to choke on tears. "Please, tell me you are better?"

He lowered his head, his body hiccuped from tears. Whisper banged her staff against the ice shackles that held onto Rageskin. Once cleared, he fell to his knees hard. He kept his head down. Whisper knelt down in front of him. "Say something. Anything, please," she begged.

"He's still in there," he sobbed. "I can feel him wanting to regain control but you fixed me. I can hold him." He looked up at her, tears streaming down his eyes, turning to steam. "Forgive me. Please forgive me for what I did to you. It wasn't me, it was Draegar. It was like I was watching from behind my eyes with no control of my body."

She placed a hand on his shoulder. "Of course I forgive you. I love you, you raging idiot."

He tried not to chuckle at her joke name for him. "I love you, too." They embraced in a quick hug. Thunder rolled across the sky, startling them, and they released. They stood up and examined the battlefield. The Eclipsire and Selenthrax were beginning to gain the advantage. There were less Inferoths and Zeyphrions in the sky fighting. They could see a green glow in the distance and a blue glow standing near it. Whisper looked at their own glows.

"Think the boys got a god to help them out?" she said.

"Time to find out." Rageskin said as they took off into the sky.

STREAM AND MUDBALL had found each other while fighting off Eclipsires. Stream had a blue aura to him while Mudball shined with a green hue. Mudball fired his crystals at a Selenthrax that had tried to sneak in while they were not paying attention. Rain splattered off them but they did not get wet.

"This feels weird and cool at the same time," Mudball said. "I know Tuzu is helping me but this energy is such a strange feeling."

"I know," Stream agreed. "Having Futurarteon in my head is something else. I can see where a dragon is going to be before they are there. Kinda handy with the fight."

Two Eclipsires fell nearby them. A red and yellow glow came down from the sky.

"Rageskin! Whisper! You're alive!" Mudball exclaimed. "I haven't seen you guys since the fight started."

"And it looks like you have a god helping as well," Stream commented.

"Yeah," Whisper said. "Same for you guys?"

"Yup," Mudball said. "Haven't figured out what to do with them yet but yeah."

They surveyed the landscape. All the clans were fighting together. They watched as Solari joined the battle with a few Selenthrax that had defected from their clan. Florastryx buzzed about, blinding who they could with their acid breath. The Eclipsire began to gain an edge. Gaiajade breath lit up the area. Stream closed his eyes to focus on his magic.

"Any thoughts?" Rageskin asked. "We have this power, we need to help out the others. We are losing the battle."

Stream slowly opened his eyes. He could see various futures at once, each result from every decision that was to be made. Images flashed quickly in his mind. Horror and death dominated at first. He kept changing decisions until he finally saw how they could win. He opened his eyes with a bright glow to them.

"That is not creepy at all," Mudball commented.

"I see how we can win. Whisper, use Exalithor to heal everyone quickly. Even the most recently dead if their ash is still within them. Rageskin, use Draegar to put a fighting spirit into everyone. There is a lot of fear holding dragons back. I'll get various dragons into places they need to be. Once we have done this, we will take out Melthorn."

"What about me?" Mudball asked.

"Use your imagination," Stream said as blue wings made of Futurarteon's energy sprouted from his back. "You will know what to do." He flapped his wings and took off as did Rageskin and Whisper. Mudball watched as their godly energy began to work quickly according to Stream's plan. The battlefield began to glow from their collective energy that resonated from those that they helped.

"Use my imagination?" Mudball said. "Couldn't be a little more specific. And really, wings? That's just showing off." Two Eclipsires jumped from either side of him. Mudball squeaked out a yelp. Tuzu's energy poured into the ground between him and the Eclipsires. From the ground vegetation grew quickly, coming together to form the shape of two Gaiajades with large flowers on their backs. The green dragons fired out vines with curved thorns and wrapped the Eclipsires in a tight embrace. The vines continued up the Eclipsires and spread into their mouths. The dragons choked and stopped moving. The vines came back into the faux Gaiajades and they turned to Mudball.

"Whoa," he said. He looked at the faux dragons. "Can you talk?" They did not reply. "Okay, just plants. Just plants." He looked out to the battlefield and remembered how their numbers had been lessened. "I know what to do. Reinforcements." He smiled at his thoughts and focused. Dozens of dragons sprung from the ground, each looking like a member of the different clans. Faux Inferoths were covered in spikes and thick bark. Zeyphrions were covered in flowers with thorns. Aquanoxes had wet kelp and bioluminescent moss on them. Gaiajades that were similar to the ones he had just made. They stood like dolls waiting for a command to come to life. "Go help my friends!" Mudball shouted. The plant dragons took off. Mudball took a moment to sink in what he just did.

"That was awesome!" he celebrated. He realized he was far from the fight compared to his friends and plant army. He began to take a step when a thought came into his head. "Wait. He said 'use my imagination.'" He focused for a moment. Large branches sprouted from his back with large leaves that fanned out from the length of the branches. He stretched out the branches thinking it would hurt but realized they were made from Tuzu's energy and were not real plants. "Hee, hee, hee, I have wings." He took a running start and jumped into the air. He struggled to get lift at first but evened out. "This is awesome!" he screamed.

The plant army charged onto the battlefield, destroying the enemy as they came across them. The clans continued fighting as the rain quit, glowing as Whisper and Rageskin infused them with godly energy. The battlefield lit up. As the Selenthrax and Eclipsire dwindled in numbers, Melthorn looked on with rage.

"No, no, no! This is not how this was supposed to end. I will not stand by as my clan is slaughtered again!"

"*I gave you the power,*" Morthauron said in Melthorn's head. "*I gave you life again.*"

"You didn't give us enough power, strength," Melthorn argued. "These dragons should be dead by now. And look at them. They glow with some strange energy that is turning the tide." He growled.

"*Seems I have underestimated Auroradraca's creations.*"

"Give me more power," Melthorn demanded. "Whatever it takes."

"*Whatever it takes?*" Morthauron replied with a smile.

"Anything."

Morthauron laughed as he came into Melthorn's body. He stiffened as the god entered him. His body tried to shake but could not.

The four dragons came upon Melthorn as he relaxed. Their energy glows intermingled with each other. Stream and Mudball stood by each other, checking out their wings.

"You too?" Stream asked.

"Yup. Won't last, probably but totally worth it," Mudball replied. He lifted up one wing. "Wing bros?"

Stream smiled. He lifted a wing and slapped Mudball's like hands .

"You guys are weird," Whisper said.

"We don't have wings," Mudball replied. "What else are we supposed to do when opportunity presents itself to slap wings?"

Whisper chuckled. Rageskin looked at them. "Celebrate later. Let's end this."

The four dragons walked up to Melthorn who was oddly calm. Each breath he took was audible with a quiet growl behind each that he took.

"We will give you one last chance to quit. It doesn't have to end with your death or the end of your clan," Rageskin said. "We can find a way to coexist."

"Oh, little Inferoth, I'm not worried about dying. My clan has already done that. Besides, death never quits," he said, growling the last words.

As Melthorn began to step forward, Rageskin and Mudball fired their breaths at the same time. Gaiajade energy shot through Melthorn, creating a hole for Inferoth liquid fire to fill. Melthorn dropped to his knees, arms and tendrils falling to his side. The four dragons took a breath in relief.

"That was easy," Mudball remarked.

"Too easy," Whisper replied.

"Oh, don't say that," Mudball whined.

"This isn't what I saw," Stream said. "Not even close."

"No, no, don't. No, don't say that," Mudball continued.

The four dragons watched as the fire within Melthorn stopped. His flesh and scales began to fill in the hole and heal itself. Melthorn raised his head and took in a deep breath. He held an eerie calmness as he stood up. A black energy crackled around him.

"Such an odd feeling. To crave blood and flesh at the same time."

The four dragons looked around as they saw dead Eclipsires begin to rise again. The other dragons began to slink away from the newly-resurrected dragons.

Exalithor spoke through Whisper. "He is possessed by Morthauron. He has recreated his first dragons: The Necrodrakes." Whisper caught her breath as Exalithor returned control to her mouth. "No, not again."

Melthorn chuckled. The four dragons rushed him and pinned him to the ground. The four gods came out of the dragons' bodies. The clans watched in awe at the sight of the forgotten gods. The gods grabbed

Melthorn by the shoulders, ripped Morthauron out of his body and threw him to the ground.

"No!" Melthorn screamed as Whisper blew her ice breath onto him. His head and chest were covered in ice. Rageskin stood up and swung his sword, shattering the dragon into a million pieces. All around them, Eclipsire began to fall to the ground like their strings were suddenly cut.

"You cannot do this!" Morthauron screamed. "It is my right to rule, to create."

"You are the god of death," Exalithor said. "Yours is not to create but to bring the release of life when a creature's time is up."

"You musts let go of yours desire to makes dragons before lifes ends for Wyrm," Tuzu said.

"I will destroy all of you," Morthauron growled. "I will find a way to bring the death of a god to Wyrm."

"You cannot," Futurarteon rebutted. "We represent different aspects of the world. To destroy us would upset the balance of the universe."

The dark sky opened up, light pouring down onto the land as if the sun had risen early. Auroradraca floated down from the opening, landing near the gods.

Stream advised, "We should move. Now." The four dragons quickly moved away from the gathering of gods.

"Sisters and brothers, it is so good to see you," Auroradraca beamed. "I see you have returned to Wyrm."

"You are the reason we were forgotten to begin with," Draegar reminded. "We had to fight and claw our way back."

"And you did, through my creations. You are welcome for that."

"Arrogant as ever," Exalithor noted. "You still believe that everything we do is for you. That you are not at fault for anything."

Auroradraca squinted her eyes, her lips curling in anger. "Do not speak to me like that again, sister. I will banish you again."

"Do not address me as your sister. It is but a title you give us to feel superior."

"I could simply destroy all my creations and make sure that you are never remembered again. I will scrub this world clean and begin again."

"Yous cannots brings death," Tuzu reminded. "Yous is goddess of lifes."

"You are right, little brother. I cannot," Auroradraca agreed. She glanced over to Morthauron. "Oh, my love, how far you have fallen from my grace. Please, forgive me for the way that I have treated you. After all, I was the reason why you felt the need to create your dragons. Maybe we can relocate to a part of Wyrm that will appreciate us more."

Morthauron stood up and took her hands into his, the black and white scales clashing against each other. "It will not be easy but I am willing to be your lover once again."

"A warning to you, Auroradraca and Morthauron," Futurarteon stated, both heads speaking. "Your alliance will bring more war to this land. The fate of Wyrm will be decided by those that you choose to leave behind."

"I am a creator of life. Every decision I make affects Wyrm," Auroradraca said smugly.

"If you so choose to leave now, the Scaleforged will return."

Rage boiled into Auroradraca's face as she and Morthauron faded away. The clans were left in shock by what they had just witnessed. The four gods turned to the four dragons.

"We thank you for helping us to return," Exalithor said. "I feared we would be stuck in the void she had created for eternity."

"You're welcome," Whisper said. "And thank you for helping us. We might have lost that battle if it wasn't for you."

"Do we get to keep our magic?" Mudball asked. Rageskin elbowed him. "Ow, what was that for?" Rageskin gave him a look.

"Unfortunately, we had to take our magic back to be whole. It was stolen from us by Auroradraca," Exalithor replied.

Mudball nodded his head in agreement. "That's fair. So no wings for me? I get it."

Exalithor smiled. "I'm sorry, little one but yes. The magic you used for that is gone."

"So what now?" Stream asked. "What will you do? What are we to do?"

"You will rebuild, truly as one clan," Futurarteon said. "We will awaken the Scaleforged, the other gods in our pantheon."

The four gods faded out and were gone. The clans looked toward the four dragons. Exhaustion could be seen across their faces.

"What now?" Mudball asked. "What do we do? Who's in charge?"

"The four of us are in charge," Stream said. "We will help each other lead this new clan."

"Vision you saw?" Rageskin asked.

Stream paused. "Just feels right."

Chapter 30 Aftermath

The sun rose again on the horizon. Flowers bloomed to hug the light as it ran across the land. Dragons laid across the ground, sleeping next to others not from their clan. Florastryx were buzzing about, having gathered food from nearby for the clans. Various fruit and dead animals were put into piles. Slowly, dragons began to wake up. Thornseed dropped off his collection of fruit and went looking for Petalspear. He flew about when he saw her near a thicket of bushes near the lake edge. Petalspear was moving branches and leaves about.

"Hello, Loves," Thornseed said as he landed. "I did nots sees yous on mornings hunts. Yous okays?"

Petalspear continued about moving leaves around, never quite happy with placement.

Thornseed looked concerned. "Loves, yous okays?"

She turned to help. "Iz fine. Iz justs wants this to bez perfect." Thornseed cocked his head in confusion. Petalspear stayed between him and her project. She placed a final flower with her mouth. "Theres. Perfects." She turned to Thornseed and waved him over. He crawled over and peered over her shoulder. Three small eggs rested in a triangle of blue flowers. Thornseed smiled.

RAGESKIN AND WHISPER woke up next to each other. Rageskin stood up and helped Whisper up.

"How do you feel?" Whisper asked.

"Like myself again. No Draegar in the back of my head. It's a relief."

"Good." They looked as dragons stirred awake. "Now what?"

"We bury the dead. Even our enemies. The Eclipsire were once allies when they were the Ferrolith."

"That's honorable."

"I think father would approve of the decision."

"What about our homes? Everyone had damage done to their territory."

Rageskin surveyed the land. "This. This will be our home. Every dragon will live here in unity like we should have been this whole time. All the territories converge here. We can reroute lava for my clan, bring pieces of your islands to build new homes. We can look into the Aquanox tunnels, so what can be done. The Gaiajade fields are not too far so we can still grow crops. We will figure out the other clans and how they will fit. The Solari that defected may get the brunt of some anger but I'll keep the Inferoth in line. I suppose the Selenthrax will too. I'll just have them move the island pieces over. It's doable, I think."

Whisper looked up at him.

"What?" he asked.

"This is the Rageskin that I fell in love with."

"You can still love me after what I did? What I said?"

"Draegar had his claws in you and you were vulnerable. I can't blame you for his influence."

"I stabbed you. Several times."

Whisper thought about it. "I guess I'll have to sharpen the ends of my staff and get my revenge during training fights."

Rageskin gulped.

"AND THEN TUZU WAS LIKE 'I helps yous to defeats the bads guys, I gives yous powers.' And I was like 'yeah, that would help. Give me your powers,'" Mudball bragged to Steelheart. She laid on a large flat rock while Mudball was acting out his words. "And then I grew these dragons out of plants and they obeyed. I was like 'I'm your leader, go fight' and they growled in unison 'yes, sir' and took off to fight. Then I grew wings out of branches and leaves but they weren't real, I wish they were real but they disappeared when Tuzu left my body to beat up Morthauron."

"Wings are overrated," Steelheart said with a grin.

"Still fun to fly," Mudball replied. "Wish I knew what I was doing when my magic made you a new body. I would've given you wings. You'd be pretty with wings." He blushed. "I mean you're pretty now, just y'know, wings are cool and stuff and-" he stopped as Steelheart put her talon on his lips.

Steelheart said, "I'm happy with the body that you provided for me. When I was a Ferrolith I didn't have wings so it isn't a big deal to me. Plus, I'm the only one like me so that's pretty cool. Being trapped in the steel body after being dead really messed with my head but now I'm free to do what I want with life now."

"Are you going to leave?"

"I don't know. I have a second chance at life. I could explore, see what's out there. See what has changed since I was around last time. Probably a lot."

Mudball lowered his head. "I knew it," he thought to himself. "She's gonna leave."

"But then I wouldn't have you around. You have to be here to help rebuild and I would miss my boyfriend so much so I think I'll just stay."

"I'm, I'm, I'm your boyfriend?" Mudball stuttered. "Really? You really want to be with me?"

"Of course, silly. You are so sweet and I know I'll never find another dragon like you. You're going to be part of my second life."

Mudball beamed a smile as his crystals glowed a bright white with a tint of red forming a heart.

STREAM SWAM IN THE lake, trying not to wake other Aquanoxes. It felt good to swim, like it had been years since the last time he just swam for enjoyment. The water was cool as it jetted over his scales. He slowed down and rested on the bank. He reflected back on the images that had gone through his head when he had Futurarteon in his head. He was not sure if they would actually win. So many decisions to be made in seconds, putting dragons where they needed to be to get to this moment. It was peaceful and felt like a new beginning for him and the other clans.

"I wonder if the tablet room is still there or got crushed," Stream wondered to himself. He watched as dragons stirred awake. The water around him moved in gentle waves. A female Aquanox swam beside him and rested on the shore. She had dark scales with light stripes on her back. Her muscles moved under the skin with each movement. Stream knew she was of the tribes that dwelled in the deeper water.

"Hi," he said, not knowing what else to say. He was struck dumbfounded by her beauty.

"Hi, Stream," she said. "I'm Waterfall. Pleased to meet you."

Epilogue 1

"Please! Stop what you are doing. We mean you no harm!" Riverbank pleaded as the large beast gripped him by the throat. "You see, that is your problem," the beast responded as he snapped Riverbank's neck. He dropped Riverbank onto the sole of his ship. The towering beast stood on two legs, golden fur covering his muscular body. Around his lion head was a brown mane with braids coming out in several spots. "I mean to do you harm." The bodies of Riverbank and the other Aquanoxes littered the wooden ship. Chains left the side of the ship and went into the ocean water. Several ships surrounded him, sailing the same direction. The ships were huge and held more beasts as its crew. "We will have our revenge on the dragons of this world," he said as a roar bellowed from his mouth. Other beasts joined in his roar as one ship rose out of the water. The ship rested on the back of an enormous dragon. The chains were wrapped around the necks of a multi-headed dragon that seemed the size of a mountain. The mouths roared with the chains wrapped around the inside of their mouths.

Epilogue 2

The planet of Wyrm holds many continents and bodies of water. Draegar waited at the bottom of the deepest ocean. He stood by a trench that ran for miles in length and depth. He banged his ax on the ocean floor. The land shook from his effort. He grew impatient for a response, swinging his ax again. He peered into the trench. Pairs of lights began to glow, following the long body of a dragon. A pair of black eyes opened and glared at Draegar.

"Arise, Oceandrax, it is time."

A flood of bubbles raced to the surface as the god of oceans roared.

Tuzu wandered through the frozen land in the north of Wyrm. The winds blew the snow around. A frozen river cut through the landscape. He came across a large mountain made of ice. Snow covered the top of it and various ledges. Tuzu studied the mountain and found what he was looking for: an outline within the ice. He banged his front leg against the side. A crack broke open the mountainside. A tendril reached out from Tuzu and slithered into the mountain. The end held a thorn that picked at the inside ice until it reached the outline. Tuzu pulled the tendril back and moved himself closer to the crack.

"Glaciron, goddess of ice, it's times to awakens," he said. He waited for a response. Snow began to avalanche down the mountain as a roar vibrated through the mountain. A pair of blue eyes opened.

Exalithor stood in a vast plain, the area calm. The land was flat with grass as far as she could see. A large tree caught her eye. She walked to it. From a distance it looked like any other tree. Upon closer inspection, the bark was made of dirt and rock. She swung her tail, the tree exploding into dust. A hole stood in its place. She peered into it. The hole was deep and dark.

"Tiamarth, god of earth, time to awaken," she yelled into it. The ground shook and cracked open. A low growl vibrated through the layers of dirt, shifting the ground beneath Exalithor. She peered down the hole and was met with yellow eyes.

Futurarteon flapped their wings high above the ground. They floated in the air, scanning the clouds for their target. Their heads turned in opposite directions until their prize was found. They glided over to a large solid gray jail that bordered the atmosphere and space. They ran their talons along the front to form a rectangle. The wall fell off, falling back to Wyrm. The inside of the cage was dark. Futurarteon walked into the cage. Two sets of gray eyes glowed in the darkness.

"Goddess of wind and weather, Sylphara, dear sisters, we have foreseen the future and you will be a part of events to come. You are to awaken now."

Lightning jumped around the cage, thunder shaking the cloud, gray eyes glared back at them. Futurarteon smiled.

Glossary of Dragon clans

Aquanox - (Ah-kwah-noks) water dragons; solid forces of water for breath weapon

Ferrolith - (Fār-ō-lith) metal dragons; liquid metal that cools into shrapnel for breath

Florastryx - (Flor-uh-striks) flower dragons; acid spit

Gaiajade - (Gī-uh-jād) earth dragons; use crystals to fire solid beams of light for their breath

Inferoth - (In-fur-oth) fire dragons; napalm-like breath of liquid fire

Mistralyx - (Mist-ruh-liks) fog dragons; mist breath causes intangibility

Necrodrakes - (Nek-rō-drāk) death dragons; sludge breath

Selenthrax - (Suh-lēn-thraks) moon dragons; living darkness breath that can be manipulated

Solari - (So-lar-ē) sun dragons; raging fire breath

Zeyphrion - (Ze-fur-on) air dragons; solid forces of air for breath weapon;

Eclipsire - (Ē-klip-sēr) blood dragons; paralyzing gaseous breath